Sam

Immaginario

C.L. MONAGHAN

Dreamers change the world!

Claire

Edited by Ewelina Rutyna
Formatted by Allyson Gottlieb of Athena Interior Book Design

www.clmonaghan.com

Upcoming Titles
by C.L. MONAGHAN

Immaginario series
Andato- book two

Midnight Gunn Series
The Hollows- book one

To Mum & Dad, for their unfailing support in everything I do.
To my boys, for being my life's blood and giving me a reason to do better.
To my husband, for allowing me to find my own way and catching me when I fall.
To the people who've always been there, dream big & never surrender

*

For every woman who ever loved an Immaginario

Prologue

I remember this quote from a Dean Koontz novel, '*I admit to having an imagination feverish enough to melt good judgement*'. Well that was me, Naomi Douglas. A twenty-nine-year-old divorcee from the beautiful city of Lincoln in the east of England. I'd always been burdened with an overactive imagination, much to my parent's despair. When I was a kid, my mother would often find me asleep, holed up in an old tea chest that I used as a toy box- torch and book by my side. I don't know why I climbed in it to read, only that it added to the 'escape' somehow. I suppose it made it more exciting, like being in a dark cave or maybe I did it to block out the rest of the world, I don't know.

For some people life is all about the pursuit of happiness. For me, it's always been about escape. Escape from the mundane, the monotonous and the societal constraints that forced me to function as a 'normal' human being, whatever that was. Escape was my safety zone.

I suppose that's why I liked my job. I was a freelance proof-reader, which meant working from home and that suited me just fine. It wasn't my ideal job, I wanted to write for a living but proofing was near enough. Non-fiction mostly, catalogues, manuals, even a phone book once. It was repetitive sometimes but never boring. I was a good proof-reader and every once in a while I got lucky and landed a client with a 'fiction'. That's how I met Joe.

Joseph Ferrantino was, without doubt or debate, the most incredible man I had ever encountered. Strong, sweet, impetuous with a roguish sense of humour and sexy as hell. I knew him inside out, his every thought and mood. I knew all his innermost secrets. When he felt pain so did I, when he was happy I smiled too. Joe had been a part of my life for what felt like forever. He was the only man who had managed to hold my attention long enough to matter. Joe was *the* one. My beautiful brown eyed Italian. I loved him irrevocably, irrationally and from the moment we were introduced my heart had claimed him. There was just one horribly big, stupid inextricable problem... Joe wasn't real.

CHAPTER
one

Naomi

The shrill ring of a mobile phone snapped me from my reverie.

"Hello?... Shit!" I sat up too fast and dropped the phone as I answered. Retrieving it from the floor, I quickly checked that the screen hadn't cracked. "Hey. Sorry Mum, what were you saying?"

"I said I'll be there within the hour and we can do lunch, yes?" She paused and I nodded, forgetting to verbalise my reply. "Naomi? You still there love? Are you still in bed?" An air of disapproval punctuated the question.

"What? No! I'm up, I got distracted...work." I said, as if that last word explained all.

"Well I don't have to come if you're busy? It must be important if you're working a Sunday?"

I felt a pang of guilt. I hadn't exactly lied, I had been working…sort of. But I was still in bed and I'd been reading about him. About Joe. Laney Marsh was the author of a new series of books set in Italy, where Joseph Ferrantino, A.K.A. Joe, was the main character. A month ago the final part of the manuscript for book one had landed in my mailbox for me to 'work my magic' as Laney had put it. Except once again it was Joe that had worked his magic on me. For over a year he'd dominated my every waking thought and featured in many of my fevered fantasies. Ever since I'd proofed the first half of the book, nearly a year ago, I had not been able to get Joe out of my mind. The word 'Fangirl' was far too tame for my behaviour. I'd been desperate for Laney to finish it; now I finally had the whole manuscript and I could not put it down. Like a starving street dog gorging on his first meal in forever, I devoured every word. I'd reread the first half so much over the past twelve months that the printed A4 sheets were now tattered and grubby. It reminded me of a well-loved teddy bear that had been played with too much. I'd just been reading a rather steamy part in the story when Mum had called and now I felt bad that I wasn't as focused as I should be during the call. It'd been weeks since I'd seen Mum or even spoken to her on the phone. *Christ, what a crappy daughter I am!*

"No, it's fine Mum. I could use a break to be honest and I'd love to see you anyway. Am I cooking or are we going out?" Really hoping she chose the latter option because my flat was an absolute bomb site and no way did

I fancy spending the next thirty minutes frantically stuffing clothes and dirty dishes into random cupboards! I hopped out of bed and walked hurriedly across the lounge area towards the small kitchen, opened the food cupboard and cringed. *Jesus, no food? I really am slipping.* The empty pizza box on the side counter caught my eye. Takeaways were mostly how I survived during a reading binge.

"How about Carluccio's? My treat." said Mum. I silently fist pumped the air

"Great! I'll ring now and book. 12.30?"

"OK love. Looking forward to it, see you in a bit." Mum said goodbye and I flung my mobile on the counter top. *Damn! Sorry, Joe you'll have to wait.* I didn't have time for anything but a quick wash in the sink and shove the tangled brown mess that was my hair up in a ponytail. I looked in the mirror and grimaced. The bags under my, normally sparkly, green eyes were so big they almost warranted an excess baggage fee!

"Oh dear god! Woman put on some make up at least." My tired looking reflection instructed me. A bit of blush, lip gloss and a sweep of mascara would have to do. I rooted around for something decent and clean to wear that didn't need ironing; a little frustrated with myself, resentful even, that my domestic goddess status was seriously lacking lately. Was I being stupid? Joe was an obsession, I knew that. It seemed that all I did these days was lay in bed, drink coffee, eat fast food and binge on everything Joe. Was my life really that dull that my only pleasure was gleaned from a character in a book? No, it wasn't that. I was really into my work right now that's all.

I hadn't really socialised much since Iain, my ex-husband, had left. The divorce had left me empty. Ian's betrayal had pushed me into a slump so deep, no one thought I'd ever come out of it. I had thrown myself into my work, buried my head in the sand and barricaded myself away from the world. You couldn't say I wasn't dedicated and since I'd gained Laney as a client and been introduced to Joe, I was reasonably happy in my little flat. Mum thought I needed more friends but I had little time for socialising and anyway I had a few friends online I could chat to. The thing about divorce is that when all your real friends are couples and mostly friends of the 'groom', you inevitably lose them, albeit gradually but one by one they lost touch with me. I mean it's not like they could invite me to a barbecue knowing Iain would be there- talk about awkward.

So here I was, in my new single life of two years, reading for a living and making enough to get by. I was lonely sometimes, I mean I was only twenty-nine and I still wanted love and romance, despite what Iain had done. He just hadn't been my 'one'. The funny thing was that upon reflection, I think I'd always known it. My one was still out there, waiting for me somewhere, I knew it. Well, I hoped anyway. Otherwise I'd be stuck being infatuated with a fictitious character forever and that was just sad…but safe. Not for the first time in twelve months did I wish that Joe was real. I mean he was perfect. Perfect for me. Almost as if he'd been written just for me to enjoy but isn't that why every woman loves a book boyfriend? Joe was always there for me and he never let me down and never hurt me. All I had to do to be with him was open a page. Fictional or not, he was my perfect fit and that would have to do.

When I got to Carluccio's, Mum was already seated, she waved me over to the table, two tall glasses of iced mineral water were already poured. She rose to meet me with outstretched arms.

"You look nice honey."

"Thanks." I smiled, hugged her and sat down. "How are you? Wow, it's busy in here. Isn't Dad joining us?"

"Oh, you know me. I just carry on, don't I," she sighed and I smiled inwardly, *forever the martyr my mother,* "your father doesn't do foreign food dear, you know that."

"Has he decided when he's retiring yet?"

Mum let out a huff and gave me a wry look. "You know your father, he hates to be sitting idle."

I nodded. "I know. I thought you were going to go see Immy though? You said you were saving for flights, right?" I picked up the menu and skimmed the lunch list. "Have you looked yet?"

"For flights or for food?" She asked.

"Both." I passed her the menu. "I'm just going to order their goat cheese salad."

"Thanks love. Oh, we're looking at flights. I got that thing on the computer, Skytracker is it?"

I giggled. "Skyscanner you mean."

"Yes, that one. They're a little expensive right now so Dad put a watch on a couple and he's going to work another few months to give us a bit of extra cash."

"Extra? I thought you already had it covered?" I asked.

"Well…" she began, "Dad wondered if you'd maybe like to come with us?" She smiled, a little too sympathetically for my liking. *Ohh, here we go. Lecture time!* I'd been here five minutes that must be some kind of record. I braced myself and plastered a neutral expression on my face.

"Well of course I would, obviously. I'd love to see Immy, Mum but I have deadlines. I'm in the middle of proofing for a big client." Mum looked a little disappointed or affronted, I couldn't quite tell. She opened her mouth as if to say something, no doubt she had prepared a reply in anticipation of my reaction to her offer but then the waiter arrived and I was granted a momentary reprieve, *perfect timing!*

"Good afternoon ladies," he nodded towards us, his notepad and pen at the ready, "are you ready to order?"

"Yes please." I said.

"Not just yet." Mum said at the same time.

The waiter nodded. "Not a problem ladies, I'll return in a few minutes."

"Could I get some breadsticks please?" I asked him. I was starving. *When did I last eat?*

"Certainly Madame. I'll bring them right over." He left and Mum looked at me, placing both her hands palm down on the table.

"Love, Dad and I worry about you. You spend far too much time on your own in that flat of yours. We thought you could use a trip and I know Imogen wants to see you."

"Mum, why are you worrying? I'm absolutely fine! I'm just…"

"Busy. Yes. I know." She pursed her lips slightly and gave a little shake of her head.

"What? I am busy you know. I have deadlines, I can't just abandon my clients and bugger off to New Zealand for a family reunion. Of course, I would love to see my sister but it's just…I just can't go yet. OK?" Mum still looked undefeated. The woman was like a dog with a bone- she wasn't going to give it up easily.

The waiter returned with my breadsticks.

"We are ready to order now, thank you." Mum said. The waiter nodded. "I'll have the seafood risotto please and the side salad."

"And for you Madame?"

"Um, just the goat cheese salad thanks."

"No problem ladies. May I take your menus?" He held out his hand and I passed them over. He was about to walk away when I touched his arm, If I was going to make it through this lunch I had some extras I wanted to order,

"Can I get a glass of Chardonnay too please? Large? Thank you."

One very long hour and a half later and a few too many chardonnays, I was home. I slung my keys on the kitchen top as I walked past, flopped down on my sofa and, hugging a cushion to my face, muffled a frustrated scream.

"Arghhh! Every bloody time!" I shouted to the empty room. Launching the cushion across the room, I watched it disappear behind the chair. If only I could launch myself away, out of reach of everyone. "You'd think I was a flipping basket case for God's sake!" What was it about my life choices that made my parents think I wasn't happy? OK, maybe happy was pushing it a bit but I mean I managed, I paid my bills and I was still involved in the book industry, even if it wasn't quite how I'd expected.

I stared at the window. It was an unusually hot British summer. I could see brilliant blue sky and zero clouds. The white chemtrail of a jet engine streaked across the blue and I wondered where its lucky passengers were escaping to. How many of them actually had a job they liked and how many were just happy to get by and pay their bills? How many were in loving relationships and how many hearts were broken…like mine? Maybe Mum was right, during lunch she'd implied I was settling for second best being a proofer. Growing up, all I had ever talked about was how I'd write my own books when I was older. I lived for books. I lived for the escape. Right now I had too many questions in my head, talking with my Mum always seemed to end up this way. As much as I wanted to see my sister, the thought of spending a few weeks with my parents, with no hope of escape, wasn't exactly appealing.

I needed a shower. The heat of the day stuck to my skin like cling film, it irked me and I needed to slough it off. Shower first and then maybe, just maybe, later tonight I'd sit and have a think about my life.

My heavy sigh was lost amongst the cascade of water. The warmth of the shower enveloped me. I drew comfort from it and tried to relax but my thoughts strayed to the conversation I'd had over lunch with my mother. She encouraged me in everything I did, albeit a little overbearingly sometimes, I knew she meant well. In her opinion, I wasn't satisfied with my job, she thought me capable of more. I suppose it was nice that *somebody* did. We talked about the possibility of me writing and she- inevitably- stated her concern about my finances; given that my previous attempts at becoming an author had failed miserably. But she encouraged me to do whatever made me the happiest. I just wished she did it with a little less derision and more tact and understanding.

I wondered if Laney Marsh had ever suffered from self-doubt. No story had ever grabbed and held my attention the way that hers had. I secretly worried that my own writing would pale in comparison if I ever plucked up the courage to try again. I'd tried writing a few times before, years ago, but I'd get so far into a story and then just give up. I wasn't sure if it was because I had no faith in my creative abilities or no faith in the actual plot. Probably a bit of both. Combine the wracking self-doubt with depression and low self-esteem and I began to feel like an imposter. I couldn't be an author. I was no one. People like me did not write.

I convinced myself that I wouldn't even have time to write considering how busy I was with my client list. Laney wasn't the only client I had on my job list right now and I was falling behind schedule. I'd been so engrossed with her book I hadn't been able to concentrate on anything else. It was the same old story, whenever my mind wandered towards writing, I always found an excuse not to.

This obsession with Joe had snuck up on me with furtive vigour and had become an almost permanent state of mind for me. Let's face it, Laney Marsh had effectively ruined any chance I ever had of falling in love with a real man, her characterisation of Joe was so compelling, he *was* real to me. I highly doubted that I did have the creativity and skill to create such a dynamic character of my own. The sad truth was, I'd never know unless I bit the bullet and tried but right now, I didn't feel ready to cope with the inevitable emotional turmoil. I was such an idiot- this constant self-torture had to stop, I even doubted my doubts!

The water pounded on the back of my neck, I rolled my shoulders and stretched my arms back trying to loosen up. I could feel the tension in them begin to ease and with it my body started to let go. The Jasmine body wash I favoured lathered up spectacularly, I loved the soft, foamy feel of it on my skin and its sweet, exotic aroma always calmed me. The scented rivulets trickled over my body and down my back, gathering in little soapy puddles at my feet. I pushed the plug of the bath down with my foot and let the water from the overhead shower start to fill it. Playfully splashing and popping the bubbles with my toes I started thinking about what would happen if I were the girl in Joe's story. If it was me that he seduced and if he was in the shower with me right now? Closing my eyes I imagined his sultry, heavy Italian accent, visualised his whispering words of seduction, his lips perhaps brushing my bare shoulder. My skin tingled. What would he do to me? How would I react? I let my imagination and my fingers take me there...

'Mmm, Naomi' Joe would murmur against my neck. *'You're so beautiful amore mio… I want to touch you, feel you against me. Let me explore you.'*

My body began to respond. This wasn't the first time I had indulged my erotic thoughts about him and it wouldn't be the last. My nipples sensitised as I gently trailed soapy hands up and down my body. The Jasmine scent adding its own blend of pleasure to the mix. In my mind, these were Joe's hands that cupped my breasts and played with the aching buds at their tip. It was his steely body I Imagined pressed hard against me. I allowed myself to drift deeper into the fantasy and raised my arms above my head, interlocking them at the wrists as if Joe was pinning me against the tiled wall. Joe, kissing me, his tongue exploring, licking, tasting. I visualised one of his hands slipping down over my belly and resting on the mound of heated flesh it found. His fingers would begin an agonising tease of the sensitive area between my legs causing my breasts to heave and my stomach to tighten.

My desire for him consumed me. I willed it with every ounce of my being for it to be Joe's touch and not my own that pleasured me. My mind pleaded with the universe for Joe's softly spoken words to fuel the ache that filled me. The fine line between fantasy and reality blurred. My slow caresses became more intimate as I slipped a finger past my opening and began to explore vigorously.

'Mia bella donna, you drive me crazy. Can you feel how much I want you lover?'

"Yes, Joe. Yes." I could feel him now, his taut body next to mine and the hardness of him. I had completely let go of reality. I wanted him so much! My touch became his

touch. My body became possessed by the idea of him here, naked, with me.

'Spread your legs for me tesoro, I need to be in you…all the way inside.' I placed my foot on the side of the porcelain bath, allowing full access. Exhaling in sharp, ragged breaths I uttered a desperate solitary whisper as I brought myself to climax, "Joe…"

A girlish giggle escaped my lips as I lay on my bed- damp hair wrapped in a towel my thoughts still on my little erotic encounter. At some point during my self-indulgent role playing, I had allowed my mind to drift so deeply into the fantasy, I'd felt like I'd not been alone. Obviously I knew I had been but it was just a strange feeling- like an energy in the room. My fantasies were becoming more and more intense each time. For all the immense pleasure and enjoyment it gave me, I was starting to worry that I might be letting things get a little out of hand. I was taking fangirling to a whole new level! I hadn't had a boyfriend, as such, since Iain had left. Only a couple of one night stands and a brief two-week fling, none of which were satisfactory. I missed sex. I wanted great sex with someone but not the relationship baggage that men my age and older came with. Unfortunately, the two seemed to go together and I wasn't sure I was ready to trust anyone enough to commit just yet. Besides, who was there? I never really got chance to meet anyone these days because I hardly ever left my flat. Nah, I'd stick with the fantasy for now. Who out there could ever hold a candle to Signore Ferrantino anyway?

The setting of the sun brought little relief from the sticky summer evening. Bravery, fuelled by- yet another- large glass of Pinot Grigio, prompted me into action. I was going to do this. I was going to try and write. *Fuck it! What have I got to lose?* I picked up a pen and notepad and stared at it. *Now what?* I tapped out an impatient rhythm with the nib on the paper, chewed the pen top and continued to stare. Little doodles of five- petaled flowers and tiny houses flowed from my pen but no words came.

I'm kind of old school I suppose, or maybe it's just a habit I picked up from university, but I always draft on paper first and type it up later. The physical process of forming the letters by hand just feels more personal, I just don't get that from a computer screen. Something about pen strokes on fresh paper and the smell of the ink feeds my creativity and allows me to connect with the words. Except it didn't seem to be working in the slightest now. All I could think about that was remotely interesting was Joe. Lost in tantalising thoughts of my Italian stallion, I looked again at my notepad and noticed an idly drawn a heart with an arrow through it with the initials J and N. Rolling my eyes I scribbled it out. Leaving the pen and paper on the table I got up and made for the kitchen, nothing fuels creativity more than wine! That was my excuse and I was sticking to it.

I lingered in the kitchen chewing my lip. Taking a moment to think, I found myself questioning any ideas that popped into my head, all of them seemed completely devoid of any value. Self-doubt was a sly old fox, he was outwitting me yet again without hardly even trying! As I brought the glass and the rest of the bottle with me to the armchair I wondered if I'd ever win one of our many battles? I didn't even look at the notepad I had abandoned on the table, needing no reminder of yet another failure on my part. Who the hell was I kidding? I would never make it as a writer. It was time for this ostrich to stick her head in the sand once again.

Rifling through my tired old DVD collection, I chose a film and stuck it in the player.

"It's just you and me again Bridget Jones." Curling my legs under me, I pressed the play button and settled down for another lonely night with only myself for company.

It was late- or early- when I woke up at 2am. The bottle of pinot was empty and the DVD player had switched itself off but the TV was still on- white noise crackled in the background. I couldn't even remember watching the end of the film. God my head hurt, had I really polished off the whole bottle? My liver wouldn't thank me later.

Hauling myself out of the chair was an effort and a half, my legs were still asleep even if I wasn't. I thirstily guzzled down some water in the kitchen and headed back to clear away the evidence of yet another drinking binge.

When I picked up the notepad to put it back in the drawer- I saw it. The word 'JOE' was scrawled all over the page in various sized letters, vertically, diagonally, horizontally, even encircling the initialled heart I had drawn previously. Some were delicately written, some big and bold and several had been written over repeatedly so that the paper had worn through in places. My brow wrinkled in confusion. I didn't remember writing any of it- the handwriting didn't even look like mine.

"What the Hell?" My first reaction was to scan the room, looking around for anything that seemed out of place. I turned the page over, there was nothing. Snorting dismissively, I threw the pad back down, shaking my head and laughing nervously en-route to my bedroom. This obsession with Joe was getting borderline scary, so now I was doing things I couldn't even remember?

"That'll teach you to get drunk on a school night!" I then finished off with an "Idiot!" Just for good measure.

I crawled into bed, not bothering to get undressed, there was a lot of proofing to do tomorrow and now I had a stinking headache. It didn't take long for me to drift off back to sleep and, comfortable in my own bed, I met Joe in my dreams.

The loud banging jolted me out of my blissfully heavy slumber. What bloody time was it? Squinting at the bedside clock, its red digits blinked 10:00 AM. I had overslept. Again. Wow, my body clock was so out of sync these days. I still had a headache too- brilliant. Stuffing my head back under the pillow, I uttered a long, low groan. The banging resumed.

"Arghhh! You have to be joking!" I shouted into my mattress, fists clenching the edges of the pillowcase. Someone was at the door but how the hell did they get past the front entrance downstairs without the key code? Unless…*oh Christ, Mum*! That meant another lengthy lecture about still being in bed at this hour. Throwing back the covers I shouted "Yeah, I'll be there in a sec!" I threw on my baggy old cardigan, noticing with dread how messy the apartment was- *bloody fantastic*! I huffed out a sigh, opening the door just a few inches, ready to face Mums disapproving look and got the shock of my life. Instead, there stood Iain, my ex-husband. I felt a blush rapidly rising at the realisation that here he stood, at my door, for the first time in two years and I looked like utter crap!

"Hey sleepyhead," he teased as I poked my head around the door, trying to hide the rest of myself behind it. The corner of his mouth twitched and he raised a quizzical eyebrow at the hot mess that was me. *Great*! My hand flew to my hair as I replied in what I hoped was a confident, I-don't-give-a-damn kind of way,

"Oh, hey Iain. What can I do for you?" My mind raced. *Please don't come in, please don't come in.*

"Um, can I come in? We need to talk." And with that he stepped forward over the threshold. I reluctantly opened the door wider to let him in. His eyes swept over my messy kitchen and I groaned. His timing was bloody awful! He coughed and then said "Look, I'll get straight to the point. I know it's been a while."

"Two years" I said and he smiled awkwardly.

"Yeah. Well anyway, like I was saying, I'll get to the point. I didn't want you hearing it on the grapevine, you know?" He paused and looked at me, eyes narrowing as if he was waiting for me to provide an answer.

"Hear what?" I asked.

"Nay…" he began. *Oh God he used my nickname! The nickname he gave me.* This wasn't going to be good news. "Nay, I'm getting married." He looked at me again. I stared back in silence. Iain looked unsure what to do so he stepped towards me, raising his arms as if expecting a congratulatory hug. I stepped backwards and gave him a look of unguarded indignation. He stopped in his tracks and immediately dropped his arms to his side. We stood in a silent face off and then he slid both hands in his jeans pockets. A few more excruciating moments of silence followed as we looked awkwardly at each other. All the pain of our separation, his affair and our divorce came rushing back to me in one dirty great big punch in the gut. I had no prepared defence for the onslaught except fight or flight- fight won.

"Get out Iain." Surprised at how calmly the words came out, considering the broiling anger and hurt that filled me. He cocked his head to the side, like a dog, as if he'd not heard me correctly.

"What?"

"I said get out. Now. Right now. Just go. Just fucking GO!" I shouted the last word, feeling the familiar prickling of tears beginning to form which, made me even angrier. How many more tears would I have to shed over this man? This complete, utter arsehole who had promised me his heart forever and then betrayed me after only five years! I hated him. I hated that I still cared enough to hate him. I hated that he'd made me cry again. Iain looked momentarily stunned and opened his mouth as if to say something. Thinking better of it he turned on his heel and marched towards the door. He didn't even look back when he said,

"Jesus Naomi, I was trying to do the right thing!" He walked out, slamming the door behind him without even a second glance. *Wanker!*

I stood in stunned silence. Did that seriously just happen? Did he really just turn up after two whole years of nothing and tell me he was getting married? Married! Why the hell would he do that? *Bastard!*

"Do the right thing?" I asked the door. "The right thing, Iain, would've been to keep your dick in your 'effin pants in the 'effin first place!" I was shouting now, my voice louder with each angry word. I launched myself at the closed door and a kind of strangulated, battle cry erupted from my throat as my fists pounded on the wood.

"BASTARD! ARSEHOLE! WANKER!" I screamed, punctuating each curse with a fist pound.

I was crying, not because I was sad but because I was angry. Furious with him but also with myself for allowing him to get under my skin. Why couldn't I have just acted like I didn't care? Or at least shown some modicum of self-control when he gave me his 'good news'? More to the point, why on earth was I chastising myself for his behaviour? How dare he do that to me, how dare he just turn up like that, out of the blue, no warning and make me feel like shit.

"Fuck you Iain." I flipped my middle finger at the door and then raised my other hand and gave it a double flip! It's the very least he deserved. I realised two things as I strode angrily back to my bed, wiping tears from my burning cheeks- one, that despite the past heartbreak, I missed being loved and two, I needed to change the key code to my front door!

CHAPTER
two

Mystery Man

I kept going over things in my head, analysing this morning's events with Iain. By the time evening came around, I'd talked myself into getting my life back on track and going in a direction that I chose. Instead of just letting life happen to me, I wanted control. It was time. No more settling for second best, no more feeling sorry for myself and burying my head in the sand. This was it. My chance to really turn things around. Why should a prick like Iain get the cheese? Unfortunately my new found bravado was met with a wall of internal cynicism and serious self-doubt and I couldn't sleep.

You can't write Naomi, you're not good enough. It's just a pipe dream. Stick to what you know. Said the voice in my head. *Do you know how many people manage to publish a book? Proofing is as close as you're going to get!*

"Oh shut it Jiminy Cricket!" I shouted at the voice. But what if the voice was right? What if I wasn't good enough? Then what would happen to all my big plans? Iain's smug face flashed in my mind. Throwing the bed covers back I sat up and with renewed determination, turned on the lamp, strode over to the lounge and got out my notepad. The first thing I noticed was the page of scribble that had so mysteriously appeared on it the night before. A myriad of inked 'Joe's' lay before me. I thought I had thrown that sheet away? Maybe not. I shrugged and screwing the page up, threw it in the bin. A slightly outrageous thought formed in my mind and I promptly retrieved the paper, smoothed it out and laid it on the table. I stared at it for a few seconds and went over to my work desk, opened the filing cabinet and took out Laney Marsh's manuscript.

All The Best Boys By Laney Marsh
Copyright Laney Marsh 2016
Final Draft.

I stared at the hefty document in my right hand. The fingernails of my left hand tapped rapidly on the metal cabinet. *It's only the paper copy, no one would know.* I bit my lip. *It's only practice.* Sitting down with my red pen, I flicked through the pages of Laney's manuscript until I found the page I was looking for. This was the scene that introduced Joseph Ferrantino. I began reading,

'I noticed the silver haired man behind the bar. He was the type of man you couldn't fail to notice. Tall, lean but athletic and toned. Six feet two inches at least and much younger than his hair

colour belied. Mid-thirties at a guess. He leaned over the bar, both hands in front on the counter top, arms straight. Engaged in conversation with a woman, he smiled and chatted with her, no, flirted with her. I could tell that from the way she played with her hair and laughed over enthusiastically at whatever it was he said to her. I smiled and glanced down at the book on my table. I took a sip of my wine- red, obviously, being in Italy. It was good even though I wasn't particularly a red fan. But like they say, 'when in Rome'... well Florence in my case. I loved what little I'd seen of the city so far.

The book bar I currently sat in could quite easily become my favourite place to hang out during my stay. I certainly liked the view anyway. I smirked again, chancing a quick glance at the sexy barman. He was looking at me. No longer talking to the woman. He shot me the most bewitching smile and I felt my heart flutter. He straightened then walked out from behind the bar and started towards me. The man's eyes never left mine and his enchanting smile still held my gaze. God he was gorgeous! From the tips of his carefully messed up hair, right down to his self-assured walk, every inch of him screamed sex. My nervous fingers played with the stem of my wine glass as he approached. He stopped in front of my table and looked first at me and then down at the book in my hand. He said,

"Love is a condition in which the happiness of another is essential to your own."

"Hmm?" was all that came out of my mouth.

"Robert Heinlein." He nodded towards my book. I looked down at my copy of Stranger in a Strange Land by Robert A. Heinlein.

"Oh! Yes, you're right." I said, amazed. Gorgeous and literary, I thought. "Wow, you really know your books."

"It is one of my favourites." His deep Italian accent floored me. Could this man get any sexier? "Do you like science fiction?" He asked. *"Because if you do I can recommend you some classics."* He offered, hitting me with a smile more dazzling than the sun.

"Thank you! Yes. I do um, like science fiction. That'd be great, thanks." I beamed at him knowing my smile was nowhere near as bright and fetching as his.

"Why are you here bella donna?" He stepped closer and pulled out the chair opposite me. *"Posso sedermi con te?"* He asked. I had no idea what he just said but my insides melted.

"Um…" I crinkled my brow slightly and gave a little shake of my head. *"I'm so sorry, um, no speako Italiano."* I explained. He let out a small laugh. Oh my God even his laugh was sexy! I was definitely visiting this place again.

"I asked you if I could sit with you bella?" He raised an eyebrow questioningly. I nodded without hesitation. *"I asked you why are you here? Are you on business or holiday?"*

"Holiday. For two weeks. I'm spending the whole two weeks in Florence." I informed him. *"I arrived yesterday."* I added, hoping this would convey that I was at the beginning of my stay and therefore had plenty of time to get to know him. I flashed him what I hoped was an encouraging smile. Not that he seemed like he needed any- he was bold as brass so far.

I chanced a closer look at his face as he sat and adjusted his chair. His mouth captured my immediate attention. His lips were full, sumptuous and downright kissable and accentuated by his strong chin. His face was angular but slim, with high cheekbones. He sported a casual scruff and short moustache that matched his salt and pepper hair. My eyes travelled upwards to his and I took in a sharp breath as two deliciously, deep set, pools of hazel brown looked directly back at me. Wow!

"What is your name?" he asked.

"Melissa" I replied.

I crossed out Melissa and replaced it with 'Naomi'. As soon as the words appeared on the paper in the bright red ink, I felt a rush of adrenaline. I felt like a naughty child and I rather liked it. Filled with rebellious determination, I turned a few pages and found another scene. As I read through it I began crossing out whole sentences and rewriting them as I would've written it, unashamedly including myself in the story.

Melissa became me and gradually, paragraph by paragraph, Joseph Ferrantino became mine. Granted, it was only in the literary sense, although I had claimed him in my heart long ago but it felt good nonetheless. I supposed if no one was going to see it what harm could it do? I was just practicing my writing skills and giving myself an extra treat at the same time. I knew it was a little crazy, claiming a fictional character as my own and even crazier writing myself into his story. I didn't know what would happen if Laney ever found out. I'd probably get sued or put in an institute for the mentally insane, but it felt satisfying seeing his name next to mine in print. Rereading what I'd written gave me an insurmountable feeling of childish euphoria. I made no apologies for indulging my most intimate fantasies. Right now, at this very moment in time, in my heart and in my own weird way, I had started to create a life with my perfect man.

It was nearing dawn when I stopped. I had spent at least two hours writing and reviewing, changing things I didn't like and moving scenes around. It hadn't taken long for me to get back into the swing of things. I found myself smiling as I wrote because for the first time in two years I felt a flicker of happiness. I shuffled off to bed and climbed in, realising that for all I was exhausted, I felt at peace for once. No anxiety, no frustrations. It was bliss. My head hit the pillow and I felt myself start to drift off.

"Goodnight Joe" I managed to whisper. As my eyes closed and my breathing steadied, just for a brief moment, I thought I heard someone reply,

"Buonanotte Naomi, amore mio."

A small, contented smile graced my lips for a second before what was left of the early hours claimed me.

When I opened my eyes again the clock had moved forward three hours. My dreams had been particularly vivid, I distinctly remembered a man's voice calling my name. I loved it when I remembered my dreams. I always tried to analyse them. I was convinced the human brain had some secret ability that we hadn't tapped into yet and that the universe talked to us, sent us signs that most failed to notice. I believed my dreams were trying to tell me something. I guess you could say I believed in magic of sorts. I wasn't religious in the traditional sense. I didn't believe in God, heaven and hell. I was more of a spiritual soul. I liked to think I had a secret connection with the earth and everything in it. Mum said I was born in the wrong decade that I was a bit of a dreamer at heart and would've made a perfect hippy. She was probably right, although I couldn't see myself dancing naked round a fire singing folk songs or wearing floral mix dresses and daisies in my hair. But, I liked to walk in the woods or barefoot on a deserted beach and listen to the wind and the waves. It was people I didn't particularly connect with.

After my nasty divorce, I became a bit of a social recluse, although I laughed and joked outwardly when I did manage to get out and visit people, inside I just wanted to go home. I had a handful of friends and acquaintances but in general I preferred my own company. These days I suffered badly with depression and social anxiety. Sometimes I couldn't even face walking out my front door. Perhaps that was one of the reasons I still loved reading so much. On a bad day all I had to do was open a book and forget the world.

When Laney Marsh's part manuscript had appeared in my mailbox a year ago, I had been ecstatic. It'd been ages since I'd had a fiction to proof and it'd come just at the right time. My sister Immy had moved across the other side of the planet and I had never felt so lonely. A good meaty romance novel was just what I needed to take my mind off the mess that was my life. Not getting much sleep wasn't helping either. I looked like a total zombie again today.

"Today is a good day young lady!" I told my mirrored self. My large satchel bag held the manuscript and my red pen, I decided to go out for a few hours, take a walk and settle in at the coffee house for an afternoon of reading and editing. Staying indoors too much was making me look like a member of the Cullen family so I grabbed my bag and headed out.

"Hey Mrs Crabtree, how are you?" I said, smiling at my elderly ground floor neighbour, who stood at the bottom of the internal stairs. She stared at me, not returning her usual cheery greeting.

"Um, everything OK?" I asked.

"No it isn't." She replied- a little alarmed. I frowned. This wasn't like her at all, she was normally full of the joys of spring.

"Oh, I'm sorry. Is it anything I can help you with? You're not unwell I hope?" I liked to keep an eye on her, she always put my post in my designated basket in the lobby for me, always had a kind word and an enquiry after my mother whenever we crossed paths. I'd hate to think of myself as a neglectful neighbour- social recluse or not.

"I heard noises last night, thought it was number 3b's cat had gotten out again and was knocking my plants over on the step." She said. Slinky, was the big fat ginger fur ball that lived in 3b with Nelly Parker. Nelly was a young lawyer who had just landed her first job at a big firm in Newark so she commuted every day. Unfortunately it meant she kicked her cat out every morning and occasionally he didn't come back till the early hours. There was no cat flap on the front door so Mrs Crabtree or one of the other residents would let him back in when they found him mewling on the front step.

"I came out to let him in," she continued. "I went to the front door and he was making a right old racket, hissing and spitting like a banshee!" She emphasised the hissing and spitting with dramatic noises of her own, re-enacting the scene for my benefit. "I thought it was maybe another tom cat and he was defending his territory, you know?" She was well into her story now, I could tell she'd been dying to tell someone whatever it was that had happened. I wondered if she'd been waiting for someone to come downstairs. "Anyway, he shot upstairs like a bat out of Hell when I opened the door, never seen the like." She tutted and shook her head, "Poor thing, he must have scared him." She dropped her voice and leaning into me, touched my arm and whispered, "Mind you, he scared me. I don't mind telling you love. Just standing there in the rain he was, soaked through, looking up at me."

"He who?" I asked. Her dramatic performance had drawn me in.

"Don't know. Not seen him before but he looked a bit odd. Just stood there looking like he did, shirt all wet." *Iain?* was the first thought in my head. Surely not though? Mrs Crabtree knew him and besides why would my ex-husband- whom I'd not seen for two years until the other day- be standing outside my building in the rain? I sighed, was he having second thoughts about his new upcoming nuptials? *Ha! Bloody typical, he was a total commitment-phobe*

"Thought it was a ghost at first, what with his hair and everything." Mrs Crabtree said.

"Wait. What?" My heart stopped. "What about his hair?" I demanded.

"White like a ghost!" She replied. "Well, least it looked to me anyway."

"Did he say anything?

"Couldn't tell you lovely. I shut the door, right sharpish I did. Didn't like the way he was looking, like he wanted to be inside. Good looking fella though, it's a shame if he's turned out a bad 'un. Get all sorts of criminals these days you know. He was a fast 'un I can tell you, the minute I'd locked the door and looked up he'd gone, quick as a flash!" Her expression turned to a look of concern when she noticed my own. "Oh dear, love. Are you alright? I haven't scared you have I?" She patted my arm. "Just I thought everyone should know, you know? Be aware, on alert so to speak."

My mind raced. *White hair. Like silver hair?* It had to be just a coincidence. Probably some old guy, or some drunk that had taken a wrong turn and thought it was his building. I told Mrs Crabtree as much but she didn't look too reassured.

"Mmm, well maybe dear but just you take care when you're in and out OK?" She asked and I nodded.

"I will, don't worry. And so should you too." I said. She smiled at me, back to her usual happy self again and pottered off to water her plants.

I thought about this strange encounter of Mrs Crabtree's all the way to Starbucks and was still puzzling it out as I settled into a booth at the back of the coffee house, took out my notepad and pen. Today I was going to people-watch, one of my favourite things to do was to eavesdrop on conversations. However, I couldn't get my mind off the mysterious nighttime stranger, who was he? I knew for a fact now it couldn't have been Iain. The only good-looking white haired young man I knew of wasn't even real so that was impossible. Then who? It was nagging me a little. A group of people entered and went to the counter to order, the place was starting to fill up as it was almost 11.30am. It'd soon be heaving when the lunch crowd came in. I had my latte and my fruit salad and sat unnoticed in my little booth.

I tried to focus on the snippets of conversations I caught. This was great practice for writing dialogue. People never did speak how you thought they did, it always made me smile. I loved just sitting and observing how people interacted with one another. The hand gestures, the fidgets, the sideways looks fascinated me and it was a useful exercise for a would-be author. I tuned in to the random conversations as people began to filter in and started jotting them down

"She said it would be OK though right?"

"Yeah, far as I know."

"Eh, order for Laura, Grande and no cream?"

"I can't tonight sorry. Tuesday?"

"Can you stop?"

"Do you have gluten free?"

"I just need some shoes"

"Nope, that's fine."

"Yes but your Dad said…"

"Sir?"

"Espresso please.

I smiled, looking at the random sentences, tiny glimpses into people's lives.

"Grazie."

"What name on the cup?"

"Joe."

My pen froze. Did I just hear that right? I glanced down to see what I'd written and there it was, right there in print. *What name on the cup? Joe.* I daren't move. I wanted to look up and find the owner of that sultry accent but was sure I'd be disappointed. No way it could be Joe, *my* Joe. This was just the universe sending another one of those signs- signs I was on the right path and finally changing my life for the better. Like the imaginary voice I'd heard in my sleep, me writing Joe's name on my pad without knowing it and the white-haired man outside my building. *Just signs.*

The cashier called out for a Joe. I had to look, I just had to. Why couldn't I look damn it! My palms were sweating, blood pumped furiously in my ears. *Just look for goodness sake!* The sound of the door closing snapped me out of my frozen state. I looked quickly around the coffee house but saw no hint of silver anywhere and then out the corner of my eye I saw him. He was walking away, already crossing the road. I just caught a glimpse of a tall, slim figure with slicked back silver grey hair. I shot out of my seat and headed for the door just as a woman struggled through with her pram. *Are you kidding me?!* I held back the door, impatience tempered my polite smile.

"Oh, thanks," she said, dragging her shopping bags through after her.

"No problem." I replied through gritted teeth. She must have caught my tone because her expression went from exasperation to apologetic in one go.

"I'm so sorry" She said in a quiet voice. Oh god, now I felt awful! That wasn't like me at all to be rude. I looked across the road for the mystery man but there was no sign.

"No, really, it's fine. I'm the one who's sorry. That was rude of me. Let me help you?"

"Thank you. Could you just take this bag while I find a seat? Thanks."

"Yes, of course. Here, you find a seat and let me buy you a drink?" I offered.

"Really? Oh, that is so kind."

She looked a little emotional and it crossed my mind that she might be having a bad day. "What can I get you?"

"Oh, um... I'll just have a large tea please. I'll take the bag." She smiled shyly and sat down, turning to face her baby in the pram who was now screaming. "Oh god, he's hungry, sorry." She began unfastening the safety straps in the pram and arranged the baby on her lap to breastfeed. I went to the counter and ordered. The cashier took my money and I asked him,

"Hey, the guy that just left, with the silver hair?" The cashier looked at me, a polite smile on his face. "What did he look like?"

"I'm sorry Madam, I don't remember an old guy." He said

"No, he wasn't old. Around mid-thirties? Italian accent?" I prompted. The cashier shook his head. "Ordered an Espresso?" Still nothing. "But you must remember him, you served him!" My voice had risen slightly at the frustration of the guy's blank stare. He shook his head again. "OK, never mind then. I'll take a cinnamon roll too please." How frustrating. How could it be that he didn't remember a guy with such distinctive colouring, and one he'd just served? It didn't make any sense. Had I been daydreaming again?

"Here's your tea." I placed the large cup down on the mother's table. "I got you a cake too, I figured he might not be the only hungry one." I smiled and nodded towards her now content baby.

"Thank you! That is so kind of you." She beamed back. "You really didn't have to."

"Yes I did. I was rude. Sorry." I shrugged apologetically. "Enjoy the rest of your day." I went back to my booth and gathered up my things. I'd had enough of people-watching. I needed to walk and clear my head. As I walked I forced myself not to think about Joe but tried to enjoy the sunshine instead. The park should be nice right now, maybe I'd go there and get an ice cream and just sit for a while.

Lincoln was a beautiful place to live. As I turned towards the park I looked up at the old medieval buildings and noted the magnificent architecture. I really didn't appreciate this city enough. The cathedrals towers dominated the skyline above the city and I could see the flag atop Lincoln Castle fluttering in the breeze. The city's cathedral quarter was situated right at the top of one of Lincoln's most iconic streets - Steep Hill. Aptly named as one needed both a sturdy pair of lungs and legs to conquer the climb from the lower part of the city upwards. Its cobbles didn't make the task any easier either but the vast array of medieval buildings and quaint little boutique shops more than made up for it. One of my favourite places to visit was a second-hand bookshop called Readers Rest, part way up Steep Hill. It offered the weary walker a place to stop, rest and peruse the shelves for a worthy read. Lincoln really was a treasure, I smiled thinking I honestly wouldn't want to live anywhere else, *except Florence,* my subconscious piped up. Great! We're back to Joe again. I rolled my eyes. It seemed no matter how hard I tried I just couldn't get him out of my head. I really was hooked on him, or the idea of him? I wasn't sure which, maybe both. Whatever it was it surely wasn't healthy. I kept telling myself it was just a fantasy and it was harmless, I wasn't hurting anyone by indulging in it. So, why did I still get a pang of guilt whenever I thought about Laney? I really should read the emails she sent. I knew I was being unprofessional, which wasn't like me at all. I sighed. Maybe I'd read them when I get home. *Make sure you do,* said Jiminy. "Oh shut up cricket!" I shot back.

'*I stood in the deafening silence. The air around me felt alive, as if it held its breath, watching and waiting. My skin alerted me to his nearness as the hairs on the back of my neck rose in greeting for his much-anticipated touch. I closed my eyes and focused my attention on the sizzling heat that radiated at my back. He was close. The space between us thick with wanting. This was it, the moment had finally come. Joe would make me his at last. His cool breath caressed my skin like a whisper of promise. I ached for him. My whole body cried out with need, desire coursed through me lighting fires at my core, begging to be sated. The heat of his fingers left scorching trails on my skin as he ran them teasingly down my spine. I arched my back and gasped in response. In the next second his arm had slid around my stomach and he pulled me backwards into him. My knees crumbled when I felt the first touch of his lips at my neck. I was instantly ready for him and he knew it. My stomach muscles trembled as his free hand glided over my belly towards the lace trim of my underwear. I parted my legs and felt liquid heat pool in the soft fabric. Drawn to it like a beacon, he moved his hand down further. I cried out when he dipped a finger inside of me. The sound prompted an immediate response from him and he uttered a guttural cry of his own.*

"Now, Naomi. I want you, adesso amore." His hips thrust forward and I felt him behind me. "That's how much I want you tesoro, that's how much you drive me crazy. Do you feel it?"

I could hardly speak, so overcome with wanting all I could manage was a gasping "Yes!" and a nod of my head. I was done with waiting. It seemed that Joe was too, he yanked down my knickers, exposing just my bottom. Releasing me momentarily, I heard the light thud of his boxers hitting the floor behind me. The thrill of what was about to happen, was briefly tinged with the self-consciousness of being with someone new for the first time. Should I wait here or turn to face him? I wanted to turn around so badly and kiss him but in that moment of indecision his strong arms were around me again. He pressed his taught body against me. His skin burned with desire. He was so hard against my back I thought I would explode if he didn't take me now. His mouth ravished my neck rendering me useless. My toes curled into the rug underfoot, as one of Joe's hands caressed and played with my breasts. The other slipped between my open thighs, exploring the warm wetness that showed how receptive I was to his touch. His kisses moved down my back, followed by little flicks of his tongue. As he neared the small of my back he pulled my knickers down further to my ankles and I stepped out of them. Joe remained on his knees behind me. I had no idea what he was going to do to me. I felt his hand slide back up my body and he gently pressed on my back,

"Bend over." He instructed. I hesitated, unsure of what his intentions were. "Naomi..." was all he said and pushed again on my back. Slightly confused but so in need of him, I did as he said. Bending forward I rested my hands on the back of the chair in front of me. A few torturous seconds passed as I stood there, vulnerable and exposed to his gaze. Only when he buried his face between my legs did I realise I'd been holding my breath and I let it go in a loud

cry. His tongue licked me slowly and his lips kissed and sucked at my flesh as if he was kissing my mouth. The scruff on his chin grazed the delicate skin of my inner thighs as he devoured me, bringing new sensations to the fore. I thought I would die from the sheer pleasure of it. I knew I wouldn't last too much longer, I was torn between wanting him to stop so we could make love and wanting to give in to it, to reach my climax. My body gave me no choice as he suddenly flicked his tongue over my bottom at the same time as he pushed his thumb inside of me and used his fingers to caress my clit. The shock of being licked in a place no one had ever touched before had me reeling, I bucked backwards onto his mouth, my body taking over. I came so hard and so fast my legs wobbled but Joe steadied me with his free arm. My ears were ringing, I stood panting, allowing myself a few moments to get over what had happened. I'd never reacted like that with any man before. Joe had taken me to heights I'd never reached. He'd licked my backside! He wasn't finished either, he began muttering in Italian, the urgency in his voice was clear. Each mumbled phrase followed by a kiss or a teasing bite as he rose behind me. I could feel all of him as he pressed himself firmly against my rear. A small hint of panic crossed my mind, did he want me like that? I'd never done that before and I was probably too far gone to say no. The state of sexual intoxication I was in I'd most likely agree to anything but I wasn't sure I could take that so soon.

"Joe, wait..." I began in protest.

He groaned. "Tesoro, darling, no more waiting, please. I need to make you mine." Joe spun me around to face him, cupping a hand to my face, he let his thumb brush my bottom lip. "Don't you want me bella? I want to make love to you Naomi. I want to give you pleasure, only pleasure." His lips replaced his thumb and in that moment I was lost forever. The taste of me on his mouth mixed with his own divine musk was like a drug. I wanted more, I wanted all of him. I wanted his pleasure, I decided, however it came.

"Oh God, yes Joe. I want you, so much." I was breathing so rapidly between his urgent kisses on my mouth and neck I barely got the words out but he heard what he needed to hear. Bending slightly I felt his arms slide down past my ass and grab my legs. He hoisted me up in one move and I wrapped my legs around his waist. The tip of his flesh rested teasingly on mine, I felt insanely exhilarated. His chest hair tickled my nipples fuelling the fire, I was desperate now, and all I could think of was having him inside me. "Joe, please." My begging barely a whisper. The anticipation was killing me. My plea was his cue and he carried me towards the bed. Words of amore poured from his lips, I had no idea what he was saying but it drove me wild. Everything about him screamed sex, his accent was just the cherry on the top. I lay on my back, legs open and ready for him. Joe stood naked and shameless at the side of the bed, drinking in the sight of me. I couldn't take my eyes off him. He was magnificent, perfect. Every inch of him gleamed from the heat between us. He positioned himself over me, kissed me once and entered me in one swift, blissful thrust.

Mine." he whispered.

I read the scene again. Damn that was hot! I was so pleased with myself, the more I wrote, the better I felt. It was addictive. I couldn't explain the pull that Joe had on me. The small shadow of guilt I had was buried under the sheer thrill of writing my story. *My* story? I chuckled to myself. Well it kind of was mine now. No one else was ever going to read it. Creating this make-believe life, roll-play or whatever you wanted to call it had taken over me. Somewhere inside 'Jiminy' protested but I shut him out. I knew I was behind with my professional work, especially my accounts and I promised myself I'd get to it at some point but not now. Now was about me and Joe. The scene I had just written was an amalgamation of many fantasies and late night dreams I'd been having lately. The dreams seemed to increase the more involved I got with this rewrite but I wasn't complaining, I was inspired! I told myself I was getting my confidence back, beginning a new chapter in my life. That the writing was giving me new direction, a new goal and a path to success. Which, was true to a point but what I really didn't want to admit was that I just wanted to write about me and Joe, together. As crazy as it might sound to an outsider, I was in love with him. There was no point trying to pass it off as fantasy anymore, he was in my head, he was part of me and this was the only way I could ever be with him. I was sure I'd be certified insane if anyone ever found out. I was aware how mad it all was, even slightly scared by the depth of my feelings for him. But it was real, to me anyway. He spoke to me, touched me, and loved me all through the pages of a book. No one was ever going to take that away from me.

I had briefly glanced over the emails from Laney, they started out as enquiries as to how the proofread was going and was I able to meet the deadline, and then progressed to genuine concern for my lack of correspondence and finished with, '*If I do not hear from you by the end of the month I must conclude that you are unable to complete the task and I will be forced to end our contract with no issue of payment.*' I had to admit, the last one had worried me. I hadn't realised just how long it had been since I had last contacted Laney. We never communicated via phone or in person, she was a self-professed recluse and only ever got in touch via email.

The paper manuscript she'd sent came with a P.O box number only, no return address. She liked her privacy for sure. I was worried because I needed payment to clear my bills and pay my rent, not because of what I'd done to her manuscript. That in itself made me sound like a horrible person but I really wasn't. I just felt, I don't know...*alive* when I was writing it. I couldn't explain it, it felt right, maybe not in principle and certainly not on a professional level but it was right for me. I just knew it and because of that, I had to carry on.

I had quickly sent a reply with some lame-arsed excuse of an ongoing stomach bug and a dodgy internet service as my reason for not being in touch. Hoping that would be enough to buy me some time, I made a mental note to send a genuine report of proofing back to her as soon as I could muster. The sane, logical part of me felt bad because, essentially, Laney had sent Joe to me. So, it was my duty to at least do the job she was still, hopefully, paying me for. I say the sane part of me because, when I took a moment to think about how far I had let myself sink into this absurd fantasy, I realised just how cuckoo I must be. Maybe I *should* go talk to someone? A therapist or something? I knew I was being irresponsible and half of me just didn't care and that was worrying. I could see Mum and Dad were right to be concerned, maybe I did need a break. That family holiday in New Zealand began to look quite appealing. Thoughts of my sister Imogen filled my head and I suddenly needed her. I checked the time on my phone, it was late here so it would be early morning in New Zealand. I clicked the Skype icon on my laptop and clicked the call button next to Immy's profile, praying that she would answer.

"Hey you! Long-time no speak." I smiled at the camera on the screen, giving my sister a wave when she came into view.

"I'm sorry, do I know you?" She quizzed back.

"Har har! That's original." I said wryly. "How's things? Any gossip?"

"Well to be fair, sister dear, it has been a while since I've seen that beautiful mug of yours. I was beginning to think you'd dropped off the face of the earth!" She laughed. I missed her laugh. "Let's see, gossip huh? Well, the firm have renewed my contract for another two years, so I guess I'll be staying here for a while…and they gave me a pay rise which, is enough for me to move further into the city, so yeah." She was positively beaming.

"Wow! Immy, that's brilliant. I'm happy for you, really. Mum and Dad will be too. Have you spoken to them? Mum said they were making plans to visit. Hey, would you mind if I decided to tag along? I mean nothing definite but you know, just in case." I shrugged my shoulders.

"Yeah, I spoke to them already. They're coming as planned now. Mum mentioned about you coming…" she paused, "Um, I mean obviously you're welcome and we'd love to see you, you'd love it here!" She paused again, I sensed her trepidation.

"OK. Spit it out, I feel a 'but' coming on. What is it?" I admit I felt a little rejected. I mean I know I hadn't been exactly keen on the idea when Mum mentioned it but I had hoped Immy's inevitable excitement at us all visiting together would ignite my own. Now I felt quite deflated.

"No, Naomi, of course you can come! It's just that it's only a small two-bedroom apartment and the sofa isn't big enough. I'm not sure where you'd sleep." I was confused. Could I not just share her room? Her next sentence explained why that wasn't an option. "I met someone, Sis. His name's Fletcher, he works at my firm and well…he kind of moved in so…" she pulled an apologetic face.

"Well could he not just move out for a few weeks?" The retort flew out of my mouth before I could stop it. I regretted it instantly. This wasn't how I'd wanted the conversation to go at all. I needed my sister. I needed to offload on her and her news had blindsided me. "Sorry, Imogen. I didn't mean it like that. I'm just… look it doesn't matter, it was just a thought. I wasn't seriously thinking about coming this time anyway. I can't afford time off work, you know? I ran my palm over my face and scrunched my eyes up. Why did I feel like crying?

"Hey, what's wrong?" came her crackled reply. The camera feed wobbled. "You called me for a reason, didn't you?" She had a look of sympathy and concern, not what I expected after I'd just snapped at her. I really wished I could hug her right now. I felt the tears brimming in the corners of my eyes.

"Why did you have to move so far away?" I sobbed. "I miss you babe. There's no one to bloody talk to here," the tears spilled from my eyes and I let them, "everything's turning to shit and I don't know what to do."

"I heard about Iain, the wanker. Mum told me, she'd seen the announcement in the paper."

"God, is there anything Mum doesn't know about! I swear she has radar or sixth sense or something."

"She's worried about you. So am I now. You were in a good place, what happened? Do you need to see someone? Counselling again?"

"No, I just. I don't think so. I'm just having a bad time is all. Work's getting on top of me a little and some other stuff on my mind." My stomach knotted, should I tell her about Joe? Would she think I'd gone crazy? *Of course she would!* "I just needed a sympathy chat with my sister that was all."

"Well then you should call more often." She teased softly. "I might be on the other side of the world but I'm always here for you, you know that. Why is work getting you down anyway? I thought you liked it. Didn't you get the rest of that story you liked? The Italian guy?" *Oh if only you knew.* I laughed suddenly at the irony of it all,

"Yeah, it's turning out to be a bit more than I can handle. It's…intense."

"Nothing you can't handle though?"

"I guess. It's making me want to write again. I'm feeling a bit overwhelmed by it, the work and the fact that Iain has moved on with his life and you're settling down and have this great job and you live in New Zealand for God's sake! And, where am I? Nothing's changed for me Immy. Where's my happy ending? I'm just fed up with everything, you know?"

"Well, it's great that you want to write though? I mean you always wanted that so do it. What's stopping you?"

"Nothing. It's complicated. I can't explain it now." The laptop screen flickered and the camera feed momentarily froze. "Immy? You still there?" A crackling sound began, like when a TV emits white noise. The screen jumped again and allowed a brief distorted picture of my sister to come through. She appeared to be waving at me. I couldn't work out if she was waving to indicate she was still there or waving goodbye. "I can see you, sort of, can you see me?" More waving. She was out of her seat now, leaning toward the camera. She appeared to be shouting at me. *What the hell is wrong with her?* "What? I can't hear you!" I shouted back. She stopped waving and started frantically pointing at me. The picture remained distorted and jumpy and the sound had gone altogether. I hated Skype sometimes. "Listen, Imogen. I'm going to turn it off, OK? I don't know if you can hear me but it's not working. I'll call you later!" I saw her shaking her head and gesturing towards me. She looked upset. *Jesus, calm down drama queen! It's only Skype.* I blew out a frustrated breath and pressed the shutdown button on my laptop. I waited a few moments for the screen to turn black, as I reached up to close the lid, I saw my reflection and a man with silver hair standing right behind me.

CHAPTER
three

Joe

It happened again. That strange sense of acute awareness,
a tangible, palpable energy in the air around me. Or was it
in me? I wasn't sure. I was afraid to open my eyes to see
where I had ended up this time. These dreams I kept
having were nothing like how normal dreams should be.
When they happened, it was like my real life was just a
distant memory. The sense of who I was became foggy
and vague compared to how I felt during these brief
episodes. I was me but different somehow, it was
impossible to comprehend. I know who I am. I know how
I live my life and I could tell you about a thousand
different memories from my past but it would feel like a
narrative, not a memory.

I stood still and prepared myself for what I would see when I opened my eyes. Heat emanated from my skin and the hairs on my arms rose to attention. A dull thudding beat out a steady rhythm in my chest. It took me a moment to realise it was my heartbeat. I knew that and yet its sound, although recognisable, seemed new to me.

I remembered something of another dream I'd had of a dark, rainy street and an old woman with a screeching ginger cat. It felt similar to how I felt now, more real and more vivid than any of my own memories. This time I knew I was indoors. Even though my eyes remained shut, I had a sense of my surroundings. The resounding silence that filled my ears was charged with anticipation. An audience of one, waiting for the show to begin.

My eyelids moved. Dim light from a lamp filtered in through the slits, easing me gently into the scene before me. I had been right, I was indoors. The shadows on the lamp lit walls told me it was night. A woman sat at a desk in front of a laptop. She was not moving. Her hand rested on top of the computer lid as if she was about to close it. Suddenly, sound replaced the silence; a short, sharp intake of breath from her, as her eyes locked onto mine through the reflection on the screen. What now?

The seconds ticked by and we continued to stare at each other, indirectly through the reflection. Her hand remained poised on the lid of the laptop, it twitched briefly and she blinked, keeping her eyes closed a second longer than is usual. I felt sure she was ready to slam the lid shut and rid herself of this vision of me. Was she afraid of me? I suppose even in a dream a woman would be frightened of a stranger appearing in her room. Who was she? I wondered. *Naomi,* came the reply in my head.

"Naomi?" I didn't realise I'd spoken until I saw her eyes widen in the reflection. Barely a whisper came from her exquisite mouth as she responded. She shook her head vigorously and rubbed her palms over her face, a few urgent mutterings reached me but I couldn't determine the language only that she was upset

"Perdono?"

"No, no no! This isn't real Naomi. You're dreaming or hallucinating or some-bloody-thing!"

English! She speaks English. Did I speak English?

"Mi scusi signorina, are you alright?" *It seems that I did!* As dreams went, this was a strange one but I tried to take my lead from her. I wondered what the purpose of it was. I always thought a dream was your subconscious trying to work out a problem but right now, I had no idea what this particular one had to do with anything. I wished she would turn around, I was starting to feel uncomfortable watching this woman from behind. It was too hard to tell what was going on just looking at her back and her reflection in the screen.

"It's not real, wake up! It's not real. No, no, no…" She was almost shouting now.

A frown crossed my brow, she - Naomi, really did seem upset. I felt dreadful for causing her distress. Was she yelling at *me* to wake up? I had to admit I wouldn't be too sorry to leave this dream but for the fact I liked looking at her. She was pretty, even in this anguished state her long brown hair tousled and slightly wild looking, fell around her face and just past her shoulders. She had a small but well-proportioned frame, petite and cute. I couldn't tell what colour her eyes were because I had only seen them reflected on the black screen so far. I found myself really wanting to see them.

She rose from her chair, her back facing me. I found myself emulating her anticipatory stance, full of nervous tension. Her hands balled into fists and her shoulders rose and fell heavily as she inhaled and exhaled attempting to calm herself. Turning slowly on her heel, I came face to face with the prettiest pair of olive green eyes.

"Joe?"

And then it ended. Blackness and nothing. In an instant she disappeared from my vision and with it went my whole sense of awareness.

CHAPTER four

Don't Believe The Psych!

I couldn't think what to say. The beanbag chair became uncomfortable and I began to rub my thumb in circles on the palm of my other hand, it was a nervous habit of mine.

"Take your time Naomi and start from the beginning. Whenever you're ready." Dr Blanchard sat across from me on a beanbag that matched mine. I think the beanbags were supposed to help her patients relax but I just felt stupid. Now that I was here and going over recent events in my head, I just wanted to laugh at myself. I kept trying to find a starting point to the conversation but everything sounded hilarious in my head. I felt a giggle bubbling in my chest but I smothered it down. Crikey, if I did start laughing she would definitely think me a loon!

"OK so, I've been reading this book, well it's a manuscript actually and anyway, there's this character in it, Joe, and he's... well kind of amazing, perfect really," I paused for breath, "I mean I really like him, his character I mean." I paused again and chewed my bottom lip, Dr Blanchard sat squished in her beanbag, listening politely. Her expression was neutral but I bet she was wondering what the hell I was jabbering on about. "Look, I probably just need some sleeping tablets or something, I don't know?" She still didn't speak. "It's just that I did something I shouldn't have, I didn't mean to, I just... I was practicing that's all and things got a bit out of hand so, I don't know...maybe it's the guilt making it happen. Do you think?" I asked Dr Blanchard.

"The guilt is making what happen exactly?" She wasn't looking at me anymore but was scribbling something down on her pad.

"The visions." I stated.

"Can you tell me more, Naomi?"

"I keep seeing him. Hearing him. Weird stuff is happening and I think I'm having some sort of mental breakdown."

"Seeing who?" She was still scribbling.

"Joe." I said simply. Dr Blanchard finally looked up and cleared her throat.

"So, you think you're seeing a fictional character, is that right?"

"Yes." I said.

"And you feel guilty because you did something? Can you tell me what?"

"Well, I re-wrote the manuscript, the original. I changed it to…" oh Christ! How could I say 'to include myself' without sounding like the biggest narcissist in the world? I didn't sound crazy, I just sounded like an idiot. *Well, here goes nothing!*

"…to include myself." I cringed inwardly.

"Because you like Joe so much?" Dr Blanchard asked.

"I suppose so." I muttered at the floor. The doctor's pen flew furiously across her notepad, the constant scraping noise of pen on paper began to irritate me.

"I see. How does that make you feel?"

"Ridiculous." I stated. Dr Blanchard nodded without even looking at me and continued to write more notes. *I'm going to ram that bloody pen where the sun doesn't shine,* I thought.

"Naomi, can you tell me what happens when you have a vision? Do you pass out? When does it happen exactly?"

"No, I've never passed out. Um let me think, I had the thing on the notepad with the names," I began ticking them off on my fingers as I recounted the incidents, "I was asleep then but I saw it when I woke up, I'm not sure if that counts?" Dr Blanchard smiled at me and inclined her head to signal for me to continue. "Then I heard him *and* saw him at Starbucks that time but… Oh! My neighbour saw him too, at least I think she did. She saw a man with silver hair outside our building."

"Joe has silver hair?"

"Yes. Salt and pepper I think it's called."

"Mmm. Please continue."

"Oh and I think I heard him speak once when I was falling asleep." I counted off three so far. "The time in the shower when I, ugh…" *Oh dear God, shut the fuck up Naomi!*

"When you what?"

I swear my cheeks were on fire. I shook my head,

"Nothing, it doesn't matter."

The doctor put down her pen and leaned forward, as much as she could do, in her beanbag. She looked almost bent double. I fought another urge to giggle.

"Naomi, if this is going to work, you have to trust me. You came to me for help but I can't help you if you're holding back. I can assure you, whatever it is you think you can't say, I've heard it all. The human mind is a complex thing, it can make you think all sorts of weird and wonderful things. Whatever you need to tell me to help you feel better, just say it." She ended her sermon with a reassuring smile. Although I didn't as much feel reassured as patronised. Suddenly, I didn't want to share my most intimate 'Joe' experiences with her.

"No, really. It's nothing. I made a mistake with that time."

She nodded at me again and wrote something else down. That damn pen would most definitely be visiting somewhere unpleasant very soon.

"OK, anymore incidents…that you feel you *can* share?" My eyes narrowed into a frown. *Sly bitch.*

"I saw him, face to face. In my flat. He spoke to me…in Italian." I added. *There, put that in your pipe and smoke it!* The irony of the smugness with which I'd delivered my admission wasn't lost on me. Somehow I'd gone from needing her to confirm that I'd been hallucinating, to wanting to prove her wrong, to prove to her Joe was real. Or maybe this was just another sick trick my subconscious was playing on me. Maybe I really was going crazy!

"What did he say?"

"I've no idea, I don't speak Italian. He did say my name though and asked if I was alright."

"But you don't speak Italian."

"No, he said that in English." Was she insinuating I was lying now? My foot began tapping on the floor in rapid succession, the speed of my thumb circling my palm increased.

"Are you anxious, Naomi?"

"A little yes." I shoved my hands under my legs.

"Why do you think you feel like that?"

"I don't know! You tell me? You're the fucking psych!" I blurted out.

"Are you feeling angry right now?" She had assumed a neutral, relaxed pose, her pen and pad were on the side table and her hands rested palms down on the beanbag next to her knees. I didn't reply. "Do you think you're angry at me?"

I shrugged, "Maybe."

"Is it because I'm not telling you what you want to hear?"

"What do I want to hear?"

"I think you're hoping I tell you that it's all OK and that you just need some rest, that Joe isn't real and you're just under a lot of pressure right now. Am I right?" She waited for my reply but none came, "The thing is Naomi, there are clearly some issues or you wouldn't have come back to see me. It's been over a year since our last session, I'm concerned that your ex-husband's engagement may have triggered off your depression. I remember you had a difficult time dealing with your divorce. Here's what I think, I think the news has had a deeper impact on you than you realise. The fact that your fantasy man has silver hair, suggests a yearning for stability. The hair colour represents the older, wiser generation. Joe is fictional, which means he is reliable, he won't betray you or let you down. He is always there when you need him. He's as attractive as your imagination can make him and he's devoted to you," she paused to take a breath, "I think you're creating the illusion of Joe to counteract the insecurity you're feeling right now and that is not healthy."

"So you're saying I'm using Joe as an emotional crutch?" I asked.

"For want of a better phrase, yes, I'd say that seems very likely." I hated to admit it but what she said sort of made sense, "I'd like you to come back and see me next week. I'll go over my notes and then we can discuss the issue further and see how to progress. How does that sound?" I blew out a breath and just nodded. "In the meantime I'd recommended you get out and socialise, be around friends and family and make sure you rest, obviously," she smiled, "maybe take that holiday to New Zealand too," she added as an afterthought.

I wiggled my way out of the beanbag chair with the help of Dr Blanchard, she was obviously an expert at getting out of the damn things. I still felt ridiculous. I thanked her and made another appointment with her secretary on the way out.

On my way back home, I mulled over her observations. The more I thought about it, the more it made sense that I would use Laney's book and Joe as my support. Hadn't books always been my means of escape? I guess I had been quite upset about Iain after all. I needed to get back in touch with Immy and ask her about visiting again. Hopefully Skype wouldn't be an arse this time and I could find out what she'd been shouting at me for the last time we'd spoken. I really should speak to Mum and Dad too, see if they were still willing to shout me a plane ticket. Mum would probably give me the 'I told you so' look but I suppose I could stomach it when the prospect of a three-week holiday on the other side of the world was on offer. Besides, if it got me out of the doldrums it'd be worth it. They weren't so bad as parents go, I wasn't being fair to them at all, and they loved me and had always been there to catch me, even in my darkest days after Iain.

I began to feel excited about visiting Immy and couldn't wait to get home to Skype her. I didn't even pause for coffee when I got in but went straight to the laptop. The ringing sound virtually sang from the screen and my brain flashed back to the last time I'd sat at this desk to speak to my sister. What had she been pointing like a mad woman at? I wish the sound hadn't have screwed up, it'd had bugged me not knowing. Of course I'd lied to Dr Blanchard about not passing out after a vision because, that's exactly what had happened when I had seen Joe in my flat. I realised now that I must have gotten myself in such a state, hyperventilating, that that's what caused me to lose consciousness shortly after. I wasn't going to let anyone be privy to that little nugget of information though, I didn't want to look too much like an idiot, admitting you were in love with a made-up person was bad enough.

No one was picking up at Immy's end. I let it ring a couple more times then hung up. Checking the time, I realised she was probably asleep. Disappointed, I called Mum on my mobile, again, no answer. I sent her a quick text saying to call me when she was free and found myself at a loss what to do next. There's was no escaping the huge backlog of work I had. It was with great reluctance I conceded to the task and rooted out the list of jobs I'd fallen behind on. My business accounts also needed updating, I despised accounts, tedious but sadly necessary. Did I really have to 'adult' today? This was going to need coffee, lots of coffee.

The walk to Starbucks was quite pleasant, the heatwave had dissipated a little but the weather remained warm and dry. A light breeze blew making the leaves on the trees dance and strands of loose hair tickle my face. At the coffee house I bought a large latte and a brownie, which I happily munched on the way home. Not exactly great for my waistline but treats were essential when facing an afternoon of number crunching and proof reading. I'd chosen one of my most boring jobs, a local business directory, to proof. It was one of my tightest deadlines so I would just have to knuckle down and get it done. I made up my mind that I'd finish proofing Laney's manuscript, as soon as possible with no more self-indulgent rewrites. Then I'd tell her I was unable to accept any future books. I needed to do some damage control with Laney, the last email she had sent hadn't exactly been friendly. Freelance work was hard won and the last thing I needed was an author sending out negative reports about my professional work ethics. Dr Blanchard was right, I'd been using Joe as a crutch to counteract all the shit that wasn't working for me in my personal life. It was time to get back to the real world and sort myself out. No Joe today. Maybe no more Joe, ever.

CHAPTER
five

An Unexpected Dinner Guest

Mum had called me back within an hour, she'd been and bought food and had invited me over for lunch on Sunday. It was only a thirty-minute walk to my parents' house and I had stopped off at the off license to buy a few bottles of specialty beers for Dad, Hobgoblin and Speckled Hen were his favourites. Mum didn't drink and as I'd decided I was off the booze for a while, I didn't buy wine. The new no alcohol policy had been decided after my talk with Dr Blanchard, it was part of my life detox and path back to normalcy, whatever that was. It'd only been a few days and even though I didn't drink that much usually anyway, I felt a little brighter and less tired today. Whether that was anything to do with the lack of alcohol or just the fact I'd made my mind up to be positive about everything, I wasn't sure but whatever the cause, it was working.

Dad opened the door a few seconds after I rang the doorbell, a big cheesy grin on his face

"Hello sweetheart! Come give you're old Dad a hug?" He opened his arms wide, welcoming me in.

"Dad. I've missed you. Why didn't you come to see me last week with Mum?" I wrapped my arms around his ample, ever expanding frame and squeezed him tight. The bottles of beer clinked together in the plastic carrier bag I carried.

"Oh! What have you brought me chuckles?" He wiggled his eyebrows in delight.

I presented the bag to him. "Beer!" I laughed. "And what is this?" I asked, patting his belly. "I thought Mum had you on a diet?"

"Ahh, yes! Salads and more salads," he pulled a face of disgust, "rabbit food! Don't tell her but I have a secret stash in the shed, shh!" He put a finger to his lips and winked at me.

"Dad, you're terrible! She'll notice at some point. That woman doesn't miss a trick."

"Yes, she will but until then I'll keep enjoying my Mars bars thank you very much. I've earned them." His belly wobbled as he laughed and I had a mad thought that he'd make an excellent Father Christmas. If he still wanted to do something after retirement, it'd be a great temporary job over the holiday season. Maybe I'd suggest it during lunch. It would certainly suit him, he was the typical rosy-cheeked, jolly old soul. Everyone always had a good word about my father. He was hardworking, loyal, stalwart old

Charlie - loved by all. My mother doted on him, even though she made out that he got under her feet most of the time, I knew she wouldn't have it any other way.

I heard her call from inside the house, "Is that our girl, Charles? Come on through love, the dinner's almost ready." The smell of roast lamb flooded my nostrils and instantly made my stomach rumble, and my mouth water.

"Oh my god, Mum that smells delicious! I'm absolutely starving." I hugged her from behind as she stood at the hob, stirring the gravy.

"Hello, Love. I did your favourite." She smiled indulgently. "I'm betting it's been a while since you ate a roast, am I right?" I nodded enthusiastically. Roast lamb was indeed my favourite and it looked like Mum had done all the proper trimmings too, roast potatoes, steamed veg and homemade gravy! My stomach growled with longing.

"Do you want me to do anything?" I offered.

"No, love. It's all ready but for the gravy. Go sit with your father and I'll shout you both when it's ready."

"OK, thanks!" I kissed her cheek and went through to the lounge. Dad was watching the footy on the telly. It was the charity shield, pre-season game between both Manchester teams.

"Who's winning, City or United?" I asked him, knowing he'd be rooting for Manchester United, he was a true red.

"Nil - Nil at the minute, playing like a bunch of blind mice though. Bloody terrible passing, I hope they improve in the second half." He shook his head at the TV. I settled onto the sofa, curling one leg under me and picked up the newspaper to glance through. Dad continued to grumble at the state of play, making some comments about the current team Manager. It made me smile, he loved his football, never missed a game if he could help it. I hated football but would engage in the commentary because it pleased him. Only a few minutes passed before Mum shouted us to the table for dinner.

"Looks amazing as always Mum." I said, she beamed at the compliment and placed the gravy boat in the centre of the table. The spread really was amazing. I only really ate a roast dinner if Mum cooked or I went out somewhere for a pub lunch. So, it was something of a treat to sit down to a home cooked meal. I tucked in enthusiastically, making noises of appreciation as I ate. Halfway through I decided to bring up the topic of their planned trip to see my sister, Imogen.

"So, I was thinking, if you don't mind and the offer of a ticket is still available, I'd like to go to New Zealand with you both?"

Dad grinned and put his fork down to pat my hand. That was his way of saying yes. Mum flashed me a brief half-smile and said,

"What happened to your deadlines? I thought you were busy."

"Yeah, I was... I am, still busy but I managed to get caught up a bit this weekend. I stayed up late the last three nights, so..."

"Oh. Well. If you still want to come I suppose it'd be nice. It means your father working a bit more overtime of course."

"Oh shush now, Linda. Of course she can come, don't be daft." My Dad looked at Mum. "I was always planning on you coming anyway sweetheart, I've already booked in a few extra hours so it'll cover the ticket, although you might have to bring your own spending money?"

"Yeah course Dad, thank you, I can cover that part obviously." I looked over at my Mother, "Mum, I promise I'll pay you back when I have the spare cash. I know you don't like Dad working much now. I appreciate it, really."

"No, it's fine, don't worry about it. We're just pleased you decided to come. Imogen will be happy too."

"Oh Crap, Immy!" I'd completely forgotten to call her back. After I'd tried to Skype her the other day and she hadn't answered, I'd seen a text from her later that day saying '*You Ok? Been worried sick! Text me ASAP.*'

"What's wrong?" Mum asked, "Is your sister alright? I haven't spoken to her for a few days."

I put my hand on my forehead and grimaced, "Yeah, she's fine don't worry. It's just something I need to clear up with her that's all. I meant to talk to her sooner and forgot. Shit."

"Darling, can you please not swear at the dinner table? It's very unladylike." Mum's chastising tone irked me slightly, I was twenty-nine not twelve. Dad smoothed it over by rolling his eyes at me and winking before stuffing another roast potato in his mouth and patting his large belly.

It turned out to quite a non-eventful and pleasant family lunch for once. Dad and I cleared the table and I told them both to go sit down and relax while I washed the dishes. I could hear Dad getting back into the game, there must only be another few minutes left. He'd missed most the second half through dinner- I wondered what the score was. Mum came through to the kitchen with her empty cup,

"Your Father's getting wound up now, penalty shootout." She tutted and gave a little shake of her head.

"Oh dear. He'll not be happy if United lose then."

"No, I'll never hear the end of it. How are you doing love?"

"Almost finished."

"Lovely, thank you dear. Don't bother drying them, I prefer to let them air dry, it's more hygienic. Tut! Just listen at him! Does he really think shouting at them will make a difference?" Her words, although intended to scold, were coloured with affection. Half the time, when I listened to them bicker with each other, I couldn't tell if they were purposeful jibes or it had just become habit after so many years of marriage. I supposed one just settled into a routine after the honeymoon period and you just got so used to each other's company. I knew they loved each other, they still held hands walking down the street and Dad still surprised Mum with the occasional bunch of flowers. She called him an old romantic, I guess I got that trait from him. Mum was a bit more pragmatic, something that I seemed to lack.

"I've just got the roasting tin to wash now, I left it to soak for a while."

"Well, when you've done that I'll serve up the trifle, Dad's been on a diet and he's done ever so well. I thought I'd let him have a little treat."

I grinned, "Oh I'm sure he'll appreciate that." She was going to kill him when she found out about his secret sweet stash!

"OH FOR GODS SAKE!" We heard Dad yell from the lounge.

"Whoops, I don't think it's going quite how he wanted it to." I made a face and Mum laughed. She made her way back to him and I reached for the roasting pan. Just as I started scrubbing, the sound of something breaking reached my ears. Then a high pitched yelp and a clattering, like something big had fallen over.

"Hey! Is everything alright?" I shouted, "Dad hasn't thrown his beer at the referee has he?" I laughed to myself, drying my hands on the towel, I started towards the front of the house to see what had happened. My guess was dad had gotten over excited and had knocked over the side table or something. Then I heard my mother begin to scream.

"Naomi! Call an ambulance! Naomi!"

My heart lurched. "WHAT? Mum, what's happened?" I was running now.

"Charles? Charles? Oh dear god no! Charles, love, wake up."

I made it to the front room and found my Mother on her knees, shaking the unmoving body of my Father. He lay face down on the floor, the side table and its contents were sprawled across the rug. The bottle of Speckled Hen had smashed and I could smell the beer. The pale liquid spread across the floor in a pool of froth next to my father's unresponsive corpse, like blood gushing from a wound. My Mother was trying to turn him over but he was a too heavy. All I could do was stare at him. His lifeless eyes were open and I was looking directly into them. I pulled out my phone and called the emergency services, my actions and speech mechanical. I was numb.

"Mum, they're on their way." kneeling beside her sobbing frame as she still attempted to rouse my Dad. "Here, move out the way Mum!" I settled by my father's side and tried desperately to revive him, putting to use all I could remember of CPR. I alternated breath with chest compressions how I thought it should be performed but nothing seemed to be working. He was gone, I knew it but I didn't have it in me to tell Mum. So I carried on, hoping I could at least give him a chance while waiting for the paramedics. Mum sat next to me on the floor and just cried his name. The ambulance arrived a few minutes later and the paramedic, after making his routine assessments and briefly trying to revive Dad, pronounced him dead and called the coroner. The paramedic and his colleague placed my Dad's body in a body bag and lifted him onto a trolley while we waited for the coroner to arrive.

Mum's sobs had gradually subsided and she was now sat on a chair in the dining room with a cup of tea, not drinking it. The paramedic came through to talk to us,

"Coroner's here Mrs Douglas." He said to Mum. She just nodded and got up to follow him.

"Do you want me to deal with it?" I asked her,

"No." was all the reply she gave. Then she paused at the door and said "Call Imogen?"

Oh Jesus! My sister. "Of course, Mum." It would be around 6am her time. She should be home. This was not a call I was looking forward to.

I rang from the landline. Every ring sounded too loud, it made me cringe.

"Mum? Why are you ringing so early? What's up?" Came Imogen's voice down the line.

"Immy, it's me."

"Naomi? Why are you at Mum's? Oh my God, what the hell happened the other night? I've been so worried about you! I was freaking out but then since no one rang or text me to tell me you were attacked or abducted I guessed it must've been a new boyfriend you forgot to tell me about. Bloody hell sis, you kept that one quiet, and there you were telling me you had no happy ending? I bet that went down well with him eh? So, what's his name?"

"What?" I was stunned. I completely forgot the purpose of my call. So Imogen had seen him too? I thought back to her mad gesturing during our last Skype session. The sound and picture had gotten distorted and I thought she'd been trying to tell me something. When I had seen Joe's reflection it had crossed my mind afterwards that perhaps Immy had seen him but that was before I'd spoken to Dr Blanchard, when I had thought he was real. Now Immy was telling me she had seen him? How was that possible? I heard my sister speaking but wasn't listening, was I imagining this conversation? Had the shock of Dad's death caused me to experience another attack of crazy? Dad's death. Dad was dead. Shit.

"Dad died, Immy." I blurted out. My sister fell silent mid conversation. "He had a heart attack. I'm… I'm here now. I was here when he…when it happened."

"Oh my God, what? No, not Daddy, no!" Her wracking sobs faded into the background and I heard a male voice in their place,

"Hello? Naomi? This is Fletcher, Imogen's partner. Can you tell me what happened? She's too upset to talk."

"Oh…hi, Fletcher." This was an awkward time to be having my first conversation with him. "Um, our Dad had a massive heart attack just after dinner. He um…he didn't make it. Listen is Immy OK? I can hear her crying. I'm sorry, Mum asked me to tell Imogen, I don't know what she wants to do? Will she be able to come home for his…funeral?"

That last word came out as a strangled sob. *Funeral.* It seemed so final. Especially when my Dad still lay on a trolley in the other room.

"I'm so sorry, Naomi. Please pass my condolences to your Mother? Imogen is devastated. I'll make sure she gets home to be with you both, don't worry."

"Thank you Fletcher. I appreciate that. Tell her I'll look after Mum and I love her please?"

"Yeah, of course. I'm going to see to her now. We'll call tomorrow, I'm sure once she's calmed down a bit she'll want to talk."

"OK, yeah. Talk tomorrow. Bye." I hung up only to hear my mother's renewed cries replace my sisters. I went back through to the lounge where the coroner was rubbing my Mother's arm sympathetically as the paramedics wheeled my Father's body out of the house. He handed her some papers and followed the body out, leaving Mum and me alone. We both watched through the window as the ambulance drove away, taking Dad's body to the morgue. I would need to contact a funeral parlour tomorrow and begin arrangements. Where would I even begin? I had no idea and couldn't think about it now. Mum was in a state, she looked on the verge of collapse herself.

"What do you need? What do you want to do?" I asked her.

"I think I just want to lie down, love. I'm exhausted."

"Do you need me to stay over?"

"Would you?" She looked so small and vulnerable, I hardly recognised her.

"I'll make up the spare bed. You go lie down. Shout me if you need me OK?"

She nodded once and dragged her weary self-up the stairs. It was an effort just watching her. It was then that I noticed the mess, the table Dad had knocked over and the broken beer bottle still lay on the floor. I righted the table and got the dustpan and brush from the pantry. The rug reeked of stale beer. I would hate that smell forever. A newspaper rested on the arm of his chair, open at the crossword he'd half completed. The sight of his handwriting pulled at my heart so hard I felt it like a physical blow.

"Oh Dad." Clutching the paper to my chest I let the tears fall unchecked. My Daddy was gone. The only man I could ever rely on had been taken from me. I had never felt pain like it. I crawled into his armchair, hugging my knees as my heart broke. I never made it to the spare room, sheer exhaustion claimed me in the end. I cried until there was no fight left in me. As the moon and the stars peeked through cloud, my world seemed darker than ever. I would never forget the day that Death came to dinner.

CHAPTER
six

Joe

I was starting to feel like a stranger in my own life. It was
another dream about her. This one was strange. It wasn't
the dream that was out of focus, it was me. I could see her,
the one called Naomi but it was distorted, as if I were
looking through a dirty window and the sound was
muffled. Her sobs still reached my ears though. She
appeared to be curled up on a chair, it was dark but it
didn't feel or look like the room I'd seen her in before.
The sound of her cries tugged at my heart like nothing I
had known. I felt drawn to this woman and the immediate
need to comfort her overwhelmed me. I never
remembered my other dreams…at least I don't think I did,
only the ones about her. I had that same feeling as before,
I remembered my life but it didn't feel like reality. The

need to be here, with her, was stronger every time this happened. Each time I found myself experiencing these bizarre episodes, it felt more and more real. Then why did this one feel wrong?

I reached out to comfort her but my arms turned to smoke. There was little or no solidity to them and when I started moving, swirling transparent colours replaced what should have been flesh and bone. I tried to touch my hands together but one went straight through the other. When I looked at my feet they weren't even on the floor, I was floating.

"Naomi?" I said. I heard the voice in my head but it came out of my mouth like the rush of an autumn breeze, a wordless whisper of sound.

She continued to cry, her heart-wrenching sobs echoing all around me, fading in and out. I struggled to correlate the sound with where she sat, it was disconnected and disjointed. I didn't understand this dream at all, it really was the strangest thing I had ever experienced.

"Naomi, please? Can you hear me?" The attempt at speech resulted in the same incoherent gush of air as before. The frustration of not being able to communicate made me feel utterly useless. Maybe if I moved closer to her she would hear me? I was clearly supposed to interact with this woman because I dreamed about her all the time now. For what purpose, I had no idea but I knew I needed to speak with her, I wanted to speak with her. I wanted to know about her and why she was in my head.

So how was I to do this? I had no 'feet' to speak of, just a vague smoky outline that swirled about a foot off the floor. I had to find a way of moving towards her. Perhaps if I concentrated my mind instead of trying to move normally it might work. I closed my eyes and focused on moving my body forward. When I opened my eyes, instead of being closer to her, I was further away.

"Aaahh! Porco dio! - Goddamnit!" This was annoying. I was torn between wanting to comfort her and wanting to just wake up and be done with this seemingly pointless escapade.

Naomi shifted around in the chair so her face was more visible. Just like before I was overwhelmed with a feeling of recognition, of knowing more of her than I could immediately comprehend. Scouring my memories, trying to place where I knew her from, I studied her beautiful, tear stained face. Her heavily lashed lids were closed, salty droplets clung to them like morning dew. I ached to kiss her sorrow away, If only I could make her see me.

I wondered what had happened to make her so upset. The last time I'd seen her she had acted as if I were imaginary, which seemed bizarre because it was clearly the other way around, she was in *my* dream. I watched her and waited, unable to do anything else.

Her sobs subsided gradually and her breathing became shallow and regular, she had fallen asleep. Without knowing how, I found myself inching closer, it was like she *breathed* me in, and every inhalation drew me further forward. The fascination with this strangely familiar woman was intoxicating. Just as an artist knows his muse, I found that I knew every line and gentle curve of her face. Distorted as the scene before me was, if I closed my eyes, a perfect picture of her etched itself in my mind with consummate clarity. How could this be?

"Daddy..." she whimpered, "...don't go..."

She was crying over her Father then? Whatever had happened, it must have been recent, and her grief was new and raw. Glancing around the shadowy room, I noticed picture frames hanging above an obscure looking fireplace. The faces of the people in the frames drifted in and out of focus but I could discern a family portrait of four people. Two of the four were young women, the other an older couple. One of the women had the same colouring as Naomi, and although her features were indistinct, I knew it was her. Other things littered the mantelpiece: a china plate, a small vase and what appeared to be a document propped up behind it. It was unreadable at first but as I concentrated my gaze a few words stood out, *'Charles Henry Douglas,'* her father? *'Time of death...'* so, it *was* grief that caused her suffering. I understood now, I remembered the loss of my own father when I was very young. It seemed but a vague memory at this moment, I presumed because it was so long ago, and that I had been a child, I maybe wouldn't have understood what had happened. I tried to picture my father's face in my mind but all that came to me was a fuzzy silhouette of a man, nothing recognisable. It saddened me that I couldn't recall what my father looked like. How could I empathise with Naomi in her grief, if I couldn't find the source of my own? Why did it matter so much to me that I wanted to share in her sorrow?

Looking back upon her face, I puzzled it over. There was no denying there was a connection of some sort but I had yet to discover what it could be and what the reason for all of this was. Perhaps I could gain more clues from my surroundings? The thought had no sooner occurred to me when I felt that familiar blackness looming, its stealthy approach meant this was ending. A multitude of protests readied on my tongue but I never got the chance to utter them. The scene before me became murkier, colours drained into greys and a final whisper reached me through the fog- her swansong,

"Stay…"

And then I was gone.

CHAPTER
seven

There Were Never Such Devoted Sisters

Fletcher had made good on his promise and made sure Imogen got home in time for our dad's funeral. Not only that but he'd made sure she could stay for a month to help Mum and I sort out all the official, legal procedures we needed to go through, registering his death, informing the life insurance company and sorting through Dads things. This last part had surprised me as it had only been three weeks since he'd gone. I thought Mum would have wanted to hold onto it all for a while at least.

"What about this jacket Mum?" I asked her, holding it up.

"Charity bag love, it's a good jacket, I'm sure someone will be glad of it." I folded it carefully and briefly touched the tweed fabric to my face, it smelled of him. My throat closed as grief threatened to engulf me but I swallowed it down, determined to stay strong for my mother. I gave the jacket a loving stroke before placing it gently in the black bin liner my mum was using for the donations. Bags of my father's belongings started to pile up around the room, a lifetime of memories wrapped up and burrowed away in cheap black plastic. It didn't seem right. Mum sat rummaging through an old wooden box full of knick-knacks. She had something clasped tightly in her hand.

"What's that you have?" I sat down next to her on the bed and she passed me the object. "Dad's watch?"

"One of them, look" I took the box from her and looked inside, it was filled with watches.

"How come he had this many? I didn't know dad collected watches?"

"He didn't collect them, they're all the watches he's ever owned since we got married. Birthday gifts, wedding anniversaries, he kept them all."

"Wow, Mum…that's amazing, did you know he had these?" I picked a few up in turn and looked at them, my parents had been married a little over forty years so there were some old timepieces here.

"I didn't know he'd kept any of them, the sentimental old fool." She choked back a sob and dabbed at her eyes. Immy joined us on the bed and we both put our arms around our mother while she cried. This rare moment of mother/daughter/sibling solidarity was strangely comforting. Physical contact from my mother was hard won, with me anyway. Immy was the golden girl in Mum's eyes so I gleaned an almost morbid satisfaction from our shared grief. It had taken Dad's death for my mother and I to share a genuine feeling of togetherness. Dad would be smiling right now if he was here.

"Mum, do you want to keep them?" Immy asked.

"I don't think so love. What use are they to me anyway? I don't need trinkets to remember him by. He's gone but I have him in here, always." She said and placed her hand over her heart.

"Do you mind if I have them?" I needed the trinkets, I couldn't believe Mum didn't want at least one of them. I'd keep them safe for her, sure she'd change her mind at some point. In all honesty, it seemed a bit callous getting rid of Dad's stuff so soon. Or maybe it was just me struggling with letting him go. Dad had always been the more affectionate of the two so it was hardly surprising to find evidence of his sentimentality stashed away. Dad and I were the same, he loved my mother unconditionally and with his whole heart. When I loved, I loved hard and with everything I had. Unfortunately, it resulted in a lot of heartbreak for me so far but I knew of no other way to be. I hoped one day I'd be lucky like Mum and find someone who loved me the way Dad had loved her. I needed to keep those watches as a reminder that real love was attainable, even for someone like me.

"Have them if you want them dear, Dad would like that." She patted my arm, blew her nose and cleared her throat.

"Ready to carry on?" Imogen asked Mum,

"Yes, love. Lots to get done before…" she stopped short and glanced at my sister. The poignancy of the look didn't escape my notice.

"Before what?" I looked at my mother, she bit her lip. "Mum?" My mother stayed nervously silent so I raised a questioning eyebrow at my sister instead. "Well?"

"Naomi, we were going to tell you before I left for New Zealand next week. Mum wanted to give you time to…to feel better."

"Tell me what? I'm not sick. What do you mean feel better?" I got the feeling I wasn't going to like this, at all. The looks passing between Immy and Mum made me realise I was very much out of the loop. They'd clearly been discussing something that I wasn't included in. That hurt. I was the older sister for God's sake. I should be the first to know!

"Well dear, Dad and I …we…had planned to go anyway, for a holiday," She paused, a slightly hesitant placatory smile on her lips.

"To New Zealand? Yeah, I know. So, you're still going then, is that it?" I asked.

Silence.

"Oh for goodness sake!" I said, rolling my eyes. "Just spit it out, what?"

"Mum's moving," Imogen blurted, "she's coming to live with us- me and Fletcher." There was a pause where the three of us stood in awkward silence, unmoving. Mum's eyes flicked nervously over to Immy and back towards me. The tension in the air crackled and boiled under the surface, threatening to erupt. Of course, the eruption just had to be my doing, I didn't do calm very well.

"I'm sorry what? You're moving? Since when?" I was incredulous! This was massive news and yet neither my mother nor my sister had thought to even discuss it with me.

"Don't get mad Naomi." said Mum.

"I'm not getting mad!" Admittedly my voice was now raised.

"Calm down Sis!" Imogen said.

"No! I bloody won't calm down. Why am I the last person to know about this? When was this decided?" I demanded.

"Your father and I have…*had*," she corrected, "discussed it months ago. We were going to use the holiday to look around and see what we thought of the place. We had already applied for the visas and everything, just in case. We didn't want to waste time if we decided on the move, we wanted to go as soon as we could."

"And no one thought it might be a nice idea to tell me first? Are you fucking kidding me?"

"We wanted to, honestly! It's just with what's going on with you lately…you know?" Immy shrugged her shoulders in my direction.

"And what exactly *is* going on with me?" I was very curious to know. Immy shook her head.

"Now isn't really the time to discuss this Sis."

"Au contraire!" The biting sarcasm dripped from my tongue, laced with acid. "I think it's the perfect ruddy time quite frankly, I'm all ears! Really interested in what you and *Mother* have been saying about me behind my back?"

"Please stop dear, I can't deal with your issues right now." Mum begged but I was too far gone to back down. Betrayal raged inside of me and began to boil over from the volcano of fucked up emotions that was me. "Naomi!

You're twenty-nine years old, you're a grown woman with your own life and you're wasting it! I can't deal with these *outbursts* you have and now the lying too? I just don't understand you. Dad and I wanted to spend our…our last years," she couldn't finish and started crying again.

"Nice, Naomi!" Imogen scolded. She put her hand on Mum's shoulder in sympathetic gesture. They were joining forces against me. Just a few minutes ago we had sat together, the three of us in consolation and unity, I had felt like a useful and needed member of our family for once. Now it was painfully clear that had been mere illusion. I wasn't part of anything, not really, not now Dad was gone. The secret plans I had not been privy to, the conspiracy between them both that I had so purposefully been excluded from, spoke volumes. I was an outsider. I was the black sheep and my opinions meant shit. The fact that my Dad, the one person I trusted, had also chosen to exclude me, was like salt in the wound.

"Oh right. I see. I get left in the dark about my parents emigrating to another country, Dad dies and I'm only *just* hearing about it because Mum slipped up and *I'm* the guilty one? How the fuck does that work? And *lying*? What the hell am I lying about?" I was furious beyond reason, I buried the pang of guilt I'd felt for making Mum cry under the pile of resentment I felt for them both.

"You know what," Imogen said, I did not like her accusatory tone. "I've tried to be patient with you because I know how you get. It's just like before… after Iain."

"Just what the hell do you mean by that? What has that idiot got to do with anything?" Now I was really confused.

87

"I told Mum, about your boyfriend…that you won't admit to me he's real, that you're convinced he's some figment of your imagination. Remember?"

"*Joe?* This is about Joe?" I laughed. "Jesus Christ Imogen, first off, I told you that in confidence and secondly, it's Dr Blanchard that told me he's imaginary and I happen to agree with her!"

"I *saw* him Naomi! He was in your flat, standing right behind you!"

"Then perhaps it's YOU that needs your head read! Ever think of that?" I could not believe she was bringing this up in front of Mum, although by the sound of it she'd already discussed it with her anyway. My sister and I hadn't had much time alone to talk since she arrived back in England, with the funeral and everything else it'd been difficult but she'd taken me to one side one morning before our mum got up and asked me to tell her about my new man. When we'd discussed it, I concluded it must have been some strange coincidental mix up. I'd had some kind of hallucination and Imogen had seen a shadow reflected in the background that she had mistaken for a person. It was the only logical explanation. She had protested of course but I thought I had managed to persuade her it was due to the darkened room and the camera playing up on the laptop. Clearly I'd been wrong. Instead, it seems she had convinced herself and my mum that I was having a mental breakdown. *Fan-bloody-tastic!* I mean, granted, seeing imaginary book boyfriends wasn't exactly what one would call sane but still. "Why on earth would you think I'd lie about having a boyfriend? More to the point why would I make up some bullshit story about him not being real if he was real?"

"For attention." Mum stated, as if it was already a foregone conclusion.

"Attention? Are you serious? Oh my lord! I'm not a child!"

"See this is why we didn't want to tell you yet, you're so…sensitive…Mum and I thought you needed more time." Imogen said.

"Sensitive? Ha ha! Sensitive? My father just died! So please, tell me how am I supposed to be?"

"He's my Dad too." Imogen replied.

"Yeah, but apparently you're not a fuck up like me eh? *You* are mentally capable of helping plan our parent's future all by your pretty little lonesome! Right?" I raised my arms, palms up towards the ceiling, emphasising the sarcasm in my question. "Well. That's just fabulous isn't it! I might as well just bugger off home now then eh? I mean it's not like anyone needs *my* help with anything."

"Naomi, don't!"

"Don't what? Leave? Why not? I'm clearly just the spare part, crack pot daughter that nobody really gives a shit about. So yeah, I'm going home! I'm sure you can manage dearest *sister.*" I virtually spat the last word out, I wanted her to feel the depth of her betrayal. I expected that kind of thing from Mum but not from Immy. Tears threatened to fall but I refused to let them. The anger I felt pushed them aside as I stormed out of my childhood home, slamming the door behind me and shutting out my mother's sobs.

When I arrived at my flat, I let the silence welcome me home. I closed and locked the door, turned off my phone and shut all the curtains. I wanted no disturbances, no contact from anyone. The world and I were enemies right now. In here it was just me alone, with nobody getting in the way of my thinking. The weight of my mother and sister's betrayal pressed down on me so hard I felt suffocated by it. I wasn't perfect, I knew that but I was trying, really trying to make my life better. Had all my efforts been for nothing then, that my family still thought I was incapable of managing myself? I'd leaned on them, especially my parents, after Iain but they were my family, isn't that what family was for? Mum always managed to make me feel like whatever I did, no matter how much effort I expended, it wasn't quite enough. She never seemed satisfied with me somehow. I always came away feeling like I was her biggest disappointment. Dad was the only one who ever told me he was proud of me for scraping myself off the floor and starting again after the divorce. Mum just made me feel I'd let her down for falling so hard, almost as if she thought I had allowed myself to hit rock bottom. I'm sure she took it as a personal insult to her ability to raise a mentally capable adult. She made me feel like an embarrassment, that having a daughter who suffered from depression was something to be ashamed of. That's exactly how I felt now, even worse because my one ally, Imogen, had crossed over to the enemy camp! It had taken guts admitting to having hallucinations and telling her about Dr

Blanchard. I had thought they'd be happy for me that this time, I had at least recognised there was a problem and sought help. I was angry and hurt that I had again been made to feel like the crazy relative in a gothic novel, stashed away in the attic out of public view. To think that they had been treading on eggshells around me and talking about me behind my back. But then that was typical of my mother, she never gave me credit for anything. Immy, I couldn't even think about her right now, Mummy's little favourite and always had been. Well, they could go live happily ever after in New Zealand together and forget about me if that's what they wanted. I had no one and nothing now Dad was gone. I wouldn't feel guilty about being a crap, neglectful daughter anymore. I would do what the hell I liked with who I liked and nobody would be around to care.

The front door buzzer startled me. I ignored it, not feeling very sociable. It buzzed twice more in quick succession followed by one long continuous, insistent ring. I knew who it was and I really didn't want to talk to her. Now was not the time for another argument but she kept ringing the damn buzzer!

"What?" I said curtly into the intercom.

"Naomi, please let me in? I go home next week and I can't leave things like this, Mum's really upset."

"Oh, is she? So, what... you've come to get me to apologise to her? Cause that's not going to happen, so don't bother."

"No. I just don't want to leave like this. Mum's going to be on her own for a few weeks before she comes over, she's going to need you." I found *that* comment hilarious!

"Sorry dear sister, I don't know if you've noticed but I'm not mentally stable enough to look after anyone…not even myself, apparently."

"Oh come on, Naomi! You know that's not what we meant. Even you must admit you're going through the ringer again, we were just worried about you because we love you. You must see that?"

Must I? I thought. *Telling me what to think again!*

"Naomi? I brought Dad's watches."

"Ahh, emotional blackmail is it now?"

"And wine…"

I could use a drink. I buzzed her in. I waited until I heard her tentative knock on my door until I opened it. She stood there, a sheepish smile on her face, holding up a big bottle of Prosecco and an overnight bag.

"I'm not supposed to be drinking." I said. She looked disappointed. Good.

"Oh, I didn't know, sorry. Can I come in?"

"What's the bag for?" Still not letting her step past the door.

"Um, I thought I'd stay over? We could have a girlie night, like we used to?" She waggled the bottle at me and smiled.

"Fine!" OK, I'd take the wine and I'd let her think she was forgiven. "I hope that bottle is chilled? I hate warm wine." She stepped over the threshold grinning.

"I thought you weren't drinking?" She asked playfully. I just tilted my head at her with a raised eyebrow. She laughed. Placing the bottle on the kitchen counter, she walked over to the lounge and dumped her bag. I got out two mismatched wine glasses and popped the cork on the wine. I held up her glass and offered it to her, she took it from me and put it back on the counter.

"Sorry."

"It hurt Immy."

"I know. I'm so sorry. Forgive me?" She hung her head on her chest and pouted. I could never resist her when she acted daft. And although I didn't want them to, my arms wrapped around her in a big sisterly hug. Why was it that the youngest sibling always got away with everything?

"Come on you," I gave her back her wine glass and headed off toward the lounge. "So, what are we watching, Love Actually or Bridesmaids?" I held up the two DVDs for her to choose.

"Bridesmaids! I fancy a laugh."

"Bridesmaids it is then." I supposed I could forget about it for now, although I still burned with resentment inside, she was my baby sister and she was leaving again next week. For my own peace of mind, I couldn't realistically let her leave thinking there was bad blood between us. I pushed aside the hurt for tonight, for my own sake more than hers and carried on as if nothing was broken. This ostrich had her head well and truly stuck in the ground.

We curled up on the sofa, drank wine, ordered a curry and laughed at the film as if we were just two devoted sisters enjoying each other's company and nothing was wrong. But it was, for me at least. The trust was gone. It pained me to know that my own sister, my most loyal friend had spilt my most intimate secret to the one person I least wanted to know about it. It had not been her secret to tell but she'd done it anyway, regardless of her 'good intentions' she had betrayed my trust and I wasn't going to forget that in a hurry.

My sister fell asleep before the end of the film, she had drunk more wine than me and I'd been happy to let her. Her tiny snores indicated my plan had worked, I turned everything off, gathered up the empty glasses and plates and took myself off to bed. Not before covering up Sleeping Beauty with a fluffy throw rug first, I didn't want to neglect my 'sisterly duties' obviously.

I had longed for the solitude of my bedroom. Revelling in the peace the enclosed darkness offered. Reaching for my laptop, I searched for Laney Marsh's email address and composed an email, attached a file and clicked send. There. It was done. I had finally sent her the finished proof of her book 'All the best boys'. One chapter of my life was done with. I'd made the decision to never take on another fiction for proofing again. I'd keep proofing non-fiction for a while, to pay the bills, but from now on, the only fiction I'd be working on was my own. Starting with me and Joe.

CHAPTER
eight

Joe

This time I was standing at the foot of her bed while she typed furiously on her laptop. She hadn't noticed me yet, at least she wasn't crying, that was something. I remembered how frustrating the last dream had been— fuzzy and distorted. I hadn't been able to talk to her or comfort her and then it had ended as it always did, blackness and nothing. I remembered each dream the moment I stepped into another. That beautiful face I was slowly becoming enamoured with no explanation as to why, just that I was. Looking down at my body I was happy to find the murky, coloured swirls of my last dream had been replaced with almost solid looking limbs. The typing stopped and it drew my eyes back to her. Her fingers resting on the keyboard and she chewed her bottom lip as she read over whatever it was she had typed. The action drew my attention to her mouth, her lips were not full and pouty but beautifully shaped and well proportioned. The hint of teeth grazing her lip sent a wave of desire through me, I suddenly found myself wanting to kiss her. As if hearing my thought, she uttered a shaky sigh and moaned,

"Oh Joe." My name on her lips was heaven.

"I'm here bella." I replied softly but she didn't react. I realised she couldn't see me again, that was disappointing. She continued to type enthusiastically, completely engrossed in her writing. As much as I wanted to talk to her, to make her see me, there was something quite comforting about watching her work. I could study her animated expressions, the tiny crease between her eyebrows as she concentrated, the way she chewed her bottom lip and then blew out a frustrated breath that made her lips vibrate. This last action made me chuckle, I found her so endearing and totally enchanting. I grew more and more fascinated with her by the minute. I was able to sit on the end of her bed and observe her, she remained totally unaware of my presence. The way the shadows played across her cheeks as she worked, the lamplight highlighting the right side of her face, accentuating her features, was utterly mesmerising. I began to realise that I remained in this dream longer than the previous ones, they had lasted only minutes. I wasn't complaining, I hoped it lasted as long as possible, I had no desire to leave. It seemed like hours until she finally stopped. The relentless tap tapping of her fingers on the keyboard had lulled me to sleep. The sudden absence of that rhythmic sound rang out like an alarm clock, I jerked my head up and I blinked. I was still on the end of her bed but stretched out with my feet up instead of being seated. I must have fallen so deeply asleep that I'd fallen out of the dream and now was back in it again? It was odd how I had continued it seemingly from the point I had left off.

Naomi had packed away her laptop and a large pile of notes on her bedside table and was now snuggling down beneath her bed sheets. She still hadn't noticed me, I accepted the fact it wasn't going to be an interactive experience this time, if it meant being able to stay with her for longer, I didn't mind. I hoped the fact that she was drifting off to sleep didn't foretell my imminent departure however. I rose off the bed fully expecting the usual blackness that accompanied my exit but it never came. After a few more minutes of waiting I found myself at a loss over what to do with myself. I was used to it ending so this was entirely new.

Looking at her peacefully sleeping, I decided on trying to discover any possible clues to her identity. Other than her first name, I knew nothing. There wasn't much to go on here in her room and I felt uncomfortable going through her things but then again, this wasn't real and these experiences intrigued me. I wanted to know more. I needed to understand why I kept seeing this woman. A quick look around wouldn't do any harm. I scanned her bedroom but nothing immediately popped out at me, it was a simple room with a double bed, wooden floors, a rug, a built-in cupboard and set of drawers and then a bedside table with a lamp on it. There was a painting on the wall, it was a print of Monet's Lily pond. *OK, so chances are she likes Monet?* I thought.

My gaze fell back on the bedside table and the pile of notes on the top. It was an A4 notepad, I wondered if I'd be able to pick them up? In the previous dream I'd been unable to physically connect with anything but it wouldn't hurt to try, I seemed substantially more solid this time.

Pleased to find that I *could* touch things, I picked up the pad of notes and began flicking through. It appeared to be notes about Italy and Florence, my home town. Intrigued, I read more. She wrote about my book bar 'The Magnificent Medici', how did she know about that? That nagging feeling that I knew this woman returned. I looked again at the familiar lines of her chin, her cheeks and the line of her brow, it was so puzzling to know that you knew someone but couldn't remember why. I turned the page and saw my name, written all over the paper in varying sizes, horizontally, vertically, diagonally…what made me stop and catch my breath was that I recognised the handwriting, it was mine.

I dropped the pad and took a step back, a memory niggled in the back of my mind of this woman asleep on her couch and the television playing to itself as she slept. I had no time to dwell on it as the sudden knock on the bedroom door made me turn so quickly I knocked the bedside lamp and it fell to the wooden floor with a crash.

"Naomi?" A worried female voice shouted through the door.

"Porco dio!" The curse left my lips and even before the door handle turned and the woman on the bed stirred and began to wake, I felt the return of the black void.

CHAPTER
nine

Naomi

"Naomi?" I heard Imogen call and then a loud crash resounded through the room, I sat up with a start just as she barged through my bedroom door,

"What the fuck?"

"You tell me! Are you OK? I heard noises."

"I'm fine. What was that crash?" I reached over to turn on my lamp but it wasn't there.

"Where's the lamp? Can you get the light?" Immy felt on the wall by the door for the switch and I shielded my eyes as it flicked on.

"Ow! Damn, what time is it?"

"It's around three I think. What the hell happened to your lamp?"

I followed her gaze to the floor where my bedside lamp lay shattered next to my notepad.

"I must have knocked it, I don't know. Bloody hell, I only just bought that lamp! Immy, could you get me the dustpan and brush from under the kitchen sink please? I don't want to step on the floor, there's glass everywhere." She nodded and went to get it. I was bummed about the lamp, it was relatively new and it wasn't cheap. I bent over to pick up a few of the larger pieces along with my notepad, it was open on a totally different page to the one I had left it on. It was open on the page with Joe's name scribbled all over it. The weirdest thing was that I could tell the other pages had been neatly folded back on themselves. It was also a few feet from the table, no way had I done that. The strangest feeling washed over me and I shivered. I could see how I might have knocked over the lamp in my sleep but I couldn't explain the notepad. That was just downright unsettling.

Immy came back with the dustpan and brush.

"You stay there and I'll sweep towards you." She said. "I got a bag for the bits."

"Thanks." I closed the notepad and put it back on the side table. I'd been writing for hours about Joe so I guess I must've opened it on that page and just forgot.

"Brrr, it's freezing in here! Is your window open?" Immy asked. I looked,

"Nope, it is a bit cold though." I said. I held open the bag for her as she tipped in the glass and shards of ceramic and then I put in the bigger pieces and tied up the bag.

"I'll take it" she offered, "you go back to sleep."

"Thanks. Sorry I woke you."

"It's alright. I was in the bathroom when I heard noises anyway, so." She shrugged. "Long as you're OK?"

I smiled and nodded, she smiled back and closed the door but left it ajar- on purpose I was betting. So she still didn't trust me then? What on earth did she think I had done or was going to do? Half of me wondered if Mum had sent her round to keep an eye on me, rather than believe Immy's story of wanting a sisterly night in- it wouldn't surprise me. I got up and shut the door a little harder than was necessary, hoping she heard it close. Honestly, between the two of them they made me feel like I was totally failing at life. If only they could see just how hard I was trying to change my stars. But it wouldn't matter soon anyway, they would both be living their own lives in New Zealand, leaving me to get on with things in whatever way I chose. I'd miss Mum, I mean she was the only parent I had left, albeit overbearing but she was still my mum. Perhaps I'd miss my sister a little less than the first time she had gone. The thought brought a wry smile to my lips. From now on it was just me, my writing and Joe. *My* Joe. The way *I* wrote him. This was going to be my story and nothing and no one was going to get in the way. For the first time in ages, I felt in control. I accepted I had some issues but show me a person who doesn't! I'd carry on seeing Dr Blanchard, at least for a few more sessions anyway and I had a couple of regular proofing jobs in the pipeline to keep the money situation ticking over. Yep, this was me, Naomi Douglas, taking my life back and not giving a shit how it looked to anyone else on the outside. Soon I would have no one to answer to but myself and I could *not* wait!

It was after 8.30am when I awoke to the smell of sizzling bacon- Imogen was cooking breakfast. She'd made coffee and bacon, eggs and tinned tomatoes.

"Woah! What's this? I didn't know I had any of this stuff in the fridge."

"You didn't, I wanted to make us breakfast so I popped round to Tesco and got it." Immy beamed. I had to admit it was nice waking up to a cooked brekkie, I couldn't recall the last time I'd even had one.

"Cheers Imms. It looks delicious, did you put sugar in my coffee?" I asked, taking a sip

"Yeah, was I not supposed to?"

"It's fine, I take sugar. I just like a flat teaspoon that's all or it's too sweet. You got it just right though, thanks!" I smiled at her.

"I'm going to have to eat and run I'm afraid, Mum called earlier, she needs me back to finish up." There was a hesitant pause and she looked at me over the rim of her cup,

"The answer's no." I said firmly.

"Oh come on Naomi? Please? I could use your help and I'm sure Mum wants to make things up with you. I already told her you would come!" She pouted at me.

"Then you'd better un-tell her because I'm not going. Before you start, I'm not being stubborn, I just have things of my own to do."

"Like what? I thought you'd caught up on all your outstanding proofs?"

"I have, it's not proofs. I'm writing my own book." I took another sip of coffee.

"Really? That's great Naomi! I mean are you really doing it this time?"

Sheesh, thanks for the vote of confidence little sister.

"Yes, really."

"What's it about?" She asked. "How much have you done already?" I couldn't decide if she was genuinely interested or she was trying to trip me up. I decided on the latter, she'd already betrayed my confidence once and I wasn't going to let it happen twice.

"You'll just have to wait and see won't you?" I winked at her, not wanting to tell her anything about it. If she knew it was about Joe she really would think I'd flipped my lid and I could just imagine the ensuing chaos. Mum would probably want me committed!

"Aww, meanie!" She poked out her tongue and giggled. "Crikey! I'd better run, I told Mum I'd be there for 9.30, she wants to crack on today. Are you sure you won't come?"

"I might pop down this afternoon, maybe, if I get enough done." I only said that to placate her, hoping it would get her off my back and off to Mum's sooner. I was itching to get writing. She seemed satisfied with my answer thankfully and after putting her breakfast pots in the sink and grabbing her overnight bag she hugged me at the door.

"See you later maybe?"

"Yeah, I'll try." *Not a chance in hell.* I closed the door after her and virtually *ran* to my bedroom to retrieve my laptop and notes with gleeful abandon. I felt happy, really happy for once. I could spend the entire day, guilt free, concentrating on myself and doing something I loved. I had purpose.

Back in the lounge, I turned off my mobile and switched on the TV. I liked to have films playing low in the background when I worked, it helped me to concentrate strangely enough. I started flicking through the channels for a film while my laptop was warming up. Movies Gold was showing the 1953 Dean Martin/Jerry Lewis film-The Caddy. I plumped for that, it was an easygoing comedy and I liked the old films. Even more so that it was set in Italy, I noted that fact as a sign. I tuned the TV volume low so I could only just hear the dialogue in the background. The duo were performing a comedy dance sketch with hats and canes, it made me chuckle. I made myself another large coffee and, when I got the milk, I noticed other food stuff had made its way into my fridge. Eggs and bacon weren't the only things my sister had bought this morning. Well at least I wouldn't have to order takeaways for the next few days. I assumed Mum had given her money to buy food for me. It was a nice gesture but as she so fondly liked to remind me, I was twenty-nine and perfectly capable of feeding myself. I could cook quite well as it happened, I just sometimes, quite often these days, didn't feel like it. Maybe I'd cook myself a nice Italian tonight. Fucking a nice Italian wouldn't go amiss either.

"I'm coming to get you Joe!" *Yeah, you wish you were.* Settling down in front of the TV with my coffee on the low table and my laptop on my knee, I readied myself to begin. I opened my notepad and glanced over a few roughly jotted down plot ideas. I still had Laney Marsh's original manuscript with my previous 'rewrites' on so I was using that as a starting point. Although I was basically using Joe as my main character, I planned on totally re-jigging the original story, this book was going to be as unashamedly self-indulgent as I could make it and get away with. It would never be published but that didn't matter. This story was for me, it was my way back to sanity and my way of seizing control of my own life. If nothing else, it got me back into writing, which is essentially where I wanted to be. It was a win-win situation.

It was a good half an hour or more at least when I took a quick screen break, had a little stretch and glanced at the TV. I watched for a few minutes, chuckling to myself at Jerry Lewis, the guy was a nutter but funny as hell. It was then I took note of the name of Dean Martin's character, he was called Joe Anthony, *Joe!* That really did make me laugh. That confirmed it, I was definitely on the right path.

It got to the part in the film where Dean sings his iconic song 'That's Amore', I loved that song and found myself signing along when the volume on the TV suddenly shot up so loud I had to cover my ears,

"Arghhh! What the bloody hell?" I dove for the remote and turned it right down again. I must've caught the remote with my foot or something, Christ, it'd nearly deafened me. I put the remote away from my feet this time and settled back down to begin typing again, a few seconds passed and the volume rose of its own accord yet again, Dean was really blasting it out! The speakers on the TV vibrated.

"What is *up* with this thing?" I turned it down again and shook the remote to see if anything inside was broken, nothing rattled.

"Do that again and I swear I'll throw you out the 'effin window!" I threatened it and put it down on the sofa near my leg instead of on the coffee table so it was nearer, just in case it taunted me again. I glared at it for half a minute, waiting to see if it dare. It didn't, so I continued to type. Five-hundred more words in and the TV turned itself off. I looked up over the lid of my laptop at the blank TV screen.

"Fucking great! I really need a busted TV right now. Fine! Stay off then." I tried to work but the silence was quite distracting. I needed some sound.

Sighing I put down the laptop and went to find a CD, I needed something easy listening and finally settled on a compilation album called 'Lazy Afternoon'. There were some decent tracks on it, perfect for my needs. I put the disc in the player and clicked 'play' and left the case next to it, face up with the songs showing. Deciding another coffee was needed and maybe a snack, I headed for the kitchen. I'd noticed Immy had left a packet of biscuits near the kettle and I was just stuffing one in my mouth when the song that was playing skipped forward to song number two. Trust me to have a faulty TV *and* CD player! I didn't mind too much, it was a beautiful song called 'Dancing on my Own', it was a Robyn cover by a local guy made good-Calum Scott I think his name was, he'd been on Britain's Got Talent or something. I started singing while I waited for the kettle and then about a third way into the song, the volume went up. OK, now I was a little perturbed, it was one thing having the TV do it- I could discount that as a faulty remote…but the CD player too? Nope, something else was going on. My palms began to sweat, torn between wanting to go and investigate and nervous about what I might find.

"Man up, Naomi!" My heart was pounding, shuffling tentatively towards the lounge area, I held my breath. The song was still blaring out and at first glance nothing looked out of place. Then I noticed the CD case was on the floor and not where I'd left it. The TV was still off and my laptop was still on the coffee table but when I looked closer I could see something was different. Edging closer, one step at a time, adrenaline pumping, I read the three words on the screen, three words I knew I had not written.

I AM HERE.

CHAPTER
ten

Joe

She slammed the lid down on the laptop and retreated a few steps, her hands covering her mouth. I hadn't intended to scare her, I just wanted to find a way of letting her know I was here. Now I felt terrible. I had tried to get her attention by turning up the television and then turning it off but that hadn't worked, so I'd tried the music. Maybe the words on the computer had been a little too much too soon. I was desperate to communicate with her. I felt like I'd used a lot of energy up with efforts so I hoped it was enough.

She'd had no idea I had sat and listened to some of the breakfast conversation with her sister. While they had been talking, I had wandered back to Naomi's bedroom and read through some more of her notes. It seemed she knew all about me. I had found some roughly scribbled pages of what appeared to be memories of conversations between her and I, or notes from a diary written in a strange way. I had sat and tried desperately to puzzle it all out and I had come to the terrifying conclusion that I wasn't dreaming at all. I must be in a coma from some sort of illness or accident. I could only assume then, that I was in fact having out of body experiences. It's the only way I knew how to explain it. Everything fit, her tears and shock that first night she had seen me reflected in her computer, the reason she knew my name and I knew hers. It also explained why I recognised her but wasn't sure why, I must have amnesia! Unless of course out of body episodes caused your memories to be unclear? Either way I knew this must be what was happening to me.

Naomi and I were obviously in a relationship, the attraction I felt for her was solid and real and I knew I had to find a way of letting her know she hadn't lost me. As stupid as it might sound, I worried that I might be on life support and that it might be turned off if nobody thought I could be saved. I had needed to write those words on the screen. I needed to be noticed. I just thanked God that I was able to physically manipulate objects now, my energy or spirit had been weak at first. I thought back to that night when my body was just a swirling mist of coloured smoke, the difference from then to now was quiet significant, frightening even. What if I was dying and this was why my ethereal essence was stronger than it had been before? I was spending more time in this form than before too, those first experiences had last only minutes, now I seemed to be here for hours at a time. It could only mean that my physical form was slowly slipping away. I had to fight back, I wouldn't give up, especially on Naomi. She needed me. Her hands dropped from her mouth and she looked around the room in awe. Her initial fear seemingly gone.

"Dad? Is that you?"

Dad? She thought it was her father! Oh, this was not good. I would have to try and type something else, she needed to know it was me not her father. I did the same thing as before and concentrated all my efforts on moving the keys with my mind not my actual fingers. It looked like I was using my fingers but the force came from within me.

"Eh! Non funziona!" It wasn't working! This couldn't be happening now. Frustration flooded me, in desperation I tried again but nothing happened. I noticed my hands looked a little transparent once more. I must have used up too much of my energy with the TV and the music.

"Porcco Dio!" Now was not the time to do a disappearing act. I felt utterly helpless.

"Dad, are you here? Please do something else if this is you? ...I miss you." Her voice broke a touch and I felt so sad for her, on reflection maybe it wasn't such a bad thing to let her think it was her father trying to communicate. It might offer her some emotional comfort perhaps. I would have to wait until I had recovered before attempting anything else. She waited for a response for quite a few minutes before giving up and sitting rather despondently back on the sofa. I sat beside her while she stared blankly into the room. A lonely tear graced her cheek and she just let it fall. I tried to wipe it away but I couldn't. I tried to put my hand on hers to hold it. I had no idea if she could feel me or not, I hoped that she could. I would spend my time beside her, offering what little comfort I could and then hopefully, once I was able, I'd leave more messages for her.

At least an hour passed as we just sat together, doing nothing but just *being*. Eventually she moved from the sofa and began pottering around her flat, I followed when she disappeared from my line of sight, eager to stay close. She ventured to the kitchen and cooked herself some lunch, a simple pasta with a side salad. As she worked she began to hum, I recognised the tune from the film she had been watching earlier 'That's Amore'. Glad to see her happy mood I hummed along with her wishing I could cook with her. I was a good cook, I knew that. My mother had taught me although I couldn't exactly remember my mother right now. It felt like when I had tried to picture my father, just a hazy, vague silhouette. I tried not to let it bother me, I was sure it would all come back to me once I woke up. *If* I woke up.

After lunch we settled back down on the sofa, her with her laptop perched on her knees, me sitting to the left of her. I could feel the heat of her body next to mine, I wished again that she could sense my presence.

"Naomi, il mio bel fiore. Sono qui con te." *Don't give up on me.* I made a promise to myself and to her, right there and then, that I would fight with everything I had in me to find my way back to her. I brushed my hand against her cheek, barely a whisper of a touch but she shivered and rubbed her cheek against her shoulder. That small indication that she had felt me touch her gave me such encouragement. Excitement filled my veins, if I could make her feel me maybe I could eventually make her hear me or see me?

"Bella donna, voglio conoscerti di nuovo. I want to remember us." The thought of her and I together made me yearn to touch her again, to *know* her again. I desperately wanted to remember the feel of her lips on mine and the way her skin felt under my hands. I imagined we must have had some wild nights, her body was perfectly made for pleasure. Her petite but well-proportioned frame emphasised every curve. She had a body Sophia Loren would be envious of. I liked a woman with curves, flesh that I could grip onto in the throws of passion and wrap my arms around at night. My crotch twitched as the desire to possess her overwhelmed me. Well this was an interesting development, an erection during an out of body episode? That was quiet an unexpected perk and one I was more than happy to explore!

Naomi shivered and moaned, her hand went to her neck and her head went back, eyes closed. Was she sensing my desire? A wicked thought crossed my mind, maybe I could send a little good feeling her way and help guide her thoughts towards me. I had an idea that if I could keep her mind on me I might be able to contact her more easily...and I got a kick out of turning her on, it felt like something I was supposed to do. Grinning, I edged a little closer so that my lips were centimetres from her ear and then let out a slow, gentle breath. She inhaled quickly and let her hand slide slowly down over her chest exposing her neck. I concentrated as hard as I could and poured my energy into running my tongue over her exposed skin. Her breasts heaved and she inhaled hard through her teeth. Oh yes! She could definitely feel me. I had a throbbing hard on now, God I wanted her with every ounce of my being. It was unfortunate that having a hard on seemed to drain all the energy out of me. I still hadn't recovered enough from my previous attempts at communication to be able to carry on but it was encouraging to know that I could affect her physically. I hoped this meant that I could convince her that it was her lover who 'haunted' her and not her father. My life might depend on the success of my efforts.

Naomi put her computer on the coffee table and got up, walking towards her bedroom she began to strip off, removing her top as she walked. Beyond thrilled, I followed her. This was my woman but I couldn't remember what she looked like naked. A part of me felt a little guilty at invading her privacy but the voyeur in me couldn't quite resist. My conscience told me to stay back, I should not be looking when she didn't know I was here but my feet had a mind of their own and followed.

While I wrestled with my morals, Naomi threw her shirt on the bed and slipped out of her bottoms leaving her in just her underwear. My heart was beating fast with the anticipation of seeing her fully naked but she turned and went to the bathroom instead. I followed again, my erection leading the way. In the bathroom, she leaned over the bath and turned on the shower and then reached around to unclasp her bra. *Oh dear God, stop looking you pervert!* My mind screamed at me to turn away but my eyes were totally captivated. I held my breath as her breasts bounced free, her pink nipples peaked as the cool air touched their nakedness.

"Tutti gli angeli! You are mine and only mine." I vowed. I would find my way back to this angel somehow. I would not allow any other man to have the pleasure of gazing upon *my* woman. Naomi hooked her thumbs into the waistband of her pants and pulled them down, bending over as she stepped out of them, giving me the most glorious view of her peachy behind. I wanted to take her right there and then. The throbbing in my groin hammering to be free of the restrictive clothing. I grasped my cock through the fabric wishing with all my heart that I could join her in the shower. She stepped into the bath and drew the shower curtain around her, blocking my view. *Damn.* I groaned inwardly but the drawing of the curtain brought with it the realisation that she deserved some privacy. The unexpected sight of her nakedness had temporarily shoved my conscience to the back of my mind and allowed my cock to lead. I already felt like a pervert for spying on her this long but she was my lady and I just wanted to remember her...*and fuck her!* Said the voice in my head. Oh yes, I wanted to fuck her. Fuck her hard and fast, possess her and make her mine and then make love to her, gently, softly until she was spent and we fell asleep in each other's arms.

I stood at the door with my back to the wall as the steam from the shower billowed out of the room through the open doorway. In my mind I imagined the water and soap running over her naked body, I wondered if we had ever made love in the shower? Yes, we must have, it would've been impossible not to have done. I wished I could remember. Little sighs and moans reached me through the noise of the cascading water. Was she masturbating? My cock twitched again. Oh dear God this was torture!

"Oh, Joe…Joe, yes! Yes!"

The knowledge that she was pleasuring herself and thinking about me almost drove me over the edge. I banged my head backwards against the wall and swore in frustration. The shower turned off instantly.

"Hello?" She called.

As much as I was happy she had heard me, now wasn't really the time to try and get her to notice me. Given what she had been in the middle of doing, it didn't feel appropriate. *Neither is playing the voyeur!* My conscience piped up. Communicating with her now would probably scare the living daylights out of her and make me look like the biggest creep on earth.

"Who's there?" She called again.

I heard the shower curtain pull back and the slapping of wet feet on the floor. Her head poked around the door and she looked up the hallway and directly at me. My heart lurched as for a moment I thought she had seen me but then she continued to look through me. She disappeared back into the bathroom and re-emerged wearing a towel. It looked like shower time was over and I felt terrible for interrupting her private moment, although she might not be happy to know it wasn't as private as she had thought. I shouldn't have listened. This time, as she went to her bedroom, I didn't follow. I didn't wait to hear if she continued her self-pleasuring. Instead I waited in the lounge. Of all the times for the blackness to come and claim me, now would've been the most appropriate. I felt like an ass for perving on her, girlfriend or not, she was entitled to her privacy. I made up my mind I wouldn't do that again. The next time I saw her naked would be when I woke up and I could appreciate her beauty in the flesh, the way I was meant to.

CHAPTER
eleven

Stranger Things Could Happen

I tried to wrap my head around today's events. I've never believed in ghosts as such, I didn't believe in God or the concept of heaven but I always looked for signs from the cosmos. My philosophy was that everything in nature was connected. We lived on the same planet, we shared DNA with other living creatures so, it was reasonable to think we also shared an energy- a force that linked everything on earth from rock to elephant to human. Some people might argue that as a case for 'God' but it depends on what your version of God is. I liked to think I was somewhere in-between, that I just appreciated the wonders of nature for what they were. I held proclivities for scientific explanations with a side garnish of natural magic. So how could I explain what had happened earlier? Was my dad really trying to contact me? Or was it just another one of my hallucinations? I shook my head.

I thought about all the strange happenings from the volume on the TV, the music, the words typed on my laptop and the loud bang I'd heard in the shower. All of them could be scientifically explained- a faulty TV remote or electrical power surge, I could've typed those words myself and just forgotten and the bang could've been a window left open or anything like that. I was being paranoid again. Dr Blanchard's words of wisdom rang in my ears, there was nothing weird going on, and it was just me and my screwy brain looking for anything I could use as an emotional crutch. I had to learn to deal with my grief and stop looking for things that weren't there. I couldn't allow myself to listen to the part of me that waved the flag vigorously on the side of the unexplainable. These were signs I wouldn't allow myself to believe, the pain of losing my dad was still too raw and the concept of him trying to reach me from beyond the grave was just too much. He was gone and I had to deal with it.

I decided on a nap so I threw the wet towel in the laundry pile, pulled on a vest top and loose boy shorts, rough dried my hair and lay on my bed, staring at the ceiling. Eventually I dropped off and when I awoke it was early evening. I'd missed most of the day and had never made it to Mum's house. I checked my mobile and it had three missed calls from Immy. I texted her to say I had fallen asleep and to send apologies to Mum. As I'd never intended to go anyway, falling asleep meant I hadn't had to lie and make up an excuse. It felt nice knowing I had the whole evening ahead of me to work on my story. The steamy scene I'd worked on earlier had affected me more than I thought, I'd turned myself on so much that I'd had to go shower. Just a shame I got interrupted at a crucial point. Grinning, I knew I would make sure to finish myself off later and Joe would be helping! That was one little fantasy I would not deny myself.

I turned on the laptop to warm up but decided against turning on the TV or the CD player. I didn't want them going all weird on me again. I needed to concentrate, no more stupid signs! My mobile pinged to signal I had a text message. It was Immy asking if would go to Mum's tomorrow. I text back a '*Yeah, maybe x*' and left it at that, turning the phone to silent.

My notepad on my knee, I began plotting. I wanted to draft out a particular scene in the readers' cafe that Joe and I owned,

'Joe wiped all the tables down while I replaced the books on the shelves. I looked over at him as he worked. He had a towel slung over his shoulder, his tight white t-shirt had a few splash stains on it from the kitchen, despite the chef's apron that was still tied around his waist. He looked gorgeous, humming as he cleaned. Not for the first time, I thought how lucky I was that he was my man. I caught his eye, he winked and flashed me one of his killer grins. I would never tire of his smile, it was so bright it could melt the polar ice caps. I knew I was biased but he had been the catch of the town back in Italy. I thought back to our first meeting, I had fallen for him the minute I looked into those beautiful big brown eyes.

It'd taken some work mind you, he was a notorious playboy and loved the company of women, all women, no matter their dress size. Joe found so much beauty in the female form and had no problem expressing it which, of course, made him utterly irresistible to

all members of the opposite sex. On those days when you felt ten pounds heavier just from looking at a cake and your hair put birds' nests to shame, Joe could make you feel sexier than Marilyn Monroe. In the time I had known him, I don't think I'd ever seen him ignore any woman that had walked into his bar in Italy or our cafe here at home. Not in a 'man-whore' kind of way- he just paid attention. A smile, a nod, a wink of his eye, Joe would always take the time to notice you and that was his secret. The guy could cook, clean, do his own laundry, he worked hard and he played hard, his Mama must've been one hell of a woman, I wish I could've met her.

His skills in the bedroom were incomparable to anything I'd ever known. Granted, I didn't have that much to compare it to but Joe rocked my world between the sheets and out of them and I couldn't imagine ever wanting anyone else. I hoped we'd be married someday because I just couldn't imagine my life without him in it.'

I began reading through my rough notes when I heard my laptop beep. It was an old machine and took a lifetime to warm up. I'd managed to quickly jot down two paragraphs while waiting for it to be ready. After reading through the last page to remind myself where I had left off, I began typing up the notes. This was usually how I started, hand writing first and then type it up as I go. After a while the words would start to flow and then I just carried on typing. So far so good. I'd not been working on my story very long and I was totally inspired by Joe. In the past, whenever I had tried to write, I would reach a certain point and then it would all sort of fizzle out and I would give up, making me feel like a failure. This time I was on a roll, I had so much to say about Joe. Perhaps because I already knew him through Laney's story or because I was totally obsessed with him, in truth it was probably more of the latter. A part of me still felt apprehensive about stealing Laney's character but I had to bury that feeling and just write. This was a story that had to be told. I needed to immerse myself in a world where Joe and I existed together, call it therapy or whatever, it was pure self-indulgent catharsis. I didn't care, something was driving me to write it and I felt *so* good. For the first time I could remember, I felt like my life had a purpose. I had something to aim for, something of my own.

The page I had typed up was done and I took a moment to recap, I wasn't quite happy with the wording so I sat chewing my pen and pondered over how I could change it. I had hit a bit of a blank and was just sitting staring at the blinking cursor on my screen when it moved. Letters appeared on my screen and the letters formed words,

"*Do not be afraid.*"

"What the fuck?" My immediate thought was that someone had remote accessed my computer and my heart rate went up a notch. Except that didn't explain why they were talking to me. I typed something back,

"*Who the hell is this? Get off my computer you wanker! I'm running a trace on you right now!*"

"*Naomi, please, do not be afraid. I don't know how much time I have.*"

"*Is this a joke? How have you got access to my laptop? Who are you?*"

"*No joke. Need to talk. Urgent*"

I stared, aghast and confused at the words appearing on my screen. Sure I was being hacked I went to turn off the machine.

"No! Stop! Please don't turn it off, mia cara."

My hand wavered, Italian? Ok, someone was definitely fucking with me. Some psycho must have remote accessed my laptop and had seen what I had been writing about.

"This is not funny. I'm reporting this to the police you weirdo. I have your I.P number." I lied.

"No, you don't. I'm here, I can see you. Naomi, I need you to hear me."

Oh my God! They could see me? I looked around for something to cover up my inbuilt webcam and microphone, all I had was my thumb so I stuck it over the lens and reached for my phone with my other hand, ready to call someone if I needed to.

"Who the fuck are you?" I demanded, forgetting I had covered up the mic and camera.

"It's Joe."

My hand dropped from the camera, how on earth could they have answered the question when I had been covering it? I decided I needed to play along and try and trip this guy up. If I was going to report this I needed information. He must have some scary-arsed tech to be doing this sort of stuff. I needed to know what he wanted.

"OK, Joe…what do you want to talk about? What do you want from me?"

"Naomi, this is NOT a joke. I need you to tell me what happened, why am I here? Where is my body? I need you to help me before it's too late."

I frowned at the screen. This guy was crazier than me.

"I don't know what happened to you 'Joe' and only you know why you're here. What do you want?"

"I'm confused. Are we not together?"

"OK buddy, I think you're talking to the wrong person." I said out loud and then typed back,

"Sorry to break it to you mate but I think you hacked into the wrong computer. I'm not the Naomi you're looking for."

I waited for a few seconds but no reply came back. Just as I was about to shut everything off and do a major virus scan more words appeared.

"But you saw me, you knew my name. You talk about me all the time. I've read your words."

In the moment it took my heart to skip a beat, time appeared to stop. My mind raced, trying to figure out what was happening. Either this weirdo hacker had somehow rigged up secret cameras in my flat and had been spying on me and was now fucking with my head or …this *was* Joe. *My* Joe. Both seemed equally impossible. I mean for a start I barely ever left my flat and if someone had indeed broken into it- why would they? Surely one of my neighbours would've noticed, you couldn't even get past the front door without the key code. Unless it was Iain? Had he gone fruit loop on me and turned into some psycho stalker? Was I about to become the victim in a real-life horror film? I scrolled the contacts list on my mobile phone till I found Iain's number and began to text him. If it was him I'd rain merry hellfire down on his idiotic arse!

"Who is Iain?" The text on the screen asked.

"Okay, I'm now officially freaked out. How can you see that? You better give me some answers here because

I'm one call away from contacting the police!" I couldn't help but look around the room for hidden cameras as I spoke. I considered taking apart my phone to see if I could find a bugging device and then caught myself, laughing scornfully. *It's not Mission Impossible for Christ's sake!*

"Naomi, this is me Joe! I saw you in your flat talking to a woman on your laptop and I KNOW you saw me. I saw you at your Parents house, I know you lost your father, you were crying in a chair. I was here when your sister stayed over. It IS me! I don't know why I'm here like this or why you can't see me now. My memories are unclear. I just know that we're together somehow, aren't we? I feel it. Have I been in an accident? Am I in a coma? Help me Naomi, please?"

Oh dear God! Was this guy real? Was it possible that Joe was here and communicating with me? Or had I gone totally crazy? My finger's hovered over the keyboard but I couldn't think what to type. I chewed hard on my lip, wracking my brain, trying to work out how this could possibly be real. The logical part of my brain was telling me this was an illusion I had created, that I must be so angry and discouraged at the real world I had created a false one in my head. My gut told me a different story- this was real and Joe was here...somehow. My heart was at odds with my brain. Although I had wished a thousand times over that Joe was indeed real and mine, there was no possible way that could ever be true. Joe was just a made-up character in a book. The child in me, the part that still believed in the impossible, was shouting at me from the depths of my soul. And for one brief, glorious moment, I allowed myself to hope beyond hope that somehow the universe had heard my desperate plea and had sent me my Joe.

"NO, NO NO! This can't be happening. It's impossible!" I shouted. Fear clawed at me, strangulating any feeling of hope. I could feel my grip on reality slipping. I clung to the notion that this was some kind of cruel joke, it had to be. The alternative was far too wonderful yet terrifying to contemplate. *Get a fucking grip Naomi! You're losing it!*

"Naomi? Please, bella. Believe me. Help me, I need you."

'Stop it! Just stop it, whoever you are. It's not funny and it's not FAIR! You can't do this to me!" I shouted out to the room. Slamming the laptop lid down and dumping it on the table, I ran to my bedroom scared out of my wits and flung myself face down on the bed, sobbing. Someone had gotten into my head and my life. Someone cruel and vicious was taunting me. That had to be the answer because I refused to accept I was going crazy.

Hugging the pillow tight around my head and curling my knees up protectively, I tried to ignore the nagging feeling that I was not alone. I couldn't shake it, I kept my face hidden and my eyes closed tight, and hoping the feeling would go away, that it was just paranoia but I knew it wasn't. Someone or something was in the room with me. My skin prickled with the change of atmosphere in the room.

"Go away!" The muffled shout caught in my pillow and I felt my body tense in anticipation of a response, so sure was I that someone was present. No audible response came but I expected something and was almost disappointed when it didn't. I don't know why because a response would have gone someway to confirming I *was* going crazy. When I cautiously lifted my face from the pillow to peek, I was caught off guard by the sight of a drinks coaster flying across the room from my bedside table. It slammed into the wall and fell to the floor where I looked at it in wide eyed shock.

"What are you?" I whispered. "This can't be happening, this can't be happening." I kept repeating this mantra desperately trying to convince myself I hadn't lost my mind. There was a banging coming from the hallway and it took all my remaining courage to get up and investigate. Knees weak, breath shaking I peeked around my bedroom door and looked down the hall- it was empty. Another noise came from the direction of the bathroom. I could hear something clattering in the sink. One slow, daring step at a time brought me level with the open bathroom door. Steeling myself to look in, I took one deep breath in and stepped through. I was greeted by the contents of my bathroom cabinet piled up in disarray in the sink below and the words I AM JOE written in black eyeliner on the mirror. I couldn't tear my eyes away and my feet were seemingly glued to the floor, frozen but not in fear, in hope. This time I listened when the child in me spoke up. I *did* still believe in magic, I *did* still believe in a world where anything is possible if you just wanted it hard enough. As I stared at the mirror the light in the room distorted and shimmered and a tall, toned figure materialised in front of me. A beautiful sliver haired, smiling Adonis- Joe.

"Is it really you?" My voice shook with emotion.

"You see me?" He asked with hopeful urgency.

I nodded, dumbfounded. He smiled in relief and took a step towards me but I hastily stepped backwards out of the door and his face fell.

"Mia cara, please don't be afraid. I know it must be a shock seeing me like this, it's…unnerving to me also but I know there is a reason for it. I think I need your help."

His plea momentarily fell on deaf ears for I couldn't take my eyes off his. He was here, he was real and he was my Joe. Everything I thought I ever knew about the universe was now shrouded in doubt. All logic had gone out of the window. Magic was real. I had stepped back not through fear of him but afraid that touching him somehow might break this spell I was under. The disappointment etched on his face brought me back.

"Help? What do you mean?" I asked, confused. I could hardly focus on my words, mesmerised by the sight of him, I wanted so much to touch him but I was convinced he would disappear in a proverbial puff of smoke if I did.

"Have I been in an accident?" he asked tentatively.

"Um…no."

His brow furrowed in confusion and he looked away for a second. The moment his eyes left mine I craved them. I needed him to look at me.

"Joe!" The cry that left my lips sounded almost desperate but it worked, his eyes flashed up towards mine again.

"Bella…I need to know why I'm here. I've been visiting you but you couldn't see me. I was here sometimes and then I wasn't, I don't understand it. Please *help* me."

It hit me then that he had no idea who he was. A work of fiction, albeit a very solid and sentient one. Perfect and beautiful and tantalisingly real yet still a physical impossibility. I didn't know what to tell him. How could I possibly begin to explain to him that he was the result of one woman's obsession with another woman's creation?

I had to be brave and reach out for him, touch him. I needed to know for sure if the vision, standing in my bathroom, was physically there. My eyes stayed fixed on his, drowning in those hazel pools lined by long luscious lashes. I was hardly aware of my hand reaching up towards him, nor of the fact that I hadn't taken a breath for at least half a minute. When I felt fire at my fingertips I still could not look away, I only knew that the heat came from him, from his own hand as it met mine and we touched for the first time.

CHAPTER
twelve

My Joe

I remember a blinding flash of light, heat in my fingertips, a shout and then nothing. Not the usual black void that took me away from her but something altogether different, brighter and clearer. The world came slowly into focus, distant birdsong mingled with the regular beep of an alarm roused me. Air brushed my cheek and morning light filtered through my still closed eyelids. I was horizontal, warm soft fabric lay against my skin and my head rested on a soft pillow. I was in bed. I knew this but it felt strange, like I was waking up for the first time in a very long time. I relished the warm, slow comfort of the morning before I opened my eyes. Naomi lay next to me, facing me, watching me. A tear graced the corner of her eye and I watched it roll gently down her cheek, drop from her jaw bone and onto the sheet.

"You're back." Naomi whispered. "You're really here." The last part sounded almost like a question, like she couldn't believe it and needed confirmation.

"Si, amore mio. It seems I am." I had no idea what day it was or how I had ended up in her bed, waking up with her, but I was glad that I had. I felt like this was how it should be. I thought back to my last memory when she had seen me in the bathroom, when I had been just a vision. I wondered what had happened between then and now because I couldn't for the life of me remember waking up in a hospital or being transferred home. It was all very confusing and strange. I knew we would need to talk about things, Naomi would help me get things straight in my head. Perhaps talking to her would awaken some memories that my conscious had decided to bury. I guessed by her reaction that this was perhaps the first morning we had woken together since my absence, the look of disbelief in her eyes told me that she had thought this moment might not ever be possible. Again, I wondered what had happened to me, wishing I could remember it but I was thrilled that we were together now, grateful that whatever tragedy had separated us was over. All that mattered to me in this moment was Naomi. She looked so incredibly beautiful I felt an overwhelming urge to kiss her.

"How did this hap…"

I cut her off with a kiss and her words were lost as my mouth covered hers. She moaned softly and I felt her surrender completely to the moment. I slipped my arm around her and drew her close, her body moulded perfectly to mine. She fit me like a missing piece of a jigsaw puzzle and nothing else mattered. I had a million questions begging to be answered but all I wanted in this moment was her mouth. The bitter sweet taste of her lips evoked a response within me that was both natural and alien. It was like a first kiss, not like when you were young and just discovering girls but that first toe-curling, all-encompassing passionate kiss of a long awaited new love. It was extraordinary. Somewhere in the back of my mind it occurred to me that I couldn't remember what it had been like to kiss Naomi and now I was exultant in my rediscovery of her. If just a kiss had me reeling I was looking forward to the sex! Just the thought made my groin harden and I instinctively deepened the kiss. She groaned and her hand found its way around the back of my head. Her fingers entwined in my hair and she gave it a little tug pushing her small frame against mine. My hand found its way down to her thigh, lingering briefly on her pert behind. I hoisted her leg up and over my own where I gleefully caressed the bare skin of her thigh. She was wearing boy short knickers and a skimpy vest top, I could have easily slipped my hand under either of them and explored further but she suddenly pulled away from me, breathless.

"Joe, wait." She gasped, her face flushed with the tell-tale sign of desire.

"What is it il amore mio?" My hand continued its slow path up her bare leg towards the curve of her bottom and I let my fingertip slip just underneath the fabric of her knickers. She put her hand over mine and halted my game.

"I can't believe I'm saying this but…Joe, we need to talk."

"Che cosa? What's wrong Naomi?" I leaned away from her and propped my head upon my elbow, a look of concern on my face. Her tone was serious and I wasn't sure I liked it. She turned away and sat on the edge of the bed with her back to me.

"Let me make us some coffee, you do drink coffee right?"

"Of course I do," what an odd question, she should know that I do, "would you like me to help?"

"No." She replied, a little too quickly. "I'll make it, you er… rest. I won't be long." She got up swiftly and walked determinedly out of the bedroom. Something wasn't right, this didn't strike me as appropriate behaviour for a newly reunited couple. I got up and walked towards the door, I could hear the distinct sound of crockery clinking together. As I reached the hallway her voice reached me, she sounded like she was having an argument with herself. Frowning, I stood still and listened more. Some Indistinct mutterings I couldn't quite make any sense of but the tone of her monologue was clear- she was agitated, anxious even. I shouted to her,

"Is everything alright? Do you want me to help?"

"No!" She shot back sounding panicked. "I mean yes, everything is fine and no, I don't need help…thanks. I'll bring the coffee to you."

"Okay." I said and turned back down the hallway. On my way back towards the bedroom I noticed a picture hung on the end wall. From where I stood I could make out two people stood in front of an old looking stone building. Curious, I walked towards it. An instant smile of recognition broke out on my face as I neared the wall. It was a framed photograph of Naomi and I, arms around each other and wearing aprons. We stood in front of an old stone building with tables and chairs outside and a sign above the building's entrance which read 'Imp's Book Bar'. We looked so happy and as I continued to look at the picture, a memory trickled slowly into my conscious. A memory of that day, the day we opened the doors to our new business venture. How excited we had been when our first customer walked down the steps and through the entrance exclaiming their delight at such an innovative concept,

"*Oh! This is fabulous!*" The female customer had said as she had perused the books perched upon the shelves inside our cafe. "*So I can just sit and read these books while I eat?*"

I remembered now with vivid clarity the proud smile on Naomi's face as she had enthusiastically explained the concept of the book bar to walk-in customers throughout the day. I remembered the first night too, how we had made love on one of the tables after closing, so caught up in the thrill and success of our first day as co-owners of the business. My grin broadened, I was so happy that memories were finally filtering through, I was beginning to remember my life with her and it was glorious! The moment of nostalgia was interrupted by the sudden sound of ceramic hitting the floor and Naomi's gasp. Turning, I saw her standing behind me, hands to her mouth, wide eyed in shock. The two cups of coffee she had been carrying lay in a steaming puddle of broken pieces on the floor at her feet.

"Are you alright bella?" I asked. "Did you trip?"

"I…What?" she shook her head. "No. No I'm fine I just…that photograph…where did it come from?" She gestured towards the framed picture with her head, crossing her arms protectively around herself as she did so. I looked back at the picture.

"You don't remember?"

She shook her head, her face now blank.

"I hung it there so every time we walked down the hallway we would remember that day…and that night." I winked at her but her face remained impassive. "Naomi!" I took both her arms in my hands excitedly, "My memories are returning! I'm starting to remember it all, isn't that good news?" I kissed her forehead and pulled her close, enveloping her in a tight hug. I could feel her rapid heartbeat against my chest, matching my own. She must be excited too.

"Joe? What exactly do you remember?" She lifted her head to look up at me, I sensed fear within those beautiful eyes of hers.

"Bella? You look…what's wrong?"

"*What* do you remember?" She insisted and pulled further away.

"Us mia cara. Our life together, our cafe, how we met, how we fell in love. Everything!" I emphasised the last word with a triumphant smile.

"Details, Joe. I need details. I need to know exactly what you remember." Her voice shook a little and I thought it sweet that she was obviously worried about me.

"How did we meet Joe?" I reached up and stroked her arm, she shuddered and her eyes flitted closed, just for a second. "Can we sit? I need to sit down." She said and walked back towards the lounge area, stepping over the broken mugs.

"Let me clean that up first?"

"No, it's OK. Leave it. This is more important." She said without looking back. I had no choice but to follow. We sat on the sofa and she took my hand in hers.

"Tell me how we met."

"In Florence." I responded.

"More," she demanded, "what else?"

"We met in Florence, in my bar The Magnificent Medici, it's where we got the idea for the Imp."

"The Imp?" She looked confused.

"Our book bar Naomi!" I laughed. "Are you sure you're alright?"

"Oh. Right. Erm, yes…I'm fine. Tired, I guess. Keep going please." I shook my head a little and gave her a half smile.

"I first saw you in my bar in Florence. You were alone and reading a book and I thought you looked so beautiful, like someone I wanted to get to know." I squeezed her hand and lifted it to my lips to kiss it.

"What book?" She breathed as my lips touched the smooth skin on her hand.

"One of my favourite's bella, *Stranger in a Strange* land by Robert Heinlein." Her sharp gasp cut through my words and I examined her face, the smallest hint of a tear accompanied her disbelieving look.

"Impossible." It was barely a whisper but I heard it.

"Maybe you thought so at one time my love but see? I'm back, I remember things. I'm all better and I remember you, us…our love…the sex." I wiggled my eyebrows at her and bent forward to kiss the tip of her nose, a small laugh or half sob, I couldn't tell which, came from her mouth.

"I can't believe it. Joe, you're really here? I just don't understand. I feel like I've lost my mind. How can this be happening? I always dreamed of this, always but it's…"

"Impossible?" I finished her sentence and she just nodded. "Nothing is impossible mia cara, our love is strong and you never lost faith in me. I'm almost sure that's what brought me back."

"Back? Oh…yes…your *accident*. Joe, we need to talk about that."

"Not now bella, now is not the time to discuss what happened. To be honest, I've no recollection of it and I'm sure it must've been horrible for you but right now, I'd rather not know what happened. Being in that strange dream state or whatever it was, was bad enough. Every time I saw you I was confused. I knew that I knew you but I couldn't remember it all. It was not an experience I wish to repeat or discuss. Not yet anyway. Right now, I just want to hold you. I *remember* us Naomi. Let's just be happy that we are together today OK?" I stroked her cheek and leaned in for a kiss, her chin rose and our mouths met. I adored the feel of her soft lips and savoured the kiss, immediately missing it when we eventually broke it off.

"I should go clean up that coffee." She said in a dazed tone.

"Really? I thought you said this was more important?" I teased.

"It is. I just need a moment to…gather my thoughts. It'll leave a stain anyway if I don't clean it up."

"Well then let's both do it." I offered.

"Thanks. I'll get a cloth you get the dustpan under…"

"Under the sink. I know where it is." I chuckled. Naomi shook her head and almost giggled. That look of disbelief had still not left her beautiful face.

After we'd cleaned up the bits of the two broken coffee mugs and moped up the puddle of coffee from the floor, I took the bag of broken crockery and dumped it in the bin while Naomi rinsed out the floor cloth in the sink. I watched her, her back facing me, still in her sleep shorts and vest top, her hair all messy and uncombed. Seeing her like that reminded me of earlier when I had awoken in our bed, alive and with her again. I had no idea how long it had been since we had woken up together but it felt like forever and I had a sudden desire to pick her up in my arms and carry her off back to bed, just so I could lay down next to her again and look at her. I stepped up behind her and slowly slid my arms around her waist, pulling her into me. Her neck was exposed and my lips brushed the soft skin just where her shoulders met the curve of it. Naomi shuddered and her head fell back against my chest, she moaned softly. I kissed her neck again and followed the kiss with a swift sweep of my tongue eliciting another, harder moan.

"Do you like that?" I asked her, my voice husky against her skin. I could feel the stirring heat of desire in my groin again.

"Yes." She whispered breathlessly

"Want more?" I asked, my mouth already poised and ready at her shoulder. After a brief hesitation, which felt like an age, she replied,

"Yes." Her hands braced against the rim of the stainless steel sink as I lavished attention on her neck finishing with a teasing nibble of her earlobe. The sounds she made were driving me wild. I was already fully hard and Naomi wasn't being shy either, she had pushed her body tight against me so that my cock now rested at the small of her back. She was practically panting in response to my kisses on her skin. My arms still encircled her waist but the hem of her vest top had risen slightly and my thumb touched bare flesh. I began moving it in slow, soft circles on her stomach, my other hand slipped down and grabbed her hip, pulling her even tighter against me. Naomi's breathing was becoming more rapid and her eyes were closed, her head still rested on my chest and was slightly tilted to the right, giving me a perfect view of her cleavage. The way her nipples stood out against the thin cotton fabric reminded me that she wasn't wearing a bra. A distant flash of a memory came to my mind of bare breasts bouncing as she rode me and I wanted that again, now.

I moved my hand up and under her vest cupping the warm, firm flesh. Tweaking the little hard nub as I playfully bit down on her exposed neck, she writhed against me. Encouraged, I let my other hand slide around her hip and down over her shorts between her legs. I could feel the heat from her radiating through the fabric. I imagined how wet she would be and my fingers itched to explore further. I began gently rubbing her through her shorts and she shifted her feet slightly so that her legs opened wider. My cock, pushed tight against her back, pulsed with the need to be inside her. Her chest heaved with each ragged breath and suddenly her hands were in my hair. She tugged on my hair and rasped,

"Please Joe! Please!"

"What do you want mia cara? Tell me." I demanded teasingly. Her hips thrust forward in response, grinding herself on my fingers. The crotch of her shorts felt damp and I knew damned well what she wanted but I wanted to hear her say it. I needed to know she desired me as much as I did her. I needed to know that she was mine. She swallowed and spoke in a whispered rush,

"Touch me."

"Anything you say bella." I responded in a low growl and did as she demanded. Hooking my fingers under the leg of her tiny sleep shorts, I found her centre and slid my finger into her silky heat. The affect was instantaneous as she cried out, gripping fistfuls of my hair and grinding down on my finger.

"Jesus Christ, Naomi! You're soaking." I worked my finger slowly in and out of her, relishing the feel of her and the way her pelvic muscles clamped around my finger. "Kiss me Naomi." She tipped her head right back and to the side offering me her mouth, her green eyes were half open and slightly glazed over. There was no doubt that she wanted me now. The hand that had been playfully squeezing her breast now slid up her throat and I held her chin in place while my mouth explored hers. That seemed to push her up a gear. The thought that she liked that, that she trusted me enough to have my hand on her throat, excited me beyond belief. She moved her hips back and forth, fucking my fingers,

"Ohhhh bella, you are truly spectacular!" I murmured against her mouth, "I want to be inside you, Naomi. Now."

"Mmm." She moaned.

"Say it." I demanded. "Tell me to make you come." Her breath hitched and she gasped,

"I want you to fuck me, Joe. Fuck me and make me come."

That was all I needed to hear. I pulled down her shorts and she stepped out of them as I took off my own and flung them aside. She was standing, bent slightly but still gripping on to the kitchen sink. I sank down on my knees so my face was level with her beautiful peachy bottom. Starting at her ankles, I ran my hands slowly, teasingly up her legs until a hand rested on each cheek. Parting her gently I took in the sight and scent of her, a sweet tangy mix of vanilla-scented Jasmine,

"Beautiful." I murmured. I couldn't resist tasting her and plunged my tongue deep into her centre. She bucked backwards and I buried my face between her legs licking, sucking and kissing her flesh. Reaching my hand around to tease her from the front, she continued to eagerly grind herself against my face. I could tell she wouldn't last long if I carried on and my inner wickedness took over. I wanted to prolong her pleasure for as long as I could so I pulled away, wiping my hand across my mouth as I rose to stand behind her.

"Don't stop." She pleaded.

"Oh I have no intention of stopping bella, I am going to make you come I just don't want it to be yet." I let the tip of my cock slide over her entrance and she moaned again, harder this time.

"Joe!"

"Spread your legs for me, Naomi." I positioned myself and teased her with the tip of my cock, sliding it slowly up and down her centre, coating it with her silkiness. Her legs shook with anticipation and several times she tried to take me inside of her by pushing backwards whenever I neared her opening. I grinned, enjoying the tease,

"Joe, please! I want you, please? I've waited so long." She begged and I could resist her no more. Grabbing her hip with my left hand, I steadied her. My right hand clasped around the base of my length, I guided myself into her. I had only pushed forward a few inches when she took matters into her own hands and thrust her hips backwards, impaling herself on me. A guttural cry formed on her lips as she took me to the hilt. A multitude of Italian expletives came pouring from my mouth and I had to take a second to gather my senses. The baseness of her act was pure and raw and it drove me to the edge.

"You little beast! Is that how you want it? Hard?" She didn't verbalise her answer but began rocking back and forth quite forcefully, soft, animalistic grunts accompanied each thrust of her hips. I stood still for a few minutes and watched, enthralled as she rode my length. She was a fucking goddess! I felt like the luckiest man on the planet. It was truly a wondrous sight to watch a beautiful woman lose herself in a moment of raw, unadulterated passion. Especially when it was your dick she was losing herself on. God, I could've watched her ride me right till the end but some innate sense of chivalric masculinity told me *I* should be the one making *her* come and so I reached down and pulled her right leg up and to the side, hooking my arm underneath her knee and opening her wide. My other arm slipped around so my hand rested on her throat again. She twisted her head towards me, wild desire flashed in her eyes, her cheeks flushed. A little wry smile touched her lips and I knew this was how she wanted it. I knew my woman, every beautiful inch of her even though fucking her now felt like the first time. I revelled in the glory of her, wanting only to pleasure her. My own pleasure driven on by the knowledge that any minute now she would fall apart in my arms. The force of my thrusts caused her hip and the top of her thigh to bang into the kitchen counter,

"Ahh!" She cried and I momentarily slowed. "Don't you dare stop!" She said and I grinned but lowered her leg and shifted her position. I pulled her a few steps away from the sink and pushed down on her back,

"Bend over Naomi." She didn't hesitate and I guided myself inside her again, slipping in easily despite how tight she was. Placing my hands on those pert cheeks, I pulled my thumbs apart so I could watch my cock glide in and out of her. I fucked her slowly at first, sliding all the way out then driving back in to the hilt. As I gathered pace she grasped the edges of the sink, her knuckles white with the strain. She was so verbal and *loud* with her responses I struggled to maintain self-control. The cries of 'Oh god yes!' and 'fuck, harder!' that sprang from that filthy mouth of hers almost caused the gathering knot of heat in my groin to erupt. I needed to make her come before that happened. I gathered up a handful of her hair and gently pulled, causing her head to tilt back. She was breathing rapidly, her mouth open. I wanted to kiss her and leaned forwards, encircling her waist with my free arm and pulling her to me, I managed to reach her mouth, handfuls of her silken brown hair still clamped in my fist, and I kissed her deeply. I kept kissing her, biting her bottom lip and soothing it with my tongue, all the while continuing a steady pace of hard thrusts until I sensed she was close to coming.

"Ti amo, Naomi." I whispered against her lips and I meant it. "My beautiful woman. Ti amo." Her lips pressed against mine and smothered the sound of her orgasm, her body shook and I felt her muscles clamp hard around my cock. Her knees buckled and I gripped her waist tighter to hold her up. I let myself go and allowed the burgeoning sensations to overcome me. My own body responded to hers and I came hard- grunting against her mouth.

As the waves of pleasure subsided, I held her gently and rained kisses down on her face and back as we waited for our breathing to slow. We stayed like that for a minute or two in happy, sated silence until she pushed away from the sink. Pulling herself off me, Naomi turned and placed both palms on my chest. She raised her eyes to mine, olive green penetrating my very soul and said,

"I love you too Joseph Ferrantino." She planted a kiss on my chest and turned her head to rest it against me.

I kissed the top of her head while I held her and heard her utter the tiniest whisper, "*My* Joe."

CHAPTER
thirteen

Naomi

What in the actual bloody hell was going on? I'd been asking myself the same question for the entire day and I still had no answer, no logical one anyway. Joe- *my* Joe was real! No matter how many times I told myself it was a physical impossibility, there was no denying a sexy silver-haired Italian man, named Joseph Ferrantino, lay fast asleep in my bed. I had lain next to him for quite some time and listened to him fall asleep but there was no way in a million years I could sleep.

For the last few hours I had convinced myself I'd finally flipped and was having full blown hallucinations. Then I remembered some quote about '*if you thought you were crazy, you definitely weren't*' or something like that. I'd thought maybe it was some kind of chemical imbalance in my brain that was causing it. But then dismissed that theory on the basis that I'd had sex with him today, twice! As much as I had given in to those fantasies previously, they'd never left my lips raw from kissing or made my lady parts throb from the blissfully heavy pounding it had gotten. Ohhhh no, that was most definitely real, so it stood to reason that Joe was too. I just couldn't for the life of me work out how? Google had been utterly useless, every hit that came back implied I was undeniably bonkers and should probably be wearing a straitjacket as part of my daily attire. As illogical as it sounded, the only possible thing left to do was read my manuscript.

I held the folder, containing the ninety-eight pages of A4 that I had written and printed off so far, on my lap. The story was nowhere near finished and I had read over it many times but now, I sat on my sofa daring myself to open it. I argued with myself that I didn't need to read it because I already knew what it said, I'd written it after all. But I knew I had to see it for myself, I had to confirm it. Tentatively I opened the file and began reading the first page. My heart did a little skip when I got to the part about how Joe and I had met, the part I had stolen from Laney Marsh's original manuscript. It was all there in black and white, the scene in Joe's book bar, The Magnificent Medici and how he came over to talk to me at my table. Every little detail was there right down to the title of the book I had been reading. It was *exactly* the same as he'd described it to me this morning. Moreover, Joe looked exactly how Laney had described him and just how I had always imagined him. I skipped forward a few pages to the part where we had fallen in love and Joe had moved to

England to open our own book bar- The Imp. We'd decided to name it that because of the infamous Lincoln Imp associated with the city. I skipped forward again and read a sex scene, I couldn't fathom how accurate the intimate details were. I had described exactly how Joe liked to make love, the names he liked to call me and how he loved to hear me ask him for what I wanted. I closed the folder and hugged it to my chest. I don't know why I was in shock because I knew that reading it would only confirm what I had already knew. Granted, the concept of what had happened remained within the boundaries of the impossible but it was here, right in front of me in print and it was happening to me in real life. The laws of science should render this an inconceivable possibility, but the blatant reality of it was undeniable- I had woken up this morning smack bang in the middle of my own novel!

"What have you got there?" Came a sultry, sleepy voice behind me. Startled, I jumped up from my seat, the folder falling to the floor.

"Shit! Joe! You scared me. Don't go sneaking up on me like that!" I scolded and bent to retrieve the folder. I had no intention of telling him what it was. Not yet anyway, not until I'd worked out how to handle it. He chuckled,

"Aww I'm sorry bella, I didn't mean to frighten you and I didn't *sneak*, you were just a million miles away. Why are you awake?"

"Well you made me jump!" I said and then immediately melted because he gave me puppy eyes and stuck out his bottom lip in an exaggerated pout. I giggled, "That is very unfair, Joseph."

"Hmmm *Joseph*? I like it when you use my full name, it makes me feel like I've been naughty." He grinned at me and wiggled his brows suggestively.

"Well maybe you have. It's not nice to scare a lady you know." I put the folder back in my drawer and made my way around the sofa towards him. He looked stunningly dishevelled in his boxers, hair all mussed up and a wicked little glint in his eyes.

"A lady? Are you sure bella? Because what you did in our bed earlier was not very ladylike." He teased. I reached the welcome of his open arms and stepped eagerly into his warm embrace. He smelled deliciously of sex and of me and in that moment, I went past caring about the how's or the why's of Joe sudden manifestation and just embraced it. He was real and he was *mine*. I had a million questions rattling around in my head but they could wait. I had no idea how long this…*thing* would last, for all I knew I could wake up tomorrow and find him gone. But, for the rest of the night, it was just me and him so when he murmured in my ear that he'd missed me and to come back to bed, that's exactly what I did.

His arm was heavy around my waist as we spooned under the covers together but I liked it, it was comforting and a solid reminder that he was there. His breath on my shoulder made my entire body tingle and I felt the stirrings of desire again. *Good grief! I'm turning into a nymphomaniac!* I turned my head towards him. *Who could blame me if I was? Look at him, he's beautiful.* I felt like a doe-eyed teenager, in the first weeks of a new love. Except I knew this was different, I had loved him before I ever really knew him, before when he was just someone's idea of a great book boyfriend. Now that he was here, I knew that even if this were to be my one and only night with him, that if I should wake tomorrow and find him gone, I'd never love like this again. I didn't want to sleep, I wanted to make the most of him and of the time we had been granted by whatever force had brought him to me. I didn't want to waste time sleeping.

"Joe? Are you awake?" I whispered.

"Yes bella." He replied softly. I turned around to face him and kissed him slowly, my hand pushed down between us and I cupped him. I felt him stiffen immediately and he inhaled sharply

"Again?" He chuckled.

"Again." I said.

"Woman you are insatiable!"

"You don't seem to mind." I said and gave him another squeeze. He growled and his hazel eyes pinned me with a wicked look.

"You, mia cara, are in big trouble."

"I was hoping you'd say that." I grinned.

"Diavolo." was the last thing he said before he grabbed me pulled me underneath him, taking me to the exact place I wanted to be.

CHAPTER
fourteen

The Imp

The first thing I noticed was the absence of his arm around me. Panic knotted in the pit of my stomach. Joe wasn't here. Had I dreamt up a sick delusion of a fantasy scenario I had invented? I didn't dare open my eyes for fear of seeing an empty space on the pillow. I lay on my side where the warm cosiness of my bed completely contradicted the cold blanket of fear I now felt. My knees drawn up into a fetal position, I squeezed my eyes tight shut, attempting to block out the morning sun that peeked through the bedroom curtains. It was a futile attempt to stop the day from happening. When I woke up yesterday, the impossible had happened. I didn't want to wake up today and find him gone.

I heard singing and hope burst from my chest like a solar flare from the sun. He was singing! He was still here, it was still real and... what the *hell* was he singing? I got out of bed and walked barefoot down the hallway towards the kitchen, shrugging on my cardigan as I walked. As I neared the kitchen I could hear the clink clunk of crockery and the smell of fresh coffee wafted past me. God, his singing was dreadful! He sounded like a cat being strangled.

"Well, it's nice to know you have at least one shortcoming." I laughed and poked my head around the door.

"Buongiorno amore mio!" He beamed at me and opened his arms out for a hug. My eyes widened, slightly taken aback by his chosen attire. He was butt naked aside from a checked apron that tied around his waist and neck. The chef's hat he wore cocked to one side, making him look both damned sexy but equally as comical.

"What in God's name are you wearing?" I wrapped my arms around him, squeezing him tight and he kissed the top of my head twice.

"It's the appropriate uniform for working in a kitchen mia cara." He winked at me, "And what do you mean by shortcoming? You don't like my singing?"

"Is that what you call it? And for your information, aprons are usually worn on top of clothes." He took on an exaggerated wounded look which immediately made me giggle.

"Naomi! You wound me with your cruel words. Everybody knows all Italians can sing like God's own angels, why are you being so wicked? You are a cruel, cruel woman. I *dress* nice for you, I cook your breakfast, service your puss…"

"Whoa there Casanova! Firstly, I'm not trying to be cruel, your singing, although wildly out of tune, is quite adorable. Secondly, I'd say you being dressed right now is somewhat of an overstatement," Joe opened his mouth in protest but I pressed a finger to his lips to stop him, "not that I'm complaining, the absolute contrary." I grinned at him and gave his bum a cheeky spank, "Thirdly, we shall discuss your services after and only after you tell me what smells so delicious? Joe! I can't believe you made me breakfast." I looked around at the various packets and cooking utensils dotted around the worktops. "What have you made?"

"Be seated bella donna and all will be revealed."

Joe ushered me from the kitchen and seated me at the table, pulling a chair out for me and proffering a low bow. I flushed a little, imagining the view from the rear. He must've noticed my reaction because he winked and slipped me the cheekiest schoolboy grin I'd ever seen. Never in my life had any man cooked me breakfast, not even Iain! Whatever it was smelled incredible and my mouth began to salivate in anticipation. Joe came back and served me a large mug of caffe latte. He placed a napkin over my lap before planting another kiss atop my head and disappearing back to the kitchen. Moments later he returned with warmed bread rolls, butter and jam and some biscuits.

"Did you make these?" I asked him, holding up the rolls.

"Si mia Signora, I always bake my own you know that. The biscotti too." He took one of the hard biscuits, dipped it in my latte and offered it to me. I opened my mouth and took a bite, it was delicious and soft, not hard like before.

"Oh wow! That's tasty Joe, these are really good." I took the other half of the biscotti from him and dipped it again.

"I made a fresh batch to take down to The Imp later." He said. I coughed.

"What?"

"Back to work today lover, as much as I know your only desire is to take me to bed and ravish me *again,* we do have a business to run. Besides, I feel great so there's no reason to delay it. I admit I'm quite looking forward to getting back there, aren't you?"

"Work? You want us to go to work?"

"Of course, why not?" *Well how about because it shouldn't even exist for starters!* Is what I wanted to say but I didn't. I couldn't think of any effective argument to the contrary without letting the proverbial cat out of the bag, so I just said,

"Um, OK. If you want to." And started slicing into a warm roll.

As we walked hand in hand up Steep Hill towards where our book bar, The Imp, was supposed to be situated, I began to feel anxious but also a little excited. What if it wasn't there? What would I say? I'd have to explain things to him, which is something I really wasn't looking forward to. I had butterflies in my stomach, but what if it *was* there, just the way I had written it in my story? That would mean I really had, by some unknown magic of the universe, managed to create my ideal life and that was huge! I mean there was no reason on earth why the cafe would be real but Joe was real enough and how else could I explain the framed picture of us on my wall at the flat. I felt like I needed to see it to believe it and now, as we breached the hill a small cobbled street lay before me. The rest of Steep Hill carried on up and to the left but right there, in full view and undeniably real, was our book bar. The window shutters were closed and there were no tables and chairs outside like in the picture but a huge sign hung above the door which clearly stated it as 'THE IMP' in big letters. A smaller phrase was painted underneath which read 'Book Bar & Cafe' then, listed as proprietors were 'J. & N. Ferrantino.' I looked again. *What! J. & N. Ferrantino? Since when are we married?* Instinctively I looked down at my left hand and uttered something totally indecipherable when I saw the tell-tale band of gold encircling the third finger. *That* had most definitely *not* been there this morning! My head swam in circles, I felt myself sinking, spinning out of control. I stumbled and Joe caught me.

"You Ok bella?"

"Um, no. Not really...I...feel." I couldn't finish because a wave of nausea hit me and I knew if I didn't sit down soon I'd be bringing up breakfast all over the cobbles.

"Hey, come here. Take my arm. Let's get you inside." Joe's concern was touching, he helped me stumble across the cobbles and sat me down on the stone steps outside the cafe while he unlocked the door. I felt so hot I could hardly breathe. The door unlocked, Joe helped me inside and sat me on one of the chairs.

"Sit here and I'll fetch you some water." I nodded and off he went at a pace to what I presumed was the kitchen area. I looked down at the wedding ring on my hand again. *A fucking wedding ring!* I know damn well it hadn't been there this morning, it had just appeared out of thin air. The thing that had me reeling, dizzy like I'd had far too much sun, was not only the fact that Joe and I appeared to be married but that I know I hadn't written any of that in my manuscript.

Joe returned with a glass of cold water and a damp cloth which he placed on my forehead.

"Drink." He instructed and I did. I could barely swallow my throat felt so tight but I managed a few sips and he took the glass from me. He pulled up a chair for himself with his free hand, his other still held the cloth to my head.

"Thank you." I croaked. The cool cloth brought welcome relief and I felt the nausea pass.

"You're as white as a sheet, Naomi. What happened? Are you sick?" Joe's brows furrowed, the joviality of this morning was gone, replaced by serious concern.

"I…I don't know. I just came over a little dizzy." I said weakly. "Maybe it was the climb up the hill." I could hardly tell him the truth, that the realisation that we did indeed own a business and that we were married but I had no recollection of a wedding, had made me almost pass out with shock!

"We were walking a little briskly." He concluded. "Maybe it wasn't such a good idea to come to work today after all. I'm sorry my love, I should've realised that you must have been through so much lately with worrying about me and on top of your father's passing too."

I jumped straight out of the chair. "Oh my god, Joe! My Dad! My Mother! How could I have forgotten that? Oh my god, I'm a fucking terrible daughter." I was frantic. How in the hell could I have forgotten that my Dad had died and since Joe's appearance, it hadn't even crossed my mind! I was the worst person on the planet.

"Calm down bella, sit down or you'll make yourself ill again."

"I can't sit down, Joe! I need to call my Mum. I haven't spoken to her since…I don't know when. I don't even know what day it is for Christ's sake!" I scrambled in my pocket for my mobile phone and searched for Mum's number. Joe placed his hand over mine to stop me.

"Love, I'm all for you calling your mother but might I suggest you use the land line or Skype? It'll be expensive on your mobile."

"What do you mean? It's just down the road? Why would I Skype her?" I looked at him in confusion.

"OK, that's it, we're going home." He stated and he stood up and pushed his chair under the table.

"Like hell we are! Not until you explain to me why I need to Skype my Mum when she lives ten minutes from this place?"

"Naomi, we're going home because you're clearly unwell and when we get home, you're going to bed and I'm calling the doctor." He tried to take my hand to pull me up but I snatched it away.

"Joseph Ferrantino! I'm not taking one step until you tell me what the fuck is going on!" My voice shook with emotion and a sickening feeling spread in my gut. He stood for a few moments, his brows creased and then softened. He sat back down and took my shaking hands in his.

"Mia cara, your Mum is in New Zealand with your sister Imogen and her family. They moved there before our wedding, we went to New Zealand for our honeymoon love. We spent two weeks with them and met baby Joshua, remember?"

"My sister has a *baby?*" He nodded and squeezed my hand. How was it that he knew all of this and I didn't? I started to cry, my elation at having Joe in my life was marred with confusion. I felt totally overwhelmed by the events of the past few days. I felt like a stranger in my own life. Except for the part about Joe and I being an item and running a book bar, this wasn't anything like I had written in my manuscript! I hadn't written about our wedding or my mum being in New Zealand or Imogen becoming a mother! It didn't make sense, none of it did. The walls in the cafe began to close in on me, I felt hot. I couldn't breathe, I needed to get out. I needed to run! I shot out of the chair and towards the door. I heard Joe shout but I wasn't listening. I knew where I was going and I ran as fast as my legs and the cobbled street would let me.

"Naomi, wait!" Joe was behind me but I left him, his voice fading as I ran, "Wait! I'll come with you!" He called but I ran and ran till my lungs burned and my heart pounded in my ears. I didn't stop running until I reached the little house with the red front door- my childhood home, the house I watched my father die in. I walked to the door and knocked, *banged* on it, until I heard a key turn in the lock. Bracing myself for the worst but willing for it to be my mother's face that greeted me, I waited.

"Yes? Can I help you?" Said the woman that was *not* my mother.

CHAPTER
fifteen

Doctor Doctor

I winced as the needle pierced my arm. Whatever liquid was in that syringe burned like the molten fires of Mount Doom.

"Will she be alright?" I heard Joe ask Dr White.

"She needs rest. The sedative will take effect soon. I'd suggest you get in touch with Dr Blanchard, her therapist, as soon as possible. Trauma can affect people in many different ways and she obviously has issues she needs to deal with." I saw Dr White pat Joe's arm and begin to pack away his equipment. Joe looked in my direction, his forced smile belying his concern.

"Naomi, I'm going to see the doctor out OK? Will you be alright for a minute?"

I nodded, already feeling the effects of the sedative. I couldn't speak because I knew that I wasn't OK. Far from it, I was drowning in a sea of confusion. My emotions were almost indistinguishable from each other. Shock blended with fear and bewilderment which gave way to grief and the whole cycle started again. This felt like a fairground ride that I couldn't get off, it just kept moving faster and faster until I wasn't sure if the world were spinning or I was.

I fought to stay awake, I needed to go over things in my head. So much had happened, so many changes in the last few days. Hell, I wasn't even sure what day it was. I felt overwhelmed. Nothing made sense, everything was fuzzy and confusing. My vision blurred and I felt my eyelids involuntarily closing.

"Joe!" I slurred, suddenly afraid of the creeping darkness that filled my vision. Afraid of what would happen when I woke up. What if something else changed? What if I woke up and found none of it had been real? I couldn't decide which was worse. I felt so out of control. But having Joe here with me was the one redeeming feature of this madness and deep down I knew that I would, if it came to it, endure everything else that this new life threw at me if it meant keeping Joe. I finally had something good and real to hold on to. I just wished my world would stop spinning.

I felt a warm hand slip into mine and give it a gentle, reassuring squeeze.

"I'm here bella. Go to sleep."

"Don't leave me." I managed to whisper.

"Never."

The sedative finally won the battle and I fell into a fitful half sleep. Not the peaceful rest that the good doctor had intended but one filled with nightmares and pain. Images of my father laid cold and unmoving on the floor, another of my mother happy in New Zealand, without me. Mum bouncing her grandchild on her knee with a laughing Immy sat beside her while I lay here…forgotten. Flashes of a wedding, my wedding to Joe that I hadn't even attended. The last image was the one that broke me…Joe *gone…* and me left with nothing and no one, just a black hole of lonely despair. I cried out and seconds later felt a warm reassuring touch at my cheek. *Not alone then?*

Unable to decide if I was asleep or just heavily sedated and hallucinating, I tried to call out to whomever had touched my cheek. I just needed to not feel alone. This time I felt a hand slip into mine and squeeze gently. Waves of fear washed over me. I was so afraid to let go and sleep fully just in case whatever magic had brought Joe to me, somehow disappeared when I lost my minute grip on consciousness.

I had no idea how long I had endured that pitiful torture but when I woke up, groggy and heavy, I knew I felt just as bad as I had before. Joe was there, sitting on the edge of my bed, *our* bed. I raised my left hand and the band of gold on my third finger taunted me. But Joe was here. I knew nothing had changed, my mother had still left me and my sister had a family I was a stranger to. But Joe was here. The more I repeated those words in my head, the more the pain in my heart lessened. Joe was here. He wouldn't let me fall, as long as I had him, I would be alright. If we were together and he loved me, I could learn to cope with all the irrational, unexplainable madness that was now my life. I needed to understand it all but there was time, I hoped. I had panicked today. The last few days had been crazy and spectacularly overwhelming but now, I understood that I would need to tackle one situation at a time. I had to because otherwise I would go under. Joe was everything I had dreamed of and more and if the only way the universe would let him be mine, was to dump a load of unexpected shit in my life, then so be it. It was naive to think I could have it all. When had anything ever worked entirely in my favour? Joe was the one good thing I had ever been given and in truth I hadn't been given him, I had stolen him and rebranded him as mine. Perhaps this was why it wasn't the perfect scenario I had envisioned. I scoffed at myself, *idiot! Only you could think being married to a hot Italian with your own business wasn't perfect!* It was true, why was I complaining? It *was* perfect it was just…too much too soon.

Joe shifted on the bed. His hand reached out to me to stroke my hair. His touch instantly reassuring. *My safety zone.*

"Bella. How are you feeling?" The concern in his eyes blatantly obvious.

"I'm OK I think. I feel a little shaky. Is there any water?"

"I'll get some, one minute." He rose and went quickly to the bathroom to fill a cup. When he returned, I had propped myself upright on two pillows. I took the water and drank it all in one go.

"You want some more?" Joe offered out his hand for the cup but I shook my head.

"No thank you." He took the cup and placed it back on the bedside table. "What time is it?" I asked.

"It's a little after 3pm." He said. "Did you get a good sleep?"

"I suppose so." I lied. "I still feel a bit groggy though."

"That's probably the effects of the sedative. The Doc thought it best to give you something to help you rest. He says it's probably all the stress of the last few weeks that finally caught up with you."

"Probably." I said, not knowing what else I *could* say. Joe looked down at his hands and he started to pick at the bedcovers.

"You scared me baby. When you ran off like that. I didn't know what to do. I had to lock the bar and then come find you. I didn't know what I would find when I reached you."

"I'm sorry." I choked back. Seeing him scared and sad like this made me feel awful. I knew I'd have to pretend like I'd had a mini breakdown or something because there's no way I could ever tell him the real reason for my outburst. Joe caught the tone in my voice and was instantly beside me, he pulled me into a crushing hug and breathed into my hair deeply.

"Don't ever do that again. Please Naomi? If you ever feel like you need to run, run to *me*. There's nothing we can't get through together OK?"

"OK" I replied meekly. The depth of feeling with which he spoke stunned me. It was clear that despite him only being an actual physical person for a few days, the situation we were in was by no means new, at least to him.

This was a fully established, committed relationship. It was a *marriage*! It would take some getting used to but I had already decided it was what I wanted. I'd just have to pretend everything was how it had always been. Joe was my husband, we had a book bar and I was *not* crazy.

"I called your mother." Joe said and I froze.

"You what? Why did you do that?" I groaned.

"Because I think she should know when her daughter is ill. Don't you?"

No! I wanted to say. *She abandoned me.* But then I remembered that everything was different now. And she had been planning on moving to New Zealand even before all of this happened.

"What did she say?"

"She wants to Skype you later when you're feeling up to it."

"What if I'm not feeling up to it?" I whined.

"Naomi," he chuckled, "come on now, don't be a coward. She's your mother and she loves you. It's just a quick call."

Then why did she leave me? I sighed heavily. "Fine. But not yet. I'm too tired and my head is fuzzy. I need all my wits about me to deal with my mother."

"You're too harsh bella. Your mama is adorable. Her heart is in the right place."

OK now I knew I was in some parallel fucking universe or something because no one could ever call my mother 'adorable'. A thought occurred to me,

"Joe? Do we have a wedding album? Of photographs. I mean."

"You know we do." His brow furrowed again but he quickly smoothed it over. *Blimey, he must think I'm bonkers.*

"Can you get it for me please?"

"Sure. If you want. Are you feeling nostalgic?" I nodded and smiled and Joe disappeared out the bedroom door. When he returned he held out a thick, brown leather covered album to me. I took it and sat nervously with it on my knee. I wasn't sure I had the mental capability or the appropriate acting skills to be able to look it with Joe sitting right there with me so I asked him to make me a coffee.

"Are you hungry bella? I can make you something special?"

"Really? That'd be lovely, thank you." I beamed at him. I was starving but it also meant it he'd be in the kitchen for a while, giving me chance to look at the album alone. I felt like I needed the space and the privacy to deal with whatever was in this album. Joe gave me a kiss on the cheek and pottered off to conjure me up some wonderful culinary masterpiece.

I stroked the album cover and slowly peeled it back. The first page gave the details and date of our wedding. I was astounded to discover we had gotten married in Lincoln cathedral! That was unbelievable…and expensive. I wondered how we had ever been able to afford that? I felt quite jealous of the fact that I had apparently gotten married in one of the most impressive medieval buildings in the country and didn't even bloody remember it! My fingers trembled a little as I peeled back another page to be presented with a large, black and white close up of Joe and I kissing. I turned to the next page and saw a full page spread of what little friends and family I had, stood together in front of the cathedral. *My* friends and family, not Joe's.

It struck me how much my dad would've loved my wedding. I pictured his face beaming with pride as he walked me down the aisle, imagined his father-of-the-bride speech and how he would've welcomed Joe into our family. The fact that both myself and my father had been denied this day hurt so much I almost couldn't stand it. The lump in my throat strangulated the whispered words I forced from my lips,

"I miss you daddy."

I kept flicking through and studying the photos, trying to absorb the fact that this had been my wedding day but it was so surreal. I could see myself, Joe and other people I recognised in the pictures but it felt like I was looking at someone else's life. It was the strangest feeling not having any recollection of what supposedly had been the happiest day of my life. It all looked so perfect and everyone was smiling, even my mother! My dress was simple and understated but elegant, exactly the sort of thing I would have chosen. Joe looked incredible in a dark navy blue suit which complimented his colouring.

"You looked so beautiful that day mia cara." The sound of Joe's voice made me jump and I quickly shut the album.

"Oh, hey. I didn't hear you come in."

"Sorry, I didn't mean to make you jump...again." He smiled. "Here is a nice hot coffee just for you and your food will be ready in about fifteen minutes." He looked rather satisfied with himself so I assumed that whatever it was that he was cooking, was going to be pretty special. My stomach growled just to remind me that I was indeed, very hungry. I inhaled deeply as delicious smells wafted in from the kitchen.

"Oh Joe, that smells amazing! What are you making?"

"It's just a little pasta dish and side salad my love." He grinned and I cocked an eyebrow at him.

"Just a little pasta? Really? Because when I make pasta it smells nothing like that!"

"That's because you are not Italian. Only Italians can cook pasta and make it smell and taste like the food of the Gods." He winked at me and I laughed.

"And only you could make arrogance look adorable." I quipped back.

"It's all part of my charm bella. There's a reason that Italians are labelled the best lovers in the world you know."

"Oh really? And what is that?"

"Because it's the truth." He shrugged laughing. "I need no other reason than that. The evidence speaks for itself don't you agree?"

I hit him with a pillow. "Oh my god! How cocky are you!" He tugged the pillow away from me and a look of pure devilment crossed his face.

"You want to talk about cocky? I can show you *cocky*." He winked.

"That is not what I meant and you know it!" I was belly laughing hard now. God he was adorable. I could forget that I didn't get to attend our wedding. I could excuse that fact that a huge chunk of my life had changed without me being aware of it. Because I had Joe and he was worth it. I would get used to my new life and everything would be fine. My mum wasn't dead-she was just not here. I supposed Joe and I could fly over and go visit her and Immy in New Zealand and I could meet my nephew or was it niece? I couldn't remember right now. But suddenly, with Joe sitting here laughing with me, things didn't seem as frightening as they had done this morning.

An alarm went off in the kitchen and Joe got up off the bed.

"That's the oven timer. Do you want to eat at the table or would you like me to fetch you a tray and you can eat it in bed?"

"Well aren't I being spoiled!"

"Yes. You are. So, which one?"

"Hmm, I think I'd like a tray please. Or is that incredibly lazy of me?"

"You're entitled to be lazy after this morning bella."

"Well, perhaps I should be lazy more often then if this is the sort of treatment I get." I teased. Joe wiggled his eyebrows and said,

"Oh this is nothing il amore mio…wait till you see what's for dessert!"

CHAPTER
sixteen

Just A Walk In The Park

A few weeks had passed in relative bliss. Joe and I had opened The Imp again and we were going to work together every day. I was slowly getting used to my new life. I'd spoken to Mum and Immy via Skype. It had been a rather bizarre experience having to pretend that everything was normal and listen to them talk about things like I should know what they were referring to. I'd tried to join in the conversation as best I could without it being obvious that I was totally clueless. I had asked a few nonchalant questions in an attempt to glean information that I could use to make my performance more plausible. But from the odd looks I'd gotten from Immy, my acting skills fell way below par.

The Imp was proving tiring work but so much fun! I'd never enjoyed socialising much and so I'd never made too many friends. The ones I'd made when I was with Iain had been his friends and had remained so after our split. I had a few old ones from my college days that kept in touch and visited now and again. But now, we had a couple of regulars who came into the book bar every day and chatted. I was getting to know my community and making new friends and found that I liked it. Of course, Joe was the big attraction, especially with all the university students. I saw the way they flirted and batted their eyes at him but I wasn't jealous. Joe being Joe, lapped up the attention and flirted right back but in an open and innocent way, with a laugh and joke. He usually winked and smiled over at me or put his arm around me and kissed my cheek, letting everyone know that he was mine. The older ladies especially loved him, even Mrs Crabtree from our building had taken to popping in at lunchtime for tea and cake and she had hardly ever gone out before. Joe had this uncanny ability to bring out the smile in everyone. Our little book bar business was booming and I was thrilled!

The one thing that spoiled it, was that I knew this picture of happiness couldn't possibly last. Joe had given me time to get over my little 'episode' and he hadn't mentioned anything further about the accident he was convinced he had been in. It played on my mind constantly, even though I tried to bury it, like a worm it always burrowed its ugly way into my thoughts. He would start asking soon, I knew it. I could see it in his eyes and on his face when he thought I wasn't looking. He wanted to know what had happened to him and I was going to have to tell him. I just hadn't banked on doing it so soon.

"Hey bella." Joe came up behind me and his arms went around my waist, pulling me into him.

"Hey you." I smiled. "I'm almost finished cleaning the tables. It was busy today wasn't it! Will you help me bring in the chairs from outside please?"

"Sure baby. I'm all done in the kitchen. I put the last of the dishes away and the pie is in the fridge for morning." He turned me around to face him and surprised me with a tender, lingering kiss. I felt that familiar tug just below my belly button that happened every time we kissed. When I opened my eyes I expected to see his cheeky smile but instead he looked rather serious.

"Come for a walk in the park with me after closing? We need to talk."

Oh God. The pleasurable tug in my belly quickly turned to a stab of fear. This was it. This was the day it would all fall apart.

"Uh huh." Was all I could manage and then thankfully his lips found mine again but not even Joe's kiss could melt away the feeling of dread that washed over me.

I spent the remaining half hour closing The Imp in absolute emotional turmoil. My mind raced. I went over and over what I could possibly say to him that didn't make me sound like a complete nutcase. I tried to think of how I could stick with the story of him having an accident, but realistically there was no way that would work in the long term. Eventually he'd need a doctor if he fell sick and then he'd find there were no medical records. Or what if one day he decided to track down evidence of his accident and couldn't find anything. I'd caught him looking at our wedding album earlier this week too. Did he not think it strange that none of his own friends or family were in any of the photographs? It was the first thing I had noticed so surely he must have too? Then again, what if I told him the truth and he believed me? I imagined how that conversation might go. *'Yes, so what happened was that I completely fell in love with you when I read about you in a book and then something magical happened and POOF! Here you are.'* How would he feel? How would he react? *Oh God.* He'd probably hate me *and* think I was a crazy basket case. There was just no way around it. I would just have to be brave and tell him everything. He deserved the truth.

My eyes constantly flicked back and forth to the small clock on the wall. When 5.30pm came Joe switched off the lights and walked me to the door. He said nothing as he turned the key in the lock. The silence was torture. When he finally turned to me he must have seen the nervous expression on my face because he took hold of my hand and gave it a reassuring squeeze.

"It's just a walk in the park bella. Come on, let's go."

We walked hand in hand to the small park not far from the little museum around the corner. It was uphill so by the time we arrived I was breathing hard. Unsure if it was caused by the climb or the growing sense of panic in my chest. Joe walked us over to a weather beaten, old wooden bench and pulled me down to sit next to him.

"Joe, I'm sorry. I…"

"Naomi, you know I love you, right?"

We had both spoken at the same time.

"Wait. What?" I didn't like the sound of that, he'd said it in a 'you know I love you *but*' sort of way.

"You go first bella."

"No, it's fine. I think I'd rather let you go first." I said, thinking that it might be easier to explain everything if I let him lead the discussion. I braced myself for the questions I knew he must be burning to ask and mentally tried to prepare my answers.

"I love you Naomi and because I love you so much. I need to ask you something but just hear me out first OK?"

Oh shit, here we go!

"OK."

"I think you should go see Dr Blanchard, your therapist, again."

"Er…what?" That was not what I'd been expecting. "Why?"

"Bella, I know you don't want to talk about what happened last week but it's been playing on my mind. I…saw some things…and I'm worried about you love. I think you might be experiencing post-traumatic stress or something like that."

This conversation was not turning out how I had feared it would. Now I wasn't sure if I should feel relieved, or worried about why Joe thought I needed therapy.

"What things have you seen? I told you, I'm fine. Really, there's no need to be worried. I've never felt so happy."

Joe chewed his bottom lip as if unsure how to proceed. He looked away from me for a few seconds and then I really did feel scared. What the hell had he seen?

"I found something. I didn't mean to read it bella. I was looking for some paper and I knew you had some in your cabinet. I found…"

"My manuscript!" I finished his sentence for him. Relief tinged with anxiety washed over me. That wasn't so bad was it? I mean it's just a story and it chronicles my life with Joe, almost like a diary really. Surely reading that wouldn't lead him to think I was gaga? Maybe it was a good thing he'd already read it, it might help soften the blow when…*if*… I told him the truth.

"Yes. I know it's private and I probably shouldn't have read it." Joe hung his head. "It caught my eye and I remembered seeing something like it when…when we weren't together." He meant when he was having his out of body experiences, or that's what he thought they were. I still had no idea what the hell had happened or how I'd ended up in my own novel.

I still didn't understand why my manuscript should be cause for concern. I tried to think back over what I had written that might upset him but I just couldn't see how it would. It had shocked me when I last looked at it and had seen how our lives together now followed my own plot line and how some things that I hadn't written, like my family being in New Zealand, had appeared. But everything had turned out great. I was happy. Surely, if Joe had read it, wouldn't it just look like I had written our story? I hadn't even finished it. In fact, the moment Joe had arrived in my life, I'd been so distracted by the sheer bizarre turn of events, and I had hardly give it much thought.

"Joe? I don't think I understand. What has reading my manuscript got to do with why you think I need a therapist?"

"Bella…I love that you have written about us. It's beautiful that you did that but…"

"But what?"

"Some of the other things that you wrote inside it…they… they don't really make any sense."

"Well, now *you're* not making any sense." I said, a little affronted. What the hell did he mean by that?

"Naomi, I'm not trying to upset you. I asked you to hear me out. Please?"

"Fine." I shrugged and Joe pulled me in for a hug. He kissed the top of my head and spoke into my hair.

"I thought coming to the park, it would be easier to talk because it was neutral ground. I see that was a mistake."

"Look, Joe. I still don't understand. Neutral ground? You're talking like it's a big thing. It's just a manuscript. I really don't see what your problem is?"

"It's not the things you already wrote…it's the things you're writing now. They're a little disturbing love."

"But I'm not writing anything! Joe, I really don't know what the hell you're talking about." This was getting beyond weird, I needed to go home and have him show me what he meant. "Can we go home? I need to see it." Joe nodded and pulled me up with him off the bench. He wrapped his arms around me and tucked my head under his chin.

"Io ti amo mia cara." He whispered softly.

"I know. I love you too. Can we just go?" I couldn't wait to get home, I knew things had already appeared that hadn't been written by me and although waking up to find I was married and my Mum had moved away had been a huge shock, I was getting used to it and everything had worked out great. So, I was more than curious to know what sort of 'disturbing' things had since materialised that had Joe in such a state of concern for my mental health.

The walk home had been quiet; we hadn't talked but every now and then Joe had squeezed my hand and given me a sympathetic smile. It had irritated me. I wasn't cross with Joe but I was agitated, I hated not being in control. I had been prepared to accept all the sudden changes in my life because I had Joe and he was everything I had ever wanted but if something or someone was messing with my situation, I had no idea how I could stop it.

I sat on the sofa while Joe got my manuscript from the cabinet, my foot tapping impatiently on the floor. When he handed me it, he asked if I wanted him to stay.

"Of course I want you to stay, I need you to show me what has upset you."

"OK." Joe sat next to me and put his arm around my shoulder protectively. This was unnerving, I looked at the manuscript on my knee and saw nothing different on the title page but it felt different in my hands. I could only describe it as how I imagine psychometry works, the moment I touched it I knew something was different- it felt...infected.

My instinctive reaction was to recoil but my curiosity overcame it. I had been living in a bubble this past few weeks and I had an ominous feeling it was about to burst and my happy little life would disintegrate before my eyes.

"Naomi? Do you want me to open it?" Joe asked.

"No Thanks, I need to do it myself." I took a big breath in and out and turned through the pages of text one by one. Nothing immediately different jumped out. The first 20k was as I had written it, just with the few unexpected changes that had occurred right after Joe appeared. Mum's move, my wedding and the birth of Immy's baby where all there but as I got to the end of my twenty thousand, things began to feel very different. I could sense it, a sickness, an invasion is the only way I could describe it. Agitation rose within me and when I turned a new page, one I knew I had not written, I had to fight for control of my emotions. New pages of text filled my manuscript, page after page of type, none of it mine. I couldn't believe what I was reading. Where had these words come from? I should've paid more attention when it started happening after Joe showed up but I'd been so swept up in the sheer magic of having Joe in my life, I'd done my usual trick and stuck my head in the sand. My manuscript had taken on a life of its own. I read through one of the new passages,

Melissa waited outside the bar for closing. She couldn't wait to see him again, it'd been months since her last trip to Florence and now she was here, waiting for Joe. She watched as the lights went out inside The Magnificent Medici and Joe stepped out of the front entrance, locking it behind him.

"Ciao Joe." I said, stepping out from the shadows. He turned towards my voice and a broad smile of recognition appeared on his face.

'Melissa? Is that you? Ciao bella! I missed you! And your beautiful smile. What are you doing here?" Joe opened his arms wide and I ran to him, the moment I reached him, he wrapped me in a hug so tight and sincere it took my breath away. God, I had missed him. I was here to stay this time and the first person I wanted to tell was Joe.'

This was not my story. This was Laney's.

CHAPTER
seventeen

Secrets and Lies

"I didn't write this." I said quietly. Silent fury bubbled inside of me and I struggled to contain it. *No! No! No! You can't have him back. You can't!*

"Naomi, of course you did bella. It's your manuscript. Baby, why are you writing things about me seeing another woman? It's a strange thing to do and a little upsetting if I'm honest. Is there something going on you're not telling me? Does it have anything to do with my accident?"

"What? No, of course not. What are you talking about?"

"Well…" Joe shifted uncomfortably in his seat. "When I was having those out of body experiences, I saw a little of your writing one time when you were asleep. The night your sister stayed here after your father had passed."

"That, was you? You knocked my notepad on the floor?" I asked and Joe nodded.

"I saw that you were writing about us, that's what gave me the clue that we were together. I wasn't sure until then but I had a feeling that I knew you. When I saw what you'd written, I thought it must be because you were sad that I wasn't there."

"You thought I was using it as catharsis?"

Joe frowned. "I don't know this word, catharsis?"

"Oh, sorry." Forgetting that English was only his second language. "It means like therapy."

"Ahh! Si, catarsi! Yes, I supposed it was like therapy for you. Now you understand me? Why I am concerned for you?"

"No, Joe. I don't"

He let out a lengthy sigh. "OK, let me try to explain. I have my memories of you and of us together and I have my memories of my life in Italia, si?"

"OK." I drew the word out, still not seeing where he was going with this conversation.

"But I also have huge gaps in my memory. I can't remember my family, my parents or friends back at home."

Oh shit, here we go. I cringed inwardly. This was going to get very awkward very quickly. I waited for him to tell me everything he'd noticed that wasn't quite right. This time I would tell him the absolute truth.

"Bella, the only thing or person who sticks out in my memories, other than you, is Melissa. But I don't know why."

Ouch.

"Now you're writing about her as if I had been seeing her back in Italy but I don't remember that. So, either it happened and I don't remember and you're somehow angry with me and this is why you're writing it all down, or…" He didn't finish.

"Or…I'm going crazy? Is that what you think?"

"No bella, ti amo. I'm not saying that. I just think we need to talk about lots of things. I need to piece together my memories and I think you have a lot of things you need to deal with. I don't think you have grieved properly for your father yet. I never hear you talk about him and you always look sad when I mention your mother and sister. You tell me you are happy but something in your eyes tells me different. I'm suggesting we go together to seek counselling."

"Joe, we don't need counselling. We do need to talk but it's not anything like you think it is. You asked me to hear you out earlier, now I need you to do the same for me OK?"

"Si, of course."

"I didn't write this." I held up my manuscript. "Well, most of it I did but not these other pages. This is someone else's work. I don't know how the hell it got there but it did. I'm going to try to figure it out but you're going to have to help me. I need you to believe me."

"I'm trying to Naomi but…how can you say it's not yours? I mean it's there in your manuscript. Did you copy it from someone?"

"No!" I said tersely and then felt an instant pang of guilt. *Liar!* "Oh shit. Look I copied the first little bit but that's all! It's not what you think." Joe was looking at me in a way I did not like, he was disappointed in me, I could tell. "Jesus Christ, I'm really not explaining this well. Let me start from the beginning." I took a deep, steadying breath and continued. "Joe… you're… not real. I mean you are *now* but you weren't before. I read about you in a book I was proofreading and…and I fell in love with you and I was upset and lonely and all I wanted was to escape for a while…so, I copied a part of the book but I started changing things in the story so it was about you and me, instead of you and Melissa." I looked at Joe for some sign that he was hearing me, that he believed me but his face had hardened, his expression unreadable. *Fuck*. I decided to just carry on and get it all out in the open as quickly as possible because if I looked into those steely eyes another second I knew I would falter. "After I started writing I kept hearing things and seeing things in the flat and, at first I thought it was my Dad's spirit or something but then you typed stuff on my laptop, do you remember?" I paused to let him answer but all he did was clench his jaw tighter, causing the muscle to twitch. I swallowed hard and bravely ploughed forward with my explanation. "Then…then that day when you appeared in my bathroom and we touched hands, something happened. Something *amazing* and magical." I was pleading with him now, willing him to see what the universe and I had contrived together.

"You came to me Joe. The universe gave you to me, you didn't have any accident and those weren't out of body experiences you were having. I wasn't sure what the hell they were but I think I know now, I think it was the magic, I think it was you beginning to manifest, to come to life... Joe?" There was a moment of heavy silence between us and then he spoke,

"Naomi, do you hear yourself?" Joe said stiffly. "You're talking like a crazy person."

"I know! I know. But I'm not crazy, *this* is crazy!" I waved the manuscript again. "It's real Joe and I don't know why but isn't it wonderful? You're here, with me and we are *happy.*"

"If we're happy then why are you writing shit about me and this Melissa?"

"It's not me! It's *Laney* the other author, your creator. I finished proofing her book but then I told her I couldn't take on any more of her work. I suppose she must be rewriting or something, I don't know but we must find her and stop her. She's changing things, I can feel it. It's all different, it's all wrong." Joe got up off the sofa and I looked up at him beseechingly. "Please Joe, we have to find her. Will you help me?" He looked away to stare at the wall. I held my breath and waited for his response. His shoulders slumped and he gave a small shake of his head and for one frightening moment, I thought I'd lost him.

"Naomi, I want to help you." *Oh thank God.* I breathed a sigh of relief.

"I'm going to book you in to see Dr. Blanchard as soon as possible."

"Wait! No, Joe. You're not listening!"

"I have listened bella. I'm trying to understand you but it doesn't make any sense, what you're saying is crazy. I want to help you, to help *us* and this is the only way that I can do that. You *must* see that?"

Annoyance and anger boiled inside of me. "Read it!" I shouted and flung the manuscript at him, it hit him in the chest and pages went everywhere. My eyes brimmed with tears and I instantly regretted my actions when I saw the hurt reflected in his. "Joe! I'm sorry I…" I reached out to him but he turned away and walked towards the door. Panic rose in my chest, "Where are you going? Please don't leave!" I cried.

"Naomi, I'm going for a walk. I've been very patient with you, put my own needs aside for *you!* I can't keep doing that without answers. There are things I need to know and if you can't see that, then we have a problem bella." Joe dropped his gaze and I felt a boulder of dread settle in my gut. "I need some air. I suggest you go to bed and get some rest, don't wait up for me." He grabbed his keys from the hook on the wall and left, closing the door behind him with a soft click. The bottom dropped out of my world. What had I done?

"Oh you stupid, stupid cow!" Why the hell did I have to go and blurt it all out like that? He was right, I did sound insane. It'd been hard enough for me to believe in and I was the one who it had happened to. Why would I think Joe would just accept it when I told him he wasn't real? Just because I wrote about it on a piece of paper? I felt like an idiot, an insensitive fool. I had hurt his feelings then told him some outrageous truths about who he was and then, to top it all off, I'd literally thrown the book at him. Now he was probably thinking about having me committed or worse, leaving me!

He'd only been gone a few minutes and I wanted him back. Instinct took over and I darted out of the door after him, running down the stairs I almost tripped over Slinky, Nelly Parker's cat from apartment 3b. Slinky let out a yowl as I stepped on his tail. I brushed him away with my foot a little too hard causing the cat to bolt upstairs. I didn't stop to see if he was alright because the need to find Joe buried any sense of concern for the stupid cat!

I reached the front door at a run, leaping from the bottom step and ran out onto the street. Looking in both directions I searched frantically for any sign of him.

"Joe!" I shouted. "Joe! I'm sorry!" A small sob erupted from my lips and I clapped a hand over my mouth trying to stop the flood of sorrow that threatened to pour from it. I stood there in the street, fighting the tears, desperately needing him to come back so I could apologise. Where would he go? *Think Naomi, Think!* The Imp! Without even a care that I didn't have a coat or, I realised, my door keys, I ran down the street in the direction of The Imp. He had to have gone there right? There was nowhere else for him to go.

By the time I was halfway up Steep Hill and heading towards the corner where our book bar was, I was panting hard. My legs were burning from the lactic acid in my muscles but I pushed on. Hope filled me with every tired footfall, it would be OK, he would be there and we'd sit down and talk. I'd agree to go to counselling, anything just to keep him with me. In the meantime, I'd try and locate Laney Marsh but I'd have to do it without Joe's help.

When I breeched the rise of Steep Hill I could see The Imp. The lights were off and the shutters were down. I felt a cold lump of despair in my chest but I banged on the door anyway.

"Joe? Are you in there? Please answer the door!" I banged on the door again and waited. Nothing. The cold lump grew and spread until it engulfed me. I stood in vain watching and waiting for Joe to open the door. I'm not sure how long I stood there, five minutes, maybe more? I waited until I began to shiver with the cold, then turned despondently for home. The walk home was desolate, I passed people on the street but they faded into the background. All I could think about was Joe. Where on earth had he gone? I quickened my pace hoping that he had just gone out for a walk, just like he said he would and was now back at our flat waiting for me.

Please be there, please be there. I chanted in my head. I couldn't allow myself to think that he might not be. When I reached the front door, I punched in the key code and bolted up the stars to my flat. It was then I remembered I'd left without my keys. I knocked on the door.

"Joe? Are you there? I forgot my keys, can you let me in?" There was no reply and I knew he hadn't come home. I rested my palms and forehead against the door and I felt a tear slide down my cheek and plop on the floor. Turning, I leaned back against the door wondering what to do next. I couldn't get inside the flat and it was no good walking around the city at night trying to find him, he could be anywhere.

I heard a soft mewling noise down at my feet, when I looked down I saw Slinky standing about a foot away. I don't know why but the return of the cat after the way I had hurt him earlier gave me hope, hope that Joe would also return. I slid to the floor and held my hand out to Slinky who immediately came forward to head-butt my open palm. His soft purrs soothed me and I scooped him up onto my lap for a cuddle.

"I'm so sorry puss. Did I hurt your tail? Hmm?" I scratched the top of his head which elicited a loud and forceful purr from the big ginger fluff ball. I was relived to find the cat was OK and had apparently forgiven me. He jumped off my lap, sauntered off down the hall and up the stairs towards his owner, Nelly's flat. It was as if he had purposefully come down just to check on me. The notion brought fresh tears to my eyes. All I could do now was sit and wait for Joe to come home. *If* he came home.

CHAPTER
eighteen

Apologies

"Naomi? Bella, wake up baby. Come on, what are you doing out here?"

I heard someone softly calling my name and felt a cold hand stroke my cheek. My heart fluttered a little in recognition.

"Joe? ...You came back!" I said, trying to drag myself into consciousness. I could hardly move, my legs and arms were so stiff. When I became fully awake I realised I had fallen asleep outside the door to our flat. I was curled up in a fetal position on the hard floor, coatless and freezing cold. I coughed a little to clear my throat. Joe was crouched down beside me- the most welcome sight I'd ever seen.

"Of course I came back. I'm sorry it's later than I planned. Why are you out here?"

"Oh Joe! I'm so sorry about our fight! I didn't mean to behave like that. I thought you might leave because I acted so crazy. I came to find you but I forgot my keys and then I waited for you to come home but you didn't. I...do you forgive me? I'll go to counselling Joe, I promise. Just please don't leave like that again." I begged him. I knew how desperate I sounded and the sound of my voice made me cringe but I couldn't help it. Joe was my world, he was the only beacon of light in my otherwise dark and lonely existence and without him to guide my way, I was blind. Relief flooded me as he pulled me up off the floor and hugged me tight. The warmth of his body felt like a blanket of comfort and safety wrapped around me. Joe was home.

"You slept out here? Jesus bella, I'm so sorry. I should've come home earlier. I went for a walk and popped into the pub for a quick pint. There were a few of our customers in there and they invited me to sit with them, we got chatting and before I knew it was midnight. I forgot to take my mobile phone with me otherwise I would've called."

"Joe, I was so scared! I thought you weren't coming home. I thought I'd lost you." I sobbed into his chest.

"You could never lose me Naomi. It was just a silly fight love, everybody has them now and again. I'm not going to leave my wife because we had a fight." He squeezed me tighter and I wanted to stay in his embrace forever. Furious with myself for nearly cocking it all up before it had hardly begun. "I just wanted to give you some space that's all. God, you must be freezing."

"I am…and really stiff." I replied.

"OK Mrs Ferrantino, let's get you inside and warmed up si?"

Joe took out his keys and let us both inside. Before I could step through the door, he scooped me up in his arms and carried me over the threshold. I clung to him like a limpet. He put me on the sofa and wrapped a throw around my shoulders.

"Thanks."

"Stay here, I'm going to run you a hot bath and get you a drink." He instructed me, kissing my lips tenderly before he went off to the bathroom. I heard the water running and then Joe came back through to the lounge and went towards the kitchen area. I heard the clink of glass and he promptly returned with two glasses of Jack Daniels, neat with no ice. I received it eagerly and took a large sip, enjoying the smooth, warming feel of the liquid as it slid down my throat.

"Better?" He asked.

"Much." I nodded enthusiastically.

"Good. Wait here, I need to go check on your bath."

I drew the throw blanket tighter around my shoulders and sipped more the bourbon. Everything was going to be OK, it had to be. There was no way I could live without Joe now. Living with depression was hard, it was always there lurking in the background waiting for an opportunity to sneak up on you and turn your world on its head. Joe was the stalwart knight who fended off the black beast that constantly circled the outskirts of my mind. For years I had fought a daily battle with that beast, often losing and succumbing to its crippling power. Joe had given me hope and love and the confidence to fight against it. Realising how quickly I had become dependent on his presence worried me a little. I fretted over the day I might wake up alone again and have nothing to fight for.

I would figure this whole mess out somehow. My very happiness depended on it. I knew I had to track down Laney Marsh, I had a feeling this happy status quo Joe and I had was in danger. If Laney was writing again and her words were appearing on my manuscript, how long would it be before things started to change with Joe and I? What if he suddenly disappeared back into the land of fiction? Or this Melissa woman became real and he developed feelings for her? I shuddered at the thought of all the possible things that could go wrong. Joe returned and took my glass, placing it on the coffee table.

"Come here you." He bent down and lifted me into his arms again to carry me through to the bathroom.

"I can walk you know."

"I know but I wanted to carry you. You, amore mio, need to be spoiled." And he set me down on the bathroom floor. I started to undress but he stopped me. "May I?" He asked.

I raised an eyebrow at him, "You want to undress me?"

"If the lady would allow it? It would be my pleasure." Joe's eyes were smouldering, looking into them sent excited shivers down my spine. I nodded in approval of his request and he began his unveiling of me. He stood at my back and lifted my arms above my head, then took hold of my shirt and pulled it slowly off over my head. Dropping the shirt he ran his hands down my arms and over my shoulders, placing soft kisses on the back of my neck. I dropped my arms as he reached around front to unbutton my jeans. He peeled down the waistband and tugged it past my hips, gently kissing my skin as he went. My pulse quickened with every touch of his lips. He surprised me when he didn't take things further, instead, when I stepped out of my knickers, he offered me his hand to guide me into the bath.

"Well, aren't we the gentleman tonight!" I teased.

"It has been known, although I can't guarantee I won't want to do some very ungentlemanly things to you later."

The bath was glorious, hot and deep and full of soft, foamy bubbles. Joe had lit a scented candle which he had placed between the two taps. He turned out the light and told me to relax for a bit. I didn't want him to go but he said I should close my eyes and just soak out the cold from my body.

"I'll be back in a little while, bella. Do you want another drink?"

"No, I'm good thanks." I wanted to stay sober. The single Jack Daniels had done its job and warmed me up but I didn't need any more. Joe closed the door softly and I sighed, sinking further into the deep water. I began to feel the chill leave my bones and the aching muscles start to ease. The candle flame flickered and made the shadows dance on the tiled wall. I let my mind relax and let go of all thoughts, just for a minute. Today had been stressful, it was now almost 1am and I started to feel sleepy, despite the impromptu 'nap' I'd had on the outside landing.

Joe came back a few minutes after and opened the door, peeking his head around it he asked if he could come in.

"Of course you can."

Joe grinned and entered the room, naked. Suddenly I didn't feel quite so tired.

"May I join you?"

I sat up and scooted forward so he could climb in and sit behind me. He sat and pushed his legs either side of me so I rested against his chest. He kissed the top of my head and reached for the sponge. After he got it good and lathered up, Joe began to gently wash me. It was the most sensual, beautiful thing I had ever experienced.

"Can I wash your hair?"

"Really? You would do that?"

"I'd like to."

"You really are incredible, you know that?"

"I know."

"Well, at least try and be a little more modest." I laughed.

"It's not in my nature bella. No one can ever love you better than I can. That's not me being egotistical, it's just the truth. I am yours, in body and soul and you are mine."

I passed him the shampoo. "Well then let's see if your shampooing skills are up to scratch shall we?"

CHAPTER
nineteen

It's All In Your Head, Alice

"Schizophrenia is often described in terms of negative and positive symptoms. Positive ones can include delusions, disordered thoughts and speech. As well as tactile, auditory and visual disturbances like the ones you have described to me today and in our past sessions. Many of the things you are experiencing are typically regarded as manifestations of psychosis. Now I'm not giving you that diagnosis today, but I would like to see how things go over the next few weeks." Dr Blanchard said. "Depending on how that goes we may have to seek both a clinical and medical examination."

"You really do think I'm crazy!" I said stunned. "I'm telling you the truth!"

Dr Blanchard gave me a sceptical, sympathetic look which I found incredibly infuriating. Why was I wasting my time here, trying to prove to her that I was telling the truth? All I had done was convince her I *had* gone loopy and now she wanted to monitor me and send me for tests to make a definite diagnosis.

"I see signs of many of the positive symptoms. However, the negative symptoms usually associated with a condition like schizophrenia aren't really apparent in you Naomi. Hence my reluctance to diagnose you. I think the death of your father and the absence of your mother have affected you psychologically, especially considering the strained relationship you had with your mother. Environmental factors can be a feature of the condition…then of course we need to rule out any possibility of substance abuse."

Dr Blanchard went on and on and I just sat there rolling my eyes. She noticed, I know she did but I was past caring. The only reason I had agreed to this charade was to placate Joe. After a while I had decided I might give it a go and tell her the truth, hoping that she may be able to shed some light on the whole situation. I had thought maybe, being a doctor of psychology, she could tell me more about the power of the mind or something like that? But no such luck, she just thought I was a proper raving looney.

I despaired at the thought of having to go through this pretence on a weekly basis for however long it took to either be diagnosed with some form of psychosis or for me to find Laney Marsh and straighten this whole thing out. Finding Laney was priority number one but it was not going to be easy keeping secrets from Joe, he was watching my every move.

Joe had been so attentive and loving, more than usual, these last few weeks. Since our fight he'd shown me such care and patience, I almost felt like a delicate little flower he was afraid would be crushed to a pulp at any given moment. As much as I loved the attention I was getting from him, I missed just being *real*. I hated that he might feel like he was treading on eggshells around me. The other thing that had changed between us was our love making, he was tender and had taken things slower in the bedroom. At first I had enjoyed it, it was sort of romantic and sweet but I was beginning to miss the raw passion that we'd had before. The Joe that I knew liked to fuck and I liked being fucked by him. I wasn't some china doll that would break with a little rough handling. The thing is, I knew why he was behaving like that and it just made me love him even more. His entire focus was on me, not once had he asked to discuss the things that were on his mind and yet I knew he must still have many questions. Things needed to be resolved and soon. One way or another I *had* to hunt down Laney Marsh, she was the only proof I had that could convince Joe, my family and Dr Blanchard that I had been telling the truth all along.

"So, does that sound alright with you, Naomi?" Dr Blanchard continued.

"Hmm?" I had totally zoned out.

"That we continue our sessions on a weekly basis for now and see how things develop?"

I nodded.

"Great, then in the meantime, I suggest you carry on with your daily routine as much as possible, rest and get plenty of sleep and do try and lay off the alcohol?"

Who the fuck are you, my mother? I gave her a placatory smile. "Yes, of course."

"Same time next week then?" She asked.

I'd rather gouge out my eyes with a spoon! "That'd be great, thanks."

"Goodbye Naomi. If you need to talk in between appointments, here's a card with my emergency number." She took a small business card from her desk and handed it to me. Jesus, I must be a special case, I was getting the emergency number! I almost laughed out loud at the sheer ridiculousness of it all. If she'd just bother to get off her arse and come down to the book bar, she would meet Joe face to face and see what I was talking about. I'd suggested as much to her but she said it 'wasn't productive for her to participate in a client's fantasies'. I'd thought that ironic because if she did happen to participate in my particular fantasies, she'd probably find it extremely 'productive', not to mention erotic.

When I got back to the flat it was around 4.30pm and Joe wasn't home yet. I'd left The Imp early so I could make my appointment with Dr Blanchard. Joe didn't lock up usually till around 5.30pm which meant he'd probably be home around 6pm. Great! That gave me and hour and a half to try and research Laney.

Laney was proving a very tough person to track down. When I had proofed for her, we'd only ever communicated via email and she only had a P.O. Box number registered as a postal address. I had contacted

Royal Mail and asked for an address connected to the P.O. box number which they had given me, albeit reluctantly. It had taken some time for me to convince the man on the other end of the phone that I had a genuine reason for wanting the address but I also informed the irritating jobsworth that I knew the law and that they were obliged to give me the connecting address because I had asked for it. I'd looked up the address online but it was registered to a different name and there was no contact phone number. I'd sent Laney a few emails but I'd gotten several mail delivery failure notices back so it was clear that she had changed her email address. The street address was quite obscure, a little village I'd never heard of somewhere in Scotland. It was too far for a quick trip and, according to Google maps, nigh on impossible to get to. It occurred to me that I had never asked Laney who her publisher was going to be, had I had that information I could've tried to contact her through those means. Right now, I was at a complete loss as to what to do next. It was looking highly likely that I would have to take a trip up to Scotland to see if the address I had was correct, but I wasn't sure how I'd get that one past the ever-vigilant Joseph.

Looking on Google maps, I could see that the little village of Crovie in Aberdeenshire was over four hundred and fifty miles away from Lincoln. It was at least an eight hour drive and once you hit the east side of Scotland, it meant travelling down a few remote roads. I wondered how I'd convince Joe to take the trip. I looked on Skyskanner and found that flights went from Doncaster airport to Aberdeen which took around four or five hours. I supposed that wasn't too bad, we'd have to hire a car and drive the rest of the way but that might be quite enjoyable. Inspired, I googled hotels near Crovie. Surprisingly Crovie, being a one street fishing hamlet, had few permanent residents, most of the cottages it seemed were now used as holiday lets. The nearest pub and grocery shop was in Gardenstown a few miles away. It was doable and absolutely necessary if I was going to track Laney down. I just had to convince Joe.

I heard a key turn in the lock and jumped, realising Joe had come home I quickly shut the laptop lid and rose to greet him with a smile.

"Hey you. You're early."

"Ciao bella. Si, it was quiet today so I thought I'd lock up early and come see you. I wanted to know how your session went?" Joe strode over to me, lifted my chin with his hand and planted a soft kiss on my lips. He pulled away then and I felt disappointed, I didn't want soft and tender, I wanted him to kiss me so hard that my lips would bruise.

"It was good, thanks. Dr Blanchard thinks I'm making progress. She wants to see me regularly for a few more weeks to see how it goes but I'm feeling great. I have an appointment for next week but after that I wondered if you fancied maybe getting away for a few days? I feel like an adventure. What do you think?"

Joe raised his eyebrows. "An adventure? What about The Imp? Can we afford to close it for that long?"

"It's just a couple of days, I need to get away for some fresh air, reset my body you know? And besides you said it's been quiet at The Imp lately so…" I knew if I implied it was for health reasons that Joe would most likely agree and it worked.

"OK. Sounds like fun. Where would you like to go?"

"Well…I was thinking Scotland. You've not been there right?" I was suddenly unsure, so much of mine and Joe's life together was a mystery.

"Scotland? That's a little far isn't it? Can't we go to Whitby or somewhere closer? It'll take us a day just to travel there."

"I love Whitby but I really fancy an adventure! Let's go somewhere totally off the beaten track. Somewhere not so touristy, just us." I hit him with my most appealing look, my eyes practically begging. "Please?"

"But it'll take so long to get there love. We can't afford to close The Imp for more than two or three days and you know there's no one to cover. I don't know." He shrugged his shoulders but I wasn't giving up.

"We could fly! Doncaster does internal flights to Aberdeen, I already looked. It's only four hours to get there. Please?"

Joe chewed his bottom lip for a few seconds and I could practically feel him teetering on the edge of indecision. "Let's think about it for a few days, si? Consider the flights and see how much it costs and then we'll decide. It would be nice to go away for a little break I suppose, but it needs to be affordable OK?"

Well, at least it wasn't a no. "OK, I'll see how much flights cost then. But Joe, I know you'll love it! Scotland is gorgeous, it's all wild and rugged."

"And cold and wet." Joe pulled a face. "Why don't we just save up for a few months and I can take you to

Italy? You haven't seen my country yet and I…" a quizzical look crossed his face, "I haven't been back since, God, I don't even remember."

"*Italy*, really?" I was momentarily distracted from my mission by the thought of travelling to Italy. But then I realised that Joe would be expecting to find family, friends and evidence that it was once his home, a dream Italian adventure would most likely turn out to be an absolute nightmare. "Italy sounds wonderful babe but that'd mean us saving for months and I really need a break now. Dr Blanchard says I need to take time out, I thought Scotland would be perfect."

"The doctor thinks it's a good idea?"

"Yes." I lied through my teeth but I needed to get Joe to Crovie come hell or high water. I'd sell my soul to the devil if it meant I could find Laney Marsh and stop her from writing.

"OK." he relented, "let's go then. Providing the flights aren't too expensive, I would say we'd drive but it's a long way. You do deserve a break." He smiled at me indulgently and I felt like a brat for lying to him but this was the only way. I went to him and planted a firm, purposeful kiss on his lips, making a mwah sound with my mouth.

"You, Joseph Ferrantino, are the best husband a girl could ever wish for." He grinned at the compliment and replied cockily

"Well, you know what they say, behind every great man is a woman waiting to beat him over the head with a frying pan if he doesn't do as he's told." He winked at me and pinched my nose between his thumb and forefinger making a honking sound, as if my nose were a horn.

"Ohhhh, you did not just say that!" I said and he backed away grinning like an idiot. "You are in deep trouble now mister. You better run!" I started to stalk him with a glint in my eye, hopeful that his playful mood might lead to some rough and tumble.

"Just so you know bella, I've hidden all of the pans!" He was openly laughing now, egging me on.

"Well then I'll just have to improvise won't I!"

"Aha! You'll have to catch me first." He quipped and stuck out his tongue. I pounced towards him and he ran off down the hallway towards the bedroom. I went after him in stalk mode. I was almost to the door when he called to me.

"Naomi? I can't offer you a frying pan but I found a handy utensil you might like to make use of. Want to see?"

"Ohhhh, really?" I said dryly and swung open the door to find Joe with a large buzzing vibrator in his hand. He waggled it at me and pressed the button to make it buzz. Oh my god! He'd found my vibrator! Heat flushed my face and I didn't know where to look.

"I don't think much to its pancake making abilities, do you?" He teased. "Shall we put it to better use and mix up some batter of our own?"

An embarrassed laugh escaped me and he waggled it again. I walked into the bedroom and closed the door with my foot. Thrilled that Joe was back to his playful bedroom antics again. Sweet and romantic was nice but right now I needed my Italian stallion and if he wanted to play master chef with my toy in our bedroom, who was I to complain?

CHAPTER
twenty

Fly Away Home

The fifty-seater plane jostled and bumped around in a pocket of turbulence. I liked flying so it didn't particularly bother me, Joe however, was as white as a sheet. I'd taken the window seat and was enjoying the view of the lush green hills and patchwork of farmlands below. Joe had each of the chair arms in a death grip, his knuckles were white and his face ashen. His forehead looked clammy and he had his eyes squeezed shut. Another air pocket made the plane lurch and I heard Joe groan.

"Are you going to be sick?" I hurriedly pulled out the paper bag from the seat pocket and opened it out for Joe. "Oh babe, I'm so sorry. If I'd known you didn't like flying we would have driven instead. Why didn't you say something?"

"Didn't know." He managed to say, and took the paper bag from me. The sound of his retching filled the small cabin and a few heads turned sympathetically in our direction. I rang for the stewardess. A moment later the slender uniformed flight attendant who had greeted us on to the plane before take-off, arrived and bent slightly over our seats, proffering her well trained smile upon us.

"Can I help you?"

"Yes, could we get another bag please?" I held out the filled paper bag to her and she took it dutifully. The contents swilling around made a slopping sound.

"Of course." She smiled, took the bag from me and turned to Joe. "Would you like a glass of water sir?"

"Thank you." Was all Joe managed to say. I patted his hand and tried to distract him with humour.

"I thought Italians were superhuman?"

"They are, it turns out flying is my kryptonite," he attempted a smile in my direction but the plane lurched again and his handsome face turned from grey to green, "oh Jesus."

"Do you want to go to the loo? You can be sick in there."

"I don't think I can get up."

Thankfully the stewardess arrived then with a handful of paper bags. Joe grabbed one and stuck his face in it seconds before he expelled more of his stomach contents. He handed her the second filled bag and took the empty ones from her. She handed him a bottle of mineral water and a napkin with a sympathetic smile.

"Won't be long now sir. About another forty minutes and we'll be landing." She looked at me. "Buzz if you need anything else."

"Thank you." I nodded and she left us. I stroked Joe's hair and put my head on his shoulder. "Poor baby. What are we going to do with you?"

"Well I would say put me in a bag and shake me up but the plane is doing a pretty good job of that already." He tried to joke but his face was still green and there was a sheen of sweat across his brow. "I think I know why I never made it back to Italy eh?" My heart constricted.

"What do you mean?" I asked tentatively.

"If I was like this flying from Italy to England, no wonder I never went back." He chuckled and relief flooded me. For a moment I had feared he was about to open up *that* conversation again and now was not a good time. I tried to deflect the conversation away from his home country and the lost memories by joking back,

"Is that the only reason?" I asked in mock indignation.

"Hmm, well there was this girl that I met. I don't quite remember her name but she had nice boobs."

I punched his arm softly. "Watch it mister, my sympathy for the sick Italian may quickly run out."

"You're kind of sexy when you're mad and bossy."

I gave him a sideways glance and smirked. "You're kind of sexy even when you smell of vomit." I giggled at his expression, especially when he covered his mouth with his hand and tried to smell his own breath.

"Oh shit, it's really bad huh?"

"Dreadful."

"Want a kiss?" He puckered up his lips and leaned in. I held him back with my hand.

"No way José! Don't you come near me until you've brushed your teeth."

"Who is this José? Do I need to be jealous?"

"You should be, he has better breath than you." I laughed and Joe came at me again, lips puckered and making kiss noises. The seatbelt sign pinged above us and the pilot made the announcement that we were beginning our descent into Aberdeen airport. A few moments later I felt the plane begin its drop through the atmosphere. I enjoyed the sensation, my belly lurched but it was rather like being on a fairground ride. Poor Joe hated it, he'd gone back to assaulting the chair arms with his death grip. I always loved looking out of the window when a plane was landing, I liked to watch the landscape and buildings unfold beneath me but right this minute, Joe needed me more. I laid my head on his shoulder again and covered his hand with mine.

"Just tell me when it's over?" He asked through gritted teeth.

"Won't be long and then we can get out in the fresh air," I glanced out of the window briefly, "and rain." I groaned.

The actual landing had been smooth much to Joe's relief. He was shaking when he stood up to retrieve our bags from the overhead compartment.

"Want me to drive when we get the hire car?" He didn't look capable of walking in a straight line right now, let alone driving. Joe stopped dead, his brow crinkled in thought.

"Do I know how to drive? I...I can't remember."

"You...don't know how to drive?" His question had caught me off guard and it didn't register that I had just confirmed that I didn't know the answer. This was something I should know. Joe looked at me in confusion. He opened his mouth to reply but people began pushing and jostling to get to their luggage and get off the plane. I'd had a last-minute reprieve for which I was extremely thankful. I just needed Joe to hold off with the questions until we found Laney, then I could tell him the truth and I'd have the proof to back it up.

As we descended the stairs from the plane on to the tarmac, the driving rain came in blustery gusts that bit and stung our faces. Joe and I ran towards the terminal building but we were soaked through by the time we reached it.

"Damn Scottish weather," Joe said as he wiped the rain from his face, "are we having an adventure yet?" He asked me dryly.

"Har har! Don't be such a pessimist. It'll be fun when we're settled in our little cottage with a roaring fire and the ocean at our doorstep."

"If you say so."

"I do. So, come on, let's go find the car hire kiosk."

We ended up with a little Vauxhall Corsa, bright red with a sunroof. That last detail made me chuckle, not much use for a sunroof around here today. I got in the driver's side and started the engine to warm up the car. Joe got in the passenger side after putting our weekend bags in the boot. He'd put my large satchel, which doubled as my handbag, between his legs in the footwell.

207

"OK, I can't get google maps up on my phone for the GPS, you'll have to dig out the A4 sheet I printed off instead." I instructed him. Joe bent and began to rummage around in my satchel, he pulled out a wad of papers bound together with an elastic band.

"You brought this? Why?"

Shit.

"Naomi?"

"I don't know. I...I can't explain right now, Joe. Can you just wait till we get to the cottage and then we can discuss it, please?" Joe examined my face for a moment and then shrugged his shoulders.

"OK. I will wait."

"Really?" I couldn't quite believe it had been that easy.

"I'm too tired and washed out to argue with you bella. I'm giving you the benefit of the doubt. We'll discuss it later. Let's get going, I'd like to get settled in." He replaced the manuscript and pulled out the A4 sheet of directions to Crovie. It was about an hour's drive and a fairly straightforward route, although some of the journey looked a little lonely. I hoped the Corsa could cope with the terrain. I'd never ventured into the wild Scottish countryside before, my only experience with this bonnie land was Edinburgh. I had no idea what to expect from this tiny fishing hamlet that lay tucked between the rugged cliffs and the open ocean. Anticipation filled me, the desire to find Laney was overpowering but I tried to enjoy some of the scenery as we travelled. Joe was unusually quiet for the most part, aside from issuing directions and asking if he could tune in the car radio, he didn't say much else. I tried putting it down to the fact that the plane journey had taken its toll on him but I knew he was biding his time to ask me why I'd brought along the manuscript. It had been a touchy subject since our argument and I had not dared to mention it again since then.

When we took the last turn off for Crovie I had to slow down and look for the car park that supposedly lay just before the hairpin bend by the village.

"There." Joe pointed to it and I pulled the car in and parked it up. The owner of our rental cottage had informed me that there was no room for cars in the village and so all vehicles had to be parked in the car park at the top of the cliff. There were three other cars parked up, I guessed they must belong to other holiday makers or perhaps to one of the five permanent residents.

The rain was still hammering down as we fished out our bags from the boot.

"How far is it?" Joe asked, the rain pelting his face.

"Um, a couple of minutes' walk down the road according to the owner."

"Thank God! We'll be like a pair of drowned rats by the time we get there. Here, let me take your bag." Joe held out his hand for my bag but I shook my head,

"It's OK, I can manage, let's just get inside. I'm freezing!" We set off down the hill, following the sign for Crovie. Thankfully, a few minutes later, the stone buildings of the hamlet came into view.

"Wow. They really weren't joking that there was no room for cars eh?" Joe and I stood at the end of the street and looked at the single row of stone cottages that clung to the bottom of the cliff, their gable ends all turned towards the ocean. Realistically, you couldn't even call it a proper street since there was no road whatsoever, just a footpath that ran in front of the cottages which doubled as a small walled sea defence. Only a few feet separated the stone walls from the beach. The tide was out now but I could imagine the waves must lash relentlessly at the wall on windy days such as today.

"That'll be fun in a storm," Joe said, "which one is ours?"

"It's the old mission hall. It doesn't have a number but I don't think it'll be hard to find somehow."

We only walked about twenty meters until we found the mission hall, there were lights on inside and I knocked on the door. A few seconds later a middle-aged woman opened it and welcomed us with her broad Scottish accent.

"Och come in there now. Yous'll be freezing."

"Thank you." I said and the woman opened the door to usher us in. The cottage was warm and relatively spacious considering the little plot of land it stood on.

"Now, my name is Moira and you'll be Mr and Mrs Ferrantino, is that right?" I nodded and noticed Joe's forehead crinkle. Moira turned and walked into the lounge area, we followed her and Joe picked up both our bags.

"What's wrong?" I whispered to him.

"I don't understand a word she is saying!" He whispered back. A snort of laughter escaped me. It was hard enough for me to understand such a broad accent so no wonder Joe was struggling.

"What a dreich day eh?" Moira said. I had no idea what 'dreich' meant but considering the rain and wind, I assumed it had something to do with the weather.

"Yes, it's not very nice out there really."

"Well, I've put yous the burner on so yous can go get warm there." She motioned to the large wood burning stove that stood roaring and radiated a much welcome heat. "Now, there's plenty 'o logs in back so you'll nae run out. I've taken the liberty 'o stocking up the fridge a wee bit for you. Just some eggs and milk and the like OK?"

"That's really kind of you thank you."

"Aye well, it's a fair way to walk to Gardenstown. That's the nearest shop and you don' want te be walking in this weather. There's enough to tide you over till tomorrow. I live just three doors away so if you need any'hin else just ask."

"Great thanks."

"Here's your key. The bed's all made up for yous. We're expecting a bit of a wee storm tonight so I wouldn'y wander off too far. It can get a wee bit squally during a storm but don't worry, these houses were built solid."

"Oh. Right, OK." I said. I supposed there wasn't anywhere for us to go, I just wanted to find Laney but I couldn't ask Moira while Joe was here. Moira nodded at us both and started towards the front door. "I'll walk you out." I offered. "Joe, could you take ours bags to the bedroom please?"

"Sure. Thank you, Moira." He said, struggling to pronounce her name. I walked Moira out of the door and as she turned to shake my hand I asked,

"Who are the other permanent residents?"

"Well, we're few and far between now lassy but there's me and ma husband, Cambell. Then there's Mrs

McCreedy and her dog and The Drummonds down the bay there."

"That's it?" I asked disappointed that there had been no mention of Laney Marsh.

"Aye lass. No' many of us left now. These cottages are mostly kept as holiday lets."

"I don't suppose you know anyone called Laney Marsh?" I asked hopefully, thinking that perhaps Laney owned one of the cottages for rent instead.

"Marsh? The name's no' familiar but I can ask Cambell for you. He knows everyone, he's a nosey bugger." She chuckled.

"Thank you, that'd be great."

"What are ye wanting wi' her anyway?"

"I used to know her, sort of. I did some work for her and I have something I need to discuss with her. The address I have for her is here in Crovie."

"Och OK, well chances are lass that she's an owner then. Probably lives in Gardenstown. Cambell will know. Anyway lass, get yourself settled in and go take care o' that gorgeous wee man o' yours. I'd no' be leaving him alone if he were mine." Moira nudged my arm and winked. I giggled back at her, Joe always appealed to the older ladies. He didn't even have to do or say anything and he had them noticing him.

I said goodbye to Moira and locked the door. I found Joe unpacking our weekend bags and hanging our clothes up in the cupboard.

"Well, I hope you can tell me what she said because I don't have a clue?" Joe pulled a face which made me smile.

"Just talk about the weather and that she's put us some supplies in the fridge. Oh and she said the logs for the fire are out the back."

"She brought food? That's nice. I'm hungry, most of the contents of my lunch ended up in a paper bag."

"Ha! Oh my poor baby, want me to go make something?"

"I'll do it, you can finish hanging these up if you like? I feel like I need to be in the kitchen. I don't feel settled until I've found my way around an oven." Joe left the room and I took over the unpacking, setting out our toiletries in the bathroom and tucking the bags away in the bottom of the wardrobe. I felt encouraged now that I was here and hopefully a little closer to finding Laney. If Moira's husband came through with some information that would save me a lot of time digging around. We were only here for two nights, I hoped it was enough.

CHAPTER
twenty-one

Stormy Weather

Joe made us scrambled egg on toast and a pot of tea. We sat on the rug in front of the wood burner to eat. It was quite cosy inside listening to the wind and rain blow against the cottage windows. It got dark quickly and the early evening seemed to herald the beginning of the storm that Moira mentioned was coming.

"Are you going to tell me why we're really here?" Joe asked, catching me off guard. I swallowed the mouthful of food too fast and grimaced. I decided to be truthful in my answer.

"I brought you here because I need you to be with me when I find Laney Marsh."

"The author?"

"Yes."

"Naomi, I thought we'd been through this already?" Joe put down his fork and looked at me. I had to keep things calm and not start an argument again. I needed Joe here and I needed him on board.

"It's not what you think. I just need to find her, it's really important Joe. I know none of this makes sense to you but our life together is at risk. Everyone thinks I'm crazy but I'm not. Although it's driving me crazy not having anyone believe me." I pleaded with him in a calm manner even though my heart was thumping in my chest.

"Do you know how it makes me feel bella? When you tell me I'm not real? It hurts. It feels like you don't love me enough to want me in your life." His voice cracked a little and a lump caught in my throat. I pushed my plate aside and scooted over to sit beside him, my hand reaching for his.

"Joe no! The reason you're here is *because* I love you so much. This…" I gestured to us both with my hand, "this, what we have together is nothing less than a miracle. I have no idea how or why it happened but it did. And I'm so so grateful for it. Think about it Joe, you can't remember your accident because you were never in one. Your memories of Italy and your own family are unclear because Italy is just part of the story and your parents never existed. You remember Melissa because she is the original love interest in your story. You didn't even know if you could drive! Neither did I, isn't that something I would know?" I was on a roll now as Joe sat quietly listening, his fingers picked at the hearth rug. "I'm not trying to hurt you Joe, really I'm not. I'm trying to get things straight in my own head. I can cope with the fact we had a wedding that I don't even remember and that my family live in another country, because it means I get you." I took a cleansing breath; I was aware of how fast I was talking but I just needed Joe to hear me. "It doesn't matter to me what you were, it matters what you are. You are my everything, Joe. Without you I might as well not exist."

"Hey, don't talk like that. Your life has value Naomi, don't ever think it doesn't."

"But it's nothing without you in it."

"This all sounds totally crazy. I just…" He shook his head and I thought I saw a hint of a tear forming in his eye. "I love you Naomi. I want to be here for you, *with* you but I just can't go along with this…this *fiction.*" He let out a string of Italian none of which I understood but I could sense the desperation in his tone. My heart cried out to him.

"Joe, please," I begged, "if you love me like you say you do, help me find Laney Marsh. I promise you everything will make sense after that. *Please* Joe?" His gaze met mine and I felt his eyes searching for evidence of truth in my own. "Joe, help me fight for us? I can't do this without you. We *have* to find Laney." Silence filled the air as I waited anxiously for his response. After a few tense moments passed he faced me.

"I don't know what is going on with you baby, I really don't but I meant it when I said that I love you and I will be here for you. I will help you find this woman if only to put this ridiculous pretence to bed once and for all. Once we find her, I want you to promise me that after you've spoken to her, it ends. No more of this fantasy or whatever it is you have convinced yourself this is. You go back home and continue your sessions with the doctor." It wasn't a question; he was *telling* me. Part of me grew annoyed at being told how to behave. My rebellious streak wanted to protest but I had to tell myself that to win the war, I must win it battle by battle and so I reluctantly agreed.

Joe finished his food without another word, his eyes on his plate, paying my glances no heed. I stood and took our plates through to the kitchen area to wash them up. I was muttering angrily to myself, scrubbing the plates furiously and dumping them unceremoniously on the draining board when I heard a door bang. I shouted through to the lounge.

"Joe?" No reply came back. "Joe?" Again, no reply. Curiosity got better of me and drying my hands off on the towel, I went to investigate. The lounge was empty. I walked to the bedroom but Joe wasn't in there either. "Joe? Are you in the bathroom?" I looked in every room but Joe had gone. Panic constricted my lungs. *Shit!* Had he walked out again like he had the last time we had argued? Goddamn idiot Italian, there was a bloody storm outside! I ran to open the front door but was confronted with the onslaught of the storm. The wind was so strong it almost pushed me back from the doorway and the driving cold rain tore into my face. "Joe?" I shouted into the wind, "JOE!" Nothing. I stood in the doorway shivering, battling the wind when a terrifying thought struck me— what if it had ended? What if Laney had written more of her manuscript and now Joe had disappeared, back to where he came from? I ran to the lounge where my satchel was and yanked it open, pulling out the sheet of A4s of my manuscript. My frantic fingers flicked to the latest pages at the back and I saw new text appearing before my eyes. I stared wide eyed in horror, a defiant scream rent from me, "NO!" Seizing the last page in both hands, I tore it up. Cursing it, yelling at it whatever it was that Joe was mine. It was at that moment I heard a muffled shout from outside the cottage- *Joe?* It sounded distant and I couldn't work out which direction it had come from, front or back? "Joe, where are you?" I was desperate now. Surely he hadn't been stupid enough to go for a walk in this storm?

Running back to the door, I yanked it back open and listened. I could swear I heard shouts but it was hard to distinguish from the wailing wind. Then a thought occurred to me, I ran to the back door it and flung it open, the rear of the cottage shielded me a little from the force of the gale. It was darker here because the light of the streetlamp failed to reach round this side of the stone cottage but I could just about make out a form on the ground. "Joe!" I flew out into the rain towards him, already soaked to my skin by the time I reached him. He lay on the ground amongst a huge pile of fallen logs, face down in the mud. "Jesus Joe! What the hell happened? Are you OK?"

"Fell." Was all he could manage to say. He groaned as I heaved him up to a sitting position and his hand went immediately to his chest.

"Are you in pain?" Joe nodded and I put my arm around him to help him to his feet. "Let's get inside, it's freezing out here." Between us we managed to get back inside and I helped him hobble to the couch. His hand still clutched his chest and that had me worried. "Joe what the hell were you doing out there?" I asked in earnest while pulling off his walking boots.

"Wood. I went for wood." He croaked.

"What's wrong with your chest? Are you injured?"

"Pain. Here." He sputtered. *Oh shit, was he having a heart attack?*

"What can I do?" I asked even though I had no idea what the hell I should do. I picked up my mobile phone but there was no signal. "Shit!" I tried to think what the first aid procedure was for a heart attack but my mind was a total blank. "Joe, I need you to tell me what happened, can you do that?"

"Went for wood. Was fine. Got pain and fell." He grunted.

"Ok. How bad is the pain?"

"It's easing a little now," relief washed over me, at least it wasn't getting worse, "just need to sit a minute. I'm OK, the fire needs wood." Joe said. I looked at the wood burner which had gone from roaring flame to a few pitiful embers, if it went out we'd be freezing if this storm went on all night.

"I'll see to it don't worry. You just sit still." I quickly threw on a couple of the smaller sticks that were generally used as kindling just to get it going again. "I need to go fetch some logs, will you be OK for a few minutes?" Joe nodded

"Yes, honestly I'm fine. The pain is gone. I think I just pulled something."

I went to change my jumper, which was sodden and muddy, and then pulled on a coat. The storm raged outside and I struggled with the log basket as the wind tried twice to snatch it from my arms. I filled it up as quickly and with as many logs as I could manage before trudging back through the door. The kindling was burning nicely and I threw on a couple smaller logs. They had been stacked and covered outside in a special log store so hadn't gotten too wet on the short trip to the cottage. The ones that had fallen on the floor where Joe had lain, I had left on the ground. I could pick those up tomorrow.

I set the fire poker down on the wrought iron companion stand and went back to Joe, who now looked more like his normal self again.

"We need to get you out of those wet clothes baby before you catch a cold. Do you think you can manage it?"

"Yes, I'm OK now. Like I said, I think I must've pulled a muscle or something lifting the log basket." He said and I gave him a questioning look.

"Looked like more than a pulled muscle from where I was, are you sure you feel OK? You look a little pale."

"I'm just cold, I need to change."

"Do you need to shower or anything?"

"Probably, but right now I just want to change and get back to this fire." Joe shivered on cue and I told him to stay where he was, I'd go get his PJs and he could change into them in front of the fire.

"PJs? Are you mothering me?" He chuckled.

"A little bit." I admitted. "But let's face it, you've had quite an eventful day. Who knew flying and mud were your nemeses!"

"If this is what you call an adventure, I can't say I'm particularly enjoying it so far." His right eyebrow arched upwards.

"My poor baby." I said over emphasising my sympathy and patting his head. I got up and heard him mutter.

"Heartless wench."

When I brought his change of clothes to the lounge I held them up to the fire to warm them while he undressed. I couldn't resist looking at him, he was so beautiful. I drank him in as he pulled off his wet jumper and t-shirt in one go. His lean, muscular torso glinted in the firelight. His arms were raised above his head, tugging off the clothing, when I noticed strange red marks on his skin. The marks looked a lot like long scratches, there were two on his front that went from one side of his chest to the other in a sort of wonky X shape. I brought him his warmed pyjamas and placed them on the sofa. He turned around to pick up the t-shirt and I saw that the marks on his front mirrored the two on his back. Tentatively I reached out and touched one with my finger.

"Ow!" Joe flinched from my touch. "What was that?"

"Sorry babe, your skin looks sore. Are you sure you didn't injure yourself?"

"I don't think so." He tried to twist his head around to look but couldn't. "I'm really cold though. What do you see?"

"Scratches." I said.

"Maybe a few logs hit my back when I fell?"

"Yeah, maybe." I said but these marks didn't look like anything I'd seen. Frowning, I gathered up his wet clothes from the sofa and a tiny piece of paper fluttered to the floor. I stared at it.

"I'm going to go wash my hands and face." Joe said after he pulled on his clean top.

"OK." I replied absentmindedly. I bent and picked up the piece of paper, it was torn and had typed text on it. I moved a cushion on the sofa that had fallen forward and found my manuscript under it surrounded by the pieces of the page I had ripped up. The jagged edges looked remarkably like the red marks on Joe's body. An unpleasant feeling rose in my stomach. The piece that I held in my hand was torn right through the middle of a word…the word was Joe.

CHAPTER
twenty-two

The Truth Hurts

Holy fucking shit! A horrifying realisation settled in my mind, I had done this. I had hurt Joe by ripping up the page in the manuscript. That must've been the pain he'd felt in his chest, the reason for his fall. Joe was connected to my manuscript and I, of all people, should've known that. That manuscript was the reason for his existence and now I knew it could also be his demise. Suddenly the tenuous link I had on this new life with Joe seemed even more fragile. My scruffy pile of papers immediately became an object to be guarded, protected, something that needed to be locked in a safe where nobody would find it. If anything should happen to it I would lose Joe forever. But I was already losing him, to Laney. It became imperative that I find her and stop her from writing anything more about Joe. I had to get him and Laney together, once she met him she would see that he was real. I'd have to confess everything of course but it had to be done. I was willing to accept the consequences of stealing her character, her ideas, if it meant Joe would be safe.

I carefully scooped up the torn pieces and laid them on top of the rest of the manuscript. Cautiously, I slipped it back into my satchel and took it to the bedroom. I looked around for a safe place to stash it, the tight spot between the wall and the bedside table was the only place I could see that no one would need to go near for any reason. The table hid the satchel from sight but I still felt uneasy. Knowing the power that it held between its thin pages was terrifying and I couldn't stop myself from pacing up and down the small bedroom, wringing my hands together and gnawing at my bottom lip. I heard Joe come into the room.

"You're like a caged animal pacing the room, what's wrong?"

"Nothing, just the storm making me a bit nervous. We're so close to the sea."

"Are you afraid we'll get swept away?" Joe grinned. I attempted a small smile but it came out more of a grimace. My eyes flicked to the bedside table. Is it safe there? "Don't worry love, I'd save you. Remember I have super powers." Joe flexed his biceps at me, flashing me his playful smile.

"Oh really? Well we should be fine as long as there are no sea planes or mud in the ocean then." I joined in his banter, hoping it would distract me from my nervous pacing.

"What did I do to land myself such a sarcastic and unsympathetic wife?" Joe put his hands on his hips, shaking his head in mock chagrin. "Maybe it's a test? If I put up with you in this life I get to live in luxury in the afterlife eh?" My face dropped, a look of genuine fear replaced the playfulness.

"Don't even joke about that. That isn't funny Joe." My throat closed in a tight knot at the thought of what could happen to him now that I knew the fragility of the object that anchored him to life. He was by my side in an instant.

"Hey, I'm just playing with you. I don't plan on going anywhere anytime soon." Joe rubbed my arms with his hands trying to reassure me.

"Yeah well you shouldn't joke. You never know what's around the corner." I said, wracked with guilt that just a moment ago, it had been me that had almost sent him to meet his maker. Worry creased my brow as I began to wonder what would happen to him if the manuscript did get destroyed. Would he die like a normal person and leave behind a physical body or would he just disappear and everything would go back to the way it had been before? Would he go back to being just another fictional character in a book. I shook my head violently trying to rid my head of such morbid thoughts.

"Come here Mrs Ferrantino. Wild horses couldn't tear me away from you bella. And if the worst happened I'd come back and haunt you. You'll never be rid of me." The irony of his words wasn't lost on me and I cocked an eyebrow at him. He must've realised what he'd said because he tried to make light of it with more banter. "And you know I'm already an accomplished spirit."

"You're not helping."

"Yeah, I suppose that subject is a little sore right now huh?"

"A little. I don't want to go over old ground again right now Joe."

"I know. I'm sorry." We both sat down on the bed next to each other. "I know it's obviously a sore subject Naomi but at some point, we must talk about everything. I need to understand what happened to me and deal with it just as much as you need to deal with your issues. I'm trying so hard to be patient and give you the time you need to heal but...I need that healing time too. I'm getting on with life in the best way that I can, in the only way I know how and that's to just carry on living. I don't want to dwell on the past, it's over but I still need to know what happened. Do you understand that?"

"Yes." Was all I could manage. God what a selfish bitch! I had been so wrapped up in myself and my fear of losing him that I hadn't given too much consideration to how he must be feeling. I mean I knew that he'd had questions and that he'd been holding back for my sanity's sake but all I had concentrated on lately was trying to prove to everyone that I wasn't crazy. I'd been so hell bent on finding Laney and proving to Joe that I'd been telling the truth; I hadn't truly taken a minute to contemplate what the truth might do to him.

"I can't help you like I want to help you because I still have so many unanswered questions." Joe squeezed my hand.

"I'm sorry." I uttered weakly. I was desperate to tell him that I could give him all the answers, I could prove all of the claims I had made but at what price? He'd already told me that it hurt his feelings when I had told him he wasn't real. I had totally missed the point. Joe thought he was real. He believed wholeheartedly that I was his wife and that he'd suffered some sort of accident that had put him in a coma. He believed that he had been able to communicate with me while he'd been in a coma and that now everything was OK, or should be at least if it wasn't for me and my crazy ramblings. Knowing all of this, he had still put me first and I had allowed it. I realised in that moment that I hadn't treated Joe as a person, an actual living, breathing person with feelings and concerns of his own. I had treated him like an object, an object that I owned. What right did I have to take his beliefs and his life away from him. If I took him to Laney and proved my story, it would crush him. Everything he thought he knew, everything he believed was real would be taken from him and I would be responsible. I could not break his heart like that. But, I still needed to stop Laney from writing. If I didn't I'd lose Joe anyway, she was writing him a new story and who knows what would happen. I couldn't take that risk, could I? What if I just let it happen? Would it be the best thing for Joe, to let him drift back into his own story? He could forget me and…and what? No, that was even worse surely, to let a man feel, live and love and then send him back into oblivion? I couldn't win either way. If I wanted to keep Joe in my world I needed to play the game, I needed to stop trying to prove myself right and just go with it. I needed to love him not objectify him and accept him as a person in his own right.

Deep down I knew this way of thinking wouldn't work for too long, there would be problems when Joe needed a doctor or a dentist or if he wanted to learn to drive and could find no evidence of a birth certificate. Even something as mundane as doing our taxes for The Imp would cause problems. Then what? How would I explain all of that? Cross that bridge when you come to it Naomi, I thought. My priority now was to stop Laney Marsh. First thing tomorrow morning I was going to hunt her down and make her listen.

Joe lay back on the bed and pulled me down next to him, wrapping his arm around my shoulders so I could rest my head on his chest. I inhaled deeply. The scent of him was intoxicating and I couldn't imagine a day when I might not be able to breathe him in. I needed him like a junkie needed drugs. Joe was my fix, he had been since the day I read his name on that stupid piece of paper and fell in love with my ultimate book boyfriend.

I listened to the thud thud of his heart beating against my cheek, trailed my fingers over his stomach in small soft circles and tried to reconcile the fact that whatever Joe had started out as, whatever fucked up magic had transformed him from fiction to fact, he was now a living, breathing human being. I had no true claim on him. I had no right to him, not even when he was merely an idea, a fantasy. All I could do was hope that he loved me, truly loved me and would stay. The dark seed of doubt crept in again to taunt me, *how do you know he really loves you Naomi? Aren't his feelings forced by your own hand? You created this version of Joe, you made him love you. He had no choice.*

I swallowed painfully, the fear rising in my throat knowing that the only way to test this theory was to tell him the truth, to take him to Laney and prove to him that he wasn't real but the truth would crush him. Imagine finding out that everything you thought you knew about yourself and your life was just some crazy quirk of unknown magical circumstance. That by all intents and purposes, you should not exist and nothing about you was real, your life was a lie. Jesus, it was like a real-life version of The Truman Show...except Truman got out.

Without realising it, the tiny circles I'd been tracing on Joe's abdomen had somehow moved lower and I found my fingers gently rubbing near the waistband on his pyjama bottoms. I noticed Joe's breathing had become shallower and his chest rose and fell quickly with each breath. The large bulge in his pants twitched as if trying to gain my attention and I immediately felt a thrill of excitement course through me. This was not a contrived reaction, at least I hoped not. Surely sexual attraction was a primal, instinctual reaction to being attracted to someone? He wouldn't get a raging hard on just because I wrote him like that. Joe had reigned in his usual behaviour in the bedroom these last few weeks and had been sweet and gentle with me that had been his own choice, not mine. Didn't that prove then that he was under his own influence to some degree?

My fingers glided downwards and over his erection, causing it to jerk upwards again. Joe's hand squeezed my shoulder as he nuzzled my hair muttering in Italian. His voice, soft and sultry could not be mistaken for anything other than seductive. I knew what he wanted. I pressed my hand more firmly on to the twitching bulge and began rubbing him slowly with my palm. Low moans came from deep in his throat and he cupped my chin with his free hand, lifting my face towards him.

"Baciami." Joe murmured, his brown eyes gleamed at me from under his long, lush lashes. I at least knew what that meant - Kiss me. Without hesitation, I slid up his body and gently teased his open lips with my tongue before crashing my mouth down on his in a bruising kiss. I needed him to know that I'd had enough of the delicate treatment. I wanted the rough and ready back. I bit down on his bottom lip and sucked it causing Joe's breath to hitch sharply. His free hand grabbed a fistful of my hair and tugged, exposing my neck. I caught the flash of heat in his look before his mouth plundered the delicate skin of my neck. Yes! There he is. I wanted nothing more than for Joe to fling me over and ravage my body but I broke away from the kiss.

"Stay there." I instructed him. He gave me a quizzical smile but shrugged in agreement.

"What are you up to?"

"Shut up and you'll find out."

"Hmm, you know I like it when you're bossy amore mio." I went to the chest of drawers and pulled out a pair of black stockings, turning to Joe I ran them suggestively through my hands. I had intended to wear these along with the little lacy black Basque to entice Joe back to his old, dominant bedroom behaviour but now I had another plan. "Are you dressing up for me bella?" The corner of his mouth turned up with the hint of a devilish grin.

"No, you are." I replied, pursing my lips, my brows raised. A low chuckle erupted from his mouth.

"Well that's something I haven't done before."

"You're not wearing them silly!" Grasping his meaning, I couldn't help but giggle. "Put your hands up." Joe did as I asked, amused curiosity fuelled his compliancy. I wrapped the stockings around his wrists and tied them tightly, pushing his arms above his head to rest on the bed. His top half lay on the bed and his legs dangled over the side with his bare feet on the floor.

"Don't move." I told him. I began a seductive strip tease for him, slowly peeling off my clothes one item at a time. A small part of me felt a little self-conscious and I almost giggled a few times, I had never played this role before, letting Joe take charge was how I liked it. But this was about him and I wanted to drive him to the edge my way. Seeing Joe's expression change from amusement to ardent desire encouraged me. I suddenly felt empowered and explicitly female. Standing there naked under his gaze I was fully aware of my body and the effect it had on Joe. His cock was straining in his pants, a fleeting image of the creature bursting from John Hurt's stomach in the film Alien flashed in my head and I almost guffawed. I could imagine Joe's cock ripping through the material of his pants at any moment, screaming to be fucked.

"Do I get to play yet or are you just going to stand there staring at my crotch?"

"You don't get to do anything. You just have to stay still and shut up. If you move the game ends. Got it?" I moved slowly and deliberately towards him, leaning over him I tugged down his pants allowing his dick to spring free. It jerked and bobbed alluringly, demanding attention. I pushed Joe's legs apart with my foot and settled myself on my knees between his open thighs. Joe lifted his head to look at me.

"I said don't move." I shot him a look of what I hoped was dominance and he lay his head back down but not before I noticed the wanton look that he shot back. Satisfied that he would behave I began his slow torture, starting at his ankles I ran my hands up the inside of his leg changing to butterfly kisses and teasing nips as I neared his groin. His body tensed as my tongue lightly grazed his balls. I continued my tease by positioning my mouth a hairs width away from his dick and allowing the heat from my breath to bathe it in warmth. His dick jerked again banging against my lips and I responded with a swift lick from the base of his shaft to the throbbing tip. Joe's hips bucked and he grumbled low in his chest. I retreated a little- returning my attentions to the area of skin in his groin, nipping at the little hollow where his thigh ended.

"Merda, donna!" Joe hissed through clenched teeth. His noises only spurred me on to more daring things. Standing up, I climbed onto the bed, turned around and straddled him so his face was inches from my exposed pussy. I felt him shift beneath me and I knew he wanted to taste me.

"You move and it ends." I was enjoying this, being the more dominant partner wasn't particularly my thing, I loved nothing more than a man that took charge but the feeling of power I had over Joe and my own femininity was intoxicating. Bringing my man pleasure on my terms turned me on no end. I could see why Joe liked being the dominant one, seeing your lover in a high state of sexual yearning, mercilessly at your hands was the ultimate high.

Bending forward so I was on all fours, my bottom aligned with his face, my head faced his crotch, I hooked my feet over his outstretched arms pinning them to the bed above his head. I moved slowly back and forth above him, trailing my long brown hair over his body and giving him a full view of my rear. I could feel his hot, rapid breaths on my backside and my body began to respond, eager for his touch. I refrained from pushing myself onto his waiting mouth, even though I ached for it. This was all about him and I was going to make damn sure he enjoyed every second.

I took hold of him in my hand and lowered my mouth, teasing his tip with my tongue. I loved the feel of him and he tasted incredible. My lips followed my tongue as I slipped them down over his length until my mouth was full and then slowly pulled away again. I continued this slow tease for a few strokes, revelling in the gasps and moans that he uttered. I switched to pleasuring him with my hand and let my tongue trail further down to stimulate his groin. My tongue reached places I knew had never been touched by anyone but me and that knowledge pleased me immensely. A rush of power surged through my body when Joe began grinding his hips against my mouth, pumping my hand harder and faster until I knew he was on the verge of a climax. I pulled away before he finished and I heard his tortured cry.

"Naomi, please. Don't stop."

"Patience baby, patience."

"Christ, woman!!"

"Shh! You love it. Now be quiet" I straightened, kneeling above his face again. No more than a few centimetres separated my flesh from his lips. I could feel every tantalising hot breath on me and I knew he must feel the heat of me on his mouth. I ground my hips in tiny circular motions above him, showing myself off to him. A plethora of Italian expletives sprang from him, none of which I understood but hearing him speak his native tongue always turned me on. I could feel the desire flow from my centre, readying me for sex. I knew Joe could sense it, the cheeky swine had the gall to stick out his tongue to take a sneaky taste. Damn his mouth felt good.

"Ah ah ah! Bad boy. No touching."

"Oh Jesus bella, you are killing me!" He growled as I rose up on my knees, out of his reach. "Please Naomi, I need to touch you."

"Not yet. Now lay still." I went back on all fours and unceremoniously took him in my mouth in one swift movement. Joe's hips thrust upwards and he called out in ecstasy. I worked him with my mouth, flicking his tip with my tongue on each upstroke. The salty tang of pre-cum coated my tongue which triggered an immediate heated response between my own legs.

"Fuuuck!" He cried. "Naomi, I'm going to come."

"Mmm." I moaned against him, not ceasing my attentions. I felt him tense and his flesh pulsate. The cries of his climax barrelled through his gritted teeth and I relished every sound he made.

When he finally calmed, I withdrew from him, wiping my mouth. Turing to face an exhausted Joe, I untied his hands and flopped down beside him, looping my leg over his. We lay there, no sound other than his panting for a few minutes until Joe suddenly flipped me over on to my back and pinned me beneath him. I felt him begin to harden again and with a wicked glint in his eyes he said.

"My turn."

CHAPTER
twenty-three

Revelations

Thankfully the storm had blown itself out and we awoke to clear skies and sunshine. Joe had woken early, getting up and making tea and toast to bring for us to eat in bed. As soon as we'd finished eating he'd showered and prepared himself for the day. I got the feeling he was eager to find Laney and get it all over and done with. I hadn't worked out how I would be able to talk to Laney without Joe overhearing the conversation. Yesterday I'd wanted him to be there so he could see first-hand that I'd been telling the truth, now I knew I couldn't have him anywhere near Laney Marsh. However, I couldn't exactly tell Joe I'd changed my mind either. If I tried that he'd wonder why I'd had the sudden change of heart. After the lengths I'd gone to drag his arse here he'd never believe it. I was going to have to wing it.

It was short walk along the shore path to Gardenstown and we'd called in to see Moira and her husband Cambell on the way. Cambell told us he'd heard of a Marsh family in the area but not an address. He'd told us to ask any of the local bakers or shop owners in Gardenstown as they'd be the most likely to know Laney. I'd had to explain all of this to Joe as we walked because as much as he'd struggled to understand Moira, her husband's accent was twice as thick.

Rows of sturdy little houses greeted us as we entered the small town, nestled neatly between the wildness of the bay and sprawling cliffs, it presented its own rugged beauty to the world. Making our way slowly through the streets, it felt like Joe and I had been transported into a different time. The old town offered a much simpler life than the one I was used to in the city, I could see the appeal. From what I could remember from my research into the area, these small villages and towns were built as a direct result of the highland clearances. In the eighteenth and nineteenth centuries, aristocratic landowners forced the eviction of farming tenants from their land and enclosed all common land to raise sheep. Thousands of Gaelic families were forced into migration to the Scottish west coast, Australia and America. The stone cottages in the west coast villages stood in defiance of the tyrannical aristocrats, small time tenant farmers became fishermen and learned to survive that way, keeping the Gaelic culture alive. I knew I was romanticising it, in reality the clearances had been brutal and lasted over hundred years.

Many people had been killed defending their ancestral homes. But something about their defiant struggle called to me, it was easy to feel a part of it when you were here, walking the streets of Gardenstown. I had Scottish ancestry, my family name of Douglas was a clan name. We had our own tartan. I felt strangely at home in these streets, in amongst my ancestors. I imagined I could hear their whispers and feel their watchful gaze from beneath the veil.

"That's a very wistful look you have there." Joe said.

"Isn't it beautiful here? I was just thinking about my heritage. I have Scottish ancestry you know."

"It is beautiful." Joe agreed. "I didn't know you had some Scottish in you, maybe that's where your fiery temper comes from huh?" He nudged my arm with his elbow.

"Hey!" I replied, playfully punching his shoulder. "I'm not fiery, I'm passionate."

"Oh no bella, the passion comes from the Italian inside you."

"I don't have any Italian in me." I said quizzically.

"Would you like some?" He grinned devilishly and I rolled my eyes.

"Ohhhh smooth, very smooth."

"I can do smooth…but I prefer rough and so do you la mia bella donna." His voice low and smouldering, sent shivers down my back and straight between my legs. Joe had such a crazy effect on me. I'd never reacted to any man the way I did to him, just the thought of sex with him had me panting like a bitch in heat.

"Will you stop it! Now is hardly the time you pervert." I laughed.

"But you like my perverse side. Remember the time with the butter and…"

"Shh! Someone might hear you." I hissed, trying to smother a laugh. "Come on now be serious please, we're on a mission remember?" We approached a greengrocer's shop and I pulled Joe to a stop. "Let's ask in here, see if they know Laney." Joe was distracted with the vegetable cart outside the shop. The chef side of him couldn't resist perusing fresh produce. "Joe?"

"Hmm?" He looked up at me, a plump plum in his hand.

"Never mind, I'm going inside a moment."

"OK, you mind if I look at these? I can pick something up for dinner tonight."

"That's fine, you play with your plums, and I won't be long." Joe raised an eyebrow at my innuendo and I blew him a kiss. I approached the counter and rang the little bell beside the till. A few seconds later a man who looked in his late sixties, came through from the back of the shop. His face was slightly weather-worn and rosy cheeked. Curly grey hair sprouted out the sides of a red woolly beanie hat. He reminded me of Smee from Peter Pan, all he was missing was the iconic blue and white striped shirt and the little round specs. The notion made me smile and the old man took it as a greeting. Smiling back at me he asked me,

"What can I do for you lassy?"

"Hi. Um, I'm actually looking for someone, a lady I work with. I have an address for Crovie but it seems she doesn't live there. I was wondering if you might know of her or her family? Her name is Laney Marsh." The old man's hand went to his chin and he stroked it, his beady blue eyes scrutinised me.

"Who's asking?"

"Oh, sorry. My name is Naomi Doug... Ferrantino. Naomi Ferrantino." I smiled and held out my hand. He didn't take it but continued to stare at me. The situation felt somewhat awkward during the few moments of silence that followed. I lowered my hand and gave a little cough, clearing my throat. "It's a matter of some urgency you see, it's about her work." The old man still didn't respond so I continued. "I need to get in contact with her as soon as possible. It really is important." Not wanting to elaborate any further I stopped and looked at him expectantly, hoping for an answer.

"A' knows the Marsh family aye. No Laney though. Maybe you got the wrong address."

"Oh." I replied, a little disappointed. "I suppose it's possible she may go by another first name, she's a writer you see."

"You one o' them stalkers are ye?"

"Oh God no. Nothing like that." *Technically you are.* The little voice in my head piped up. I ignored it. "I've been erm...helping her with her book but there's a problem and I need to see her. I don't have much in the way of contact details."

"Funny. It stands to reason if yous are working together you'd have contact details eh?" The man narrowed his eyes suspiciously. Jesus! Talk about tight lipped community. This was like pulling teeth! I plastered on my sweetest smile.

"Ms Marsh is very private. She only used to communicate via email. I've been trying to get hold of her for a while but she's not answering her emails. I'm starting to get worried about her." I thought I'd try the concerned associate approach instead. It seemed to make the old man think anyway. I was just about to say something more when Joe burst through the door with his arms stuffed full of fresh fruit and vegetables, an excited expression on his face and a reel of Italian spouting from his mouth. The old man's attention was diverted from me and he beamed at Joe.

"Naomi, look at all this! Beautiful produce huh?" He bundled the produce onto the counter and gestured towards his hoard. "So fresh and juicy!" He said enthusiastically. Turning to the old man he asked, "All organic yes?"

"T'is aye. Local grown, you'll no get better sir." The pride on the man's face was obvious and he was clearly appreciative of Joe's praise. "Yous want me te bag it up for yous?" He asked Joe. Joe's brow furrowed and I interjected.

"He's asking if you want to buy it?" I turned to the man and explained. "Joe is from Italy, I'm afraid he's having trouble understanding your accent."

"Ahh! Italian eh? You'll know all aboot great grub then aye."

I continued to translate for Joe, "He says you know about great food."

"Si signore. Food is life uh?" Joe grinned heartily and the old man responded with a booming laugh and clapped Joe on the shoulder in agreement. They continued to coo over the quality of fresh, organic produce, Joe going full Italian with his over enthusiastic hand gestures, emphasising his words. I stood by patiently waiting for an opportunity to interject and push the man for information. As the old man finished bagging up our purchases I heard Joe ask him if he could recommend any local fishmongers because he planned on making us a fish dinner tonight.

"Try old Alan down by the harbour. He sells his daily catch fresh from his boat, you'll no get fresher than straight from the ocean. You tell him Drew sent ye and he'll see you right."

"I will, thank you Drew." Joe beamed and held out his hand to shake the old man's hand. Drew, didn't hesitate to give Joe's hand a hearty shake, followed by a friendly pat of his arm.

"And you lassy," Drew addressed me, "you can find the Marsh family estate atop the hill but I wouldn'y go poking around too much if I were you. Like you said, they're a private family. They don't mix much around town. Watch your step." The added warning took me by surprise a little. What did he mean by 'watch my step'? I didn't get chance to ask because another customer came into the shop and Drew went off to greet them. Joe took his bag full of groceries and walked out the shop, waving a friendly goodbye at Drew as he exited.

"What is it with you?" I demanded when we were back on the street.

"What do you mean?" Joe asked.

"That man was playing hard to get until you walked in. He wasn't talking at all."

"He seemed friendly enough to me."

"Yeah, well everyone likes you it seems!"

"Aww, bella. I can't help it, it's my natural charm." He quipped, his eyes glinting. "Don't worry my love, I like you." Joe blew me a kiss and winked.

"It's only because you bought a load of stuff." I said huffily. "I've never seen someone get so excited over a cucumber before." Joe started laughing and I pulled a face at him, he had such a natural way with people it really bugged me sometimes. I found it hard to be mad at him though, he'd managed to get the information about the Marsh's for me without even trying.

"You want me to show you how excited I can get about a cucumber later?" He wiggled his eyebrows suggestively. "I got a big one, fat and juicy…cucumbers have many uses you know, not just for eating."

"Oh my Lord! You really are perverted." I couldn't help but laugh. "Is everything about sex with you?"

"Pretty much bella. Sex and food, two very valid reasons for living." He smiled broadly. "Sooo… about that cucumber?" Joe said coyly.

"The one in the bag or the one in your pants?" I smirked.

"Both."

"Joe!" The shock on my face was genuine. I felt the first flush of heat on my face, slightly embarrassed at what he was suggesting.

"I don't ask, I don't get." He shrugged, nonchalant. "Think you can handle two?" I turned my face away, my hand covering my mouth trying to smother the nervous giggle. I had never experimented with food during sex before. Joe was pushing me to my limits constantly. I adored getting dirty with him but I wasn't sure I could handle what he had in mind. I felt him take my hand and pull me to a stop. His face was serious now, none of the impish glint in his eyes.

"Naomi, I'm sorry. I didn't mean to make you feel uncomfortable. I'm just joking around."

"It's OK, I never know if you're being serious or not. I mean…I like to try new things but…"

"You've never done anything like that." He finished for me. I shook my head, smiling shyly. "Don't worry love, we can try something a little less…perverted." He grinned and put his arm around me, pulling me in for a hug. His amused chuckle rumbled through his chest. This man sometimes made me feel like an innocent virgin. I was determined to try and keep up with him.

"Like what?" My voice muffled by his coat.

"Oh I don't know, we'll think of something." He pulled away from me and cupped my chin, raising my face to look at him. "Ti amo Naomi." His lips found mine and he kissed me tenderly, the depth of feeling I held for him threatened to overwhelm me. Life with Joe was a rollercoaster of emotion and sexual tension. It was a ride I never wanted to get off. My mind immediately went back to my mission. I had to find Laney. I had to somehow stop her writing and secure my future with Joe because I knew I could never go back to a life without him. He was my world. He made me feel like the most important person on the planet. I had never had anyone love me so openly and fervently before. Genuine or not, I was addicted to his love, to him and I never wanted to let him go.

We arrived at the harbour hand in hand. Joe talked animatedly all the way there about the feast he planned on cooking for us this evening. His passion for food rivalled his passion in the bedroom and both were equally deserving of praise. We spotted Alan's boat- The Kelpie Queen, in the harbour and Joe pulled me enthusiastically towards it.

"Hey babe? Do you mind if I go up the hill? I want to go find the Marsh estate. It's getting on and as much as I'd love to stay and talk 'fish', I really need to go." This was the perfect opportunity to go off on my own, Joe would be happy talking to Alan for a while. I could already see the light in his eyes as he scanned the crates of fresh seafood on the boat.

"Oh, yeah OK. I thought you wanted me to come with you? Wasn't that the whole point?" He frowned.

"Yeah, I know. I've been thinking about it and I think it's something I need to do on my own. It might be less threatening to Laney if I'm on my own don't you think? Besides, I don't even know if it's the right family. Chances are it's not so it'll be a wasted journey for you. You're better off staying here and choosing your prize." I nodded towards the boat. Joe continued to frown.

"I thought you needed me to meet this woman? That was the whole reason you planned the trip right? What's changed?"

"Nothing babe, I did want you to meet her. I just feel like I need to see her alone first. Is that alright?

Just…humour me, please?" I looked beseechingly at him and he caved.

"If you're sure? Do you want me to come meet you when I'm done here?"

"Um, no it's fine. I'll meet you in that little tea room over there." I pointed along the harbour to a small tea room called 'Tea for Two', Joe nodded.

"How long?"

"I don't know, about an hour, hour and a half maybe?"

"OK love. I'll pick us some fish for dinner but don't be more than an hour and a half, we have to walk back to Crovie and I don't want this fish to go off."

"I won't be, I promise. Thank you, Joe." I reached up and kissed him on the lips. "See you soon, pick us something nice." I smiled at him and he smiled back then turned and walked towards Alan's boat. I waited till I saw him approach Alan and begin talking and then I practically ran back up the street towards the path that led up the cliff to the Marsh estate.

It took about twenty minutes to find the grand entrance to the estate, a long wide driveway, lined either side by tall trees, stretched away from the ten-foot-wide wrought iron gate. The property was surrounded by a stone wall that looked about six feet high and old. I surmised it must be quite a large estate by the grandeur of the entrance. The gate was closed, I tried pushing it but it was far too heavy. I looked at the huge stone pillars that held up the gate and saw a small black box with a button in the middle. I pushed it. Nothing happened. I pushed it again three times in a row, holding my finger down on the third try. I waited and then a buzzing noise sounded and the heavy gate clanked and swung open, creaking and groaning in the process. I began the long lonely walk up the tree lined driveway. I had no idea how long it was because I couldn't, yet, see any evidence of a house.

It took a good ten minutes of fast paced walking until I rounded a corner and was confronted by a huge mansion house. It looked more like a castle with its dark grey stone walls and turreted towers. I'd seen a few pictures of grand Scottish houses and castles, this one was smaller than ones I'd seen but no less imposing. Surrounded by trees on either side, there was a circular end to the driveway leading right up to the front door. There were iron bars on the windows that looked old and rusted and some of the window panels looked thick with dirt. I looked around the front courtyard at what once must've been immaculately kept but now lay untended and unloved. Overgrown shrubbery spilled over the boarders and weeds penetrated the gravel drive. I shivered, my lip curling upwards in a grimace. If I didn't know better, I'd think I'd just happened upon a haunted house. The reality of it was probably that the family who lived here were perhaps elderly and couldn't manage the estate as they once used to, or perhaps weren't as affluent as previous generations. Looking at the house and its neglected frontage, you could easily mistake it for being abandoned. There was little to no sign of life that I could see, no lights in the windows or anything to indicate it was still lived in. This couldn't be where Laney lived surely? The impression of her I got through her writing was one of a woman similar in age to me, full of life and vibrancy. I couldn't picture her living somewhere like this. I almost turned back except for the fact that someone had opened the gate to let me in.

I approached the stone steps that led to the heavy wooden front door and lifted my hand to the iron door knocker. Before I could knock, I heard a click and the door opened slowly. I stepped back in anticipation, expecting to see an elderly maid or homeowner, instead a tall, blonde beauty stood half hidden behind the door. She smiled shyly at me, trying to avoid eye contact.

"Um…hello." I paused to smile. "My name is…"

"I know who you are." She interrupted, her voice was quiet but captivating nonetheless. "She said you'd come." Her words surprised me.

"You know me?" I admit I felt slightly perturbed by this fact. The woman nodded, her face remained dipped but she momentarily lifted her eyes to look at me. When I met her gaze, I was immediately struck by their brilliance. They were a shade of ice blue I'd never seen before, they were mesmerising. She noticed my stare and dropped her eyes to the ground again. "Do you know why I'm here then?" Again, the woman nodded. "Is Laney Marsh at home?" The woman shook her head. Disappointed I asked, "Will she be long? Is it possible I could wait inside?" After a moment of thought the woman stepped back and opened the door wider to allow me inside.

"You can wait in the library." The blonde woman told me as she began walking down the dark hallway towards the rear of the house. My shoes resonated on the tiled floor with each step, sending echo bouncing off the walls. There were no lights or lamps of any kind in the hall but I managed to follow the sound of the woman's footsteps in front.

"Is there a light or something you could switch on please? It's a bit hard to see." I asked politely, no sooner had I finished my sentence than a single light shone from an old fitting on the ceiling, casting shadows around me. That was odd, I hadn't seen the woman stop or heard her click a switch at all. "Thank you." I said tentatively. She led me to a dimly lit room, the instant I entered I knew it was the library, the unmistakable smell of old leather and paper hit me. I loved that smell, some people would call it musty but I called it home. There was something about libraries and old book shops I found incredibly overawing, the vast array of knowledge contained within the millions of pages demanded reverence but I always felt calm in those places. I could happily spend all day sitting amongst old books, surrounded by centuries of thoughts, dreams and the fantastical workings of the human mind. This was my idea of total paradise.

The dim light grew brighter as we neared a seating area in the centre of the room and it was then that I realised the sheer size of the library. It seemed incomprehensible compared to the size of the house from the outside. I'm sure I must've looked like an open-mouthed fish as I stared in wonderment at shelves piled from floor to ceiling with books, shelves that stretched back further than the light in the room could reach.

"How…?" Was all I could manage to utter.

"Please sit Naomi." The blonde said. "Can I offer you a drink?"

"Um. No thanks." I replied mindlessly. I realised then I hadn't asked the woman's name, or rather she hadn't introduced herself to me at the door." "What's your name?"

"I'm the librarian." She said. *Okaaay.*

"Oh. Right. But what should I call you?" Thinking she hadn't quite grasped my meaning.

"The librarian." She stated simply. I shrugged a shoulder and nodded slowly.

"Right." There was an awkward silence and then the librarian turned and walked towards the door.

"Wait here and don't touch anything." She said quietly and then was gone.

"Well that wasn't odd in the slightest." I said to the room. I sat upright in an old leather high-backed chair. I guessed by the style of it, it was a Chesterfield. Its green leather was soft and well worn, especially along the arms where several tiny cracks could be seen. This chair had certainly seen some use. Looking around the space where I sat, I could see a beautiful antique writing bureau, I recognised it as a Davenport. Of course, I would expect a house like this to be full of antiques so it was no great surprise to find such a beautiful piece in the library. Its presence only added to the nostalgic atmosphere. My eyes glanced over the books on the nearest shelf in front of me. All of them were old and leather bound. Huge thick, heavy volumes with gold lettering on the well-worn spines. I found them comforting, I felt strangely like I was amongst family here.

Several minutes ticked by as I waited rather impatiently for the librarian to return. I couldn't sit still any longer, the pull of the books was too strong, I had to go and look at them more closely. I often wondered what volumes huge family libraries in grand houses would hold, now was my chance to take a peek. Stepping up to the shelf I reached out my hand to touch one of the red leather spines, the moment my finger made contact I felt it- an electric pulse, like the dull thub thub of a heartbeat, emanated from the book and through my hand.

"What the hell?" I jumped back rubbing my palm on my hip. Was that static? I peered at the spine of the book that had just shocked me. There was a symbol near the top, something I didn't recognise and then underneath a string of numbers that looked like a date and finally a name.

"Erika Parker." I mumbled. I didn't recognise it as a title that I knew. I moved along the shelf to the next volume, the same sequence appeared on the spine - a symbol, a set of numbers and a name. I read it out.

"James Markham." Moving further along I continued to read out names on the spines of the books. They all looked the same except the further along the shelves I travelled, the older the books looked. I noticed the ageing covers corresponded with the numbers on each book. If those numbers were indeed dates then some of these volumes were centuries old. I could find no recognisable titles amongst them, just rows and rows of names.

I heard footsteps in the distance, it sounded like two sets. I quickly retreated to my seat and waited. The librarian entered first and stood to one side allowing the second woman to follow. This woman was older, much older but graceful and held a certain air of authority. I found myself standing to greet her.

"Hello Naomi. My name is Laney Marsh, I've been waiting for you."

CHAPTER
twenty-four

The Author

"You're Laney?" I couldn't quite hide the shocked tone in my question. Laney Marsh smiled briefly and walked towards me holding her hand out in greeting. I took it and gave it a weak shake. This couldn't be Laney, she was...old. She wasn't anything like I'd imagined.

"Not what you were expecting?" She mused.

"I...um, well no not quite." I answered honestly. Laney sat in the chair opposite and motioned for me to sit.

"I feel like you're at a disadvantage Naomi, I know why you think you are here but you are mistaken."

"How so?" This was an odd way to begin our conversation. I was thrown totally off guard. I thought I'd be here begging this woman to stop writing and attempting to convince her that her creation had come to life but something told me that was not how this was about to play out. Now that I was finally meeting her face to face, I had a distinct feeling this is exactly what she had been expecting.

"I know about Joe and I know what you think he is."

"You know? How? And what do you mean by what I think he is?" I did not like the way this conversation was going, the first feelings of trepidation fluttered to life in the pit of my stomach.

"I'll tell you how in a little while, let's start at the beginning shall we?" I just nodded in response not knowing what to say. "I am an author, Naomi. Not the kind that you know, something different. You could say I am duty bound to chronicle the lives of humans under my charge. I'm also not the only author, there are many of us, hundreds in fact but we all hold the same duty." I heard her talking but nothing this woman said made any sense.

"Chronicle the lives of humans…what the hell are you talking about?" Had I just walked into the bat shit crazy hotel or something?

"Listen and you will begin to understand." She spoke with such authority I had no choice but to shut up and listen. "We are a special guild of…*people*, who were chosen to fulfil very privileged roles. The position I hold as an author is one of great power and responsibility. I do not take my duties lightly, there are serious consequences to any authors who do not follow the rules."

"Duty bound by whom? And what guild? Are you talking about writing biographies or something?"

"The universe." She said simply.

"The universe?" I couldn't hide the scepticism in my voice. Crikey, this old bird was battier that I was!

"Yes dear, the universe. You are aware of it I take it?" She quipped, raising an eyebrow. "And, I suppose you could say biographies are a *speciality* of sorts." The corner of her mouth lifted slightly. The blonde librarian giggled and then shushed herself, clapping a hand over her mouth. "You have been on our radar for a while Naomi. We send out feelers and look for certain responses from our 'people of interest'. You had what we were looking for and so we waited for you to come to us," she paused and leaned forward, giving me an intense look, "and here you are."

"Okaaay." I said, dragging the word out. "I'm really not getting what you're trying to say here. You're telling me that you're duty bound by the universe to chronicle the lives of people on earth and that you somehow tested me and then brought me here on purpose?"

"Mmm, it's a little more in depth than that but that's more or less it, yes."

"Dare I ask why?"

"You were chosen to be one of us."

"And by that you mean…an author?"

"Eventually perhaps, yes. It depends. You would begin as a librarian. Your lifelong fascination with books coupled with certain beliefs that you hold were what peaked our interest. We've been watching you for a very long time." She paused, waiting for a response. I struggled to process what she was saying, it all sounded so far-fetched, like something you read about in a children's adventure book. It wasn't for the unexplained appearance of Joe, I'd have thought she was joking. I knew it was all connected to my damned manuscript and to Laney but I had never expected something like this and now I held no doubt that she was telling the absolute truth. Now I understood how insane my explanations to Joe must've seemed and how much he must love me to have stuck around.

"What do you mean by beliefs?"

"I mean that you are very in tune with your environment Naomi. You notice things, the little day to day occurrences that other's may pass off as mere coincidence, you understand them and you take note."

"Signs." I muttered to myself.

"Indeed. It takes a special type of person to do that. You are able to tap into the energy of the universe and interpret it. That is exactly what is needed to become an author." I frowned, there were still things I needed explaining.

"You said you tested me, what did you mean by that?"

"Occasionally, when we are sure we have a person of interest, we test them. How we do that depends on each person but for you it was the manuscript I asked you to proofread. Words are extremely powerful things. They have the power to manipulate and influence in many ways. A true author also has that power and you have proved that you do." A heavy, sinking feeling settled in my gut like a stone. *Oh God no!* The meaning behind her words suddenly hit me and I felt my already tenuous grip on reality begin to slip. She could not mean what I feared she did?

"Joe was my test?" No sooner had I spoken than I knew I was right. Her sympathetic look hammered home the awful truth. "He really isn't real?" My voice cracked, tears pricked the corner of my eyes. "No! That can't be true!" I managed to squeak out a denial before a heart wrenching sob broke away from me. "Why? Why would you do that? That's cruel!"

"It's necessary. I know exactly how you feel Naomi, I had to endure my own pain when I was chosen. The system is designed thus because you need to fully understand the power and responsibility you have as an author. Your job is to chronicle not create. You have the power to do both but you must not, under any circumstances, use your power to create. You have experienced first-hand how your words can change lives. You changed your own and you began to see the consequences. Words can have a ripple effect, they don't just influence you, they influence the world around you. We needed you to understand the severity of what could happen if you were ever to use your position as an author to start meddling in people's lives."

"What right did you have to do that?" I yelled, jumping out of my seat, fists balled and tears streaming down my cheeks. "This is my life! Joe's life! What about him? What happens to him now?" Cold fear struck at my very core. "Fuck! Is he even still alive? He's…he's waiting for me to come back…isn't he?"

"Naomi, please try to calm down and listen. Everything will make sense when you understand."

"I don't want to fucking understand! I want Joe! I love him. You have no right to take him from me!"

"You love the idea of him. You did not love a physical being, because he was never real. He was words on a page, words that touched you, manipulated and influenced your feelings. You used your gift in unison with your words to manipulate things you don't yet comprehend. It was meant to happen that way so you would begin to understand the level of power and responsibility you would hold as an author."

"Where. Is. Joe?" I demanded through gritted teeth. "I don't give two fucks about your stupid test or being an author. Joe is mine. I will not let you take him."

"Joe is still here. He is waiting for you like you planned but you have a choice to make Naomi. The universe has chosen you and there is no way of changing that now. You don't have to become an author."

"Good! Then I respectfully decline." I interjected.

"But, as with everything in the universe there has to remain a balance. Things have been changed and therefore you can either rectify it and agree to become part of the guild or you can choose to stay with Joe and your life together will continue."

"I choose the latter." I didn't even hesitate. There was nothing on earth or the bloody universe that would make me chose otherwise. Laney fell silent, contemplating me for a moment.

"You can of course choose Joe but there are certain rules that must be followed."

"Like what?" I eyed her suspiciously. Why was there always a catch? Nothing was ever bloody simple.

"If you choose to live your life with Joe he must choose this also. The moment you decide this he will become a true part of life on this plane. He will become real but it must be of his own choosing."

"Fine. I don't see a problem with that." As much as I tried to sound convinced, I wasn't. How would Joe react knowing the actual truth?

"If this is what you decide you must bring him to me so we can explain things to him fully."

"OK. What else?" Somehow I knew she wasn't finished.

"You've seen already how your life has changed as a result of Joe's existence, it has upset the balance of things and balance will always fight to be restored. You tried to create a life of happiness with someone who was never meant to be. That has consequences...and will continue to have consequences throughout your life. No one ever has a perfect life Naomi, bad things happen to good people and good things happen to bad people. That is just the way it is as always will be. That is life. What you have done is create a false reality. The ripples will travel through time and space and only multiply and grow in strength as time passes. You and Joe must be made fully aware of that fact. And you must both agree to accept these terms. However, should either one of you decide not to proceed then you will take up a position as a trainee and balance will be restored."

"And Joe?" I dared to ask, knowing already what her answer would be but needing to confirm it.

"Joe will be what he was before, a figment of your imagination, just words on a page. Until the next time."

"The next time?"

"Yes," she nodded and let her head drop, her gaze now resting on her knees, "the next time we decide to test someone." Everything suddenly fell into place.

"Oh my god! Melissa! That's why he remembers Melissa isn't it?"

"He remembers her?" Laney's head snapped up, she looked shocked.

"Yes! It all makes sense now. Melissa was the name of another woman you tested wasn't it? You just reused the manuscript?" Laney's face was impossible to read. She sat stock still with her hands clasped tightly together. A tense silence filled the space between us and I caught a hint of pained sorrow in her eyes. Laney slowly unclasped her hands and reached for the librarian who stood by her side. Laney let out a slow shaky breath, her voice barely a whisper as she said,

"I am Melissa."

CHAPTER
twenty-five

Choices

"What?" I wasn't sure I had heard her correctly, "Did you just say,"

"I am Melissa," Laney interrupted, "yes." She had regained some of her former decorum but I could sense she was still shaken underneath.

"How is that possible? Did you write the book about yourself?" I felt my stomach curdle, fighting the need to retch in disgust I continued to probe her, "But you said that was forbidden! And now you've used him to trap me? How could you do that? That's disgusting!" I glared at Laney with absolute disdain, the thought that she could use Joe, a man she created and probably loved at one time, to entrap someone else was abhorrent to me. I could never do something like that.

"It's not what you think Naomi."

"Well then how is it? Because from where I'm standing that's *exactly* how it looks." I shot her a challenging stare, demanding she explain herself. Admittedly a large part of the anger I felt towards her was born of jealousy, I had thought Joe was mine, my creation, mine to love. I had believed I was the only woman he had ever loved and yet now I found out he had been *hers* first. I swallowed the bile that arose in my throat. Laney let out a long, tired sigh. The Librarian patted her on the shoulder comfortingly and I wanted to slap her hand away. Laney Marsh deserved no such sympathy.

"Remember I told you I had faced my own test before I was chosen to become an Author?"

"*Joe?* Joe was your test too?" My fists were still balled and I dug my nails into my palms, trying desperately to detract from the pain in my heart. Laney nodded,

"I was sent that very same manuscript over fifty years ago, it's been altered a little since then to fit the time but the essence of it is the same." She said rather sadly. A stunned silence fell between us as I tried to process what she was saying. All I could think about was that Laney had been in love with Joe, *my* Joe at some point in the distant past. She has kissed him, touched him and done lord knows what with him…and even more sickening was the realisation that Joe had reciprocated. I felt the floor move beneath me and the room sway, I was going to fall. Soft, steady hands caught me and guided me back to a sitting position in the large leather chesterfield. The Librarian now stood beside me, a look of genuine concern on her face.

"He…he remembers you," I said shakily, "he told me he remembers Melissa. Does that mean he still," the next word stuck fast in my throat but I forced it out, "*loves* you?"

"I doubt it very much, it's just a ghost of a memory from the past, a past that's not even real." I detected a hint of uncertainty in her tone that set my teeth on edge.

"Just how many times has that manuscript been used?" I said through tight lips.

"I was the second I believe," Laney replied, she coughed to clear her throat before continuing, "As the novel became more popular in society, it became easier to discover more potential candidates. There are people whose task it is to create ways of finding suitable candidates, one of those tasks, amongst many others, is writing manuscripts similar to this one to send out to,"

"Lure people in!" I spat. "You're playing with people's lives here, do you know that? Do you care?"

"It's not our job to care Naomi, if we let ourselves care then we begin to take pity on the people whose lives we're trying to protect."

"Protect! That's a fucking joke. How are you protecting the homeless man who dies alone on a street? Or the child that dies in a car accident?"

"We can't protect individuals per say, you must understand that there is a balance to maintain, everything happens for a reason just the way it is supposed to protect that balance. If we started to care we would be driven to change the fate of anyone we felt pity for and that has massive consequences Naomi. You've only seen a tiny glimpse of the effects that the ripples of change can cause.

We had to do things this way because you needed to see, to understand how it must be. You cannot change fate, if you do then you must live with the consequences." Laney sat stiff backed and had regained her composure somewhat, that air of authority was back and a look of carefully contrived calmness spread across her face. I wanted to punch her.

"You turned him down didn't you." It was a statement not a question and I felt a twinge of gleeful gloating at the knowledge that I was right, I could see it in her eyes. Laney hadn't loved Joe enough to make sacrifices, she'd chosen the life of an Author over him. Well I wasn't going to make that mistake. That nagging little voice in the back of my mind attempted to remind me of the potential consequences of my choice, it tried to tell me I was being selfish but I ignored it…for now.

"I did, yes. I understood the responsibilities I had been given and chose to do the right thing." *Sanctimonious bitch!* Oh she really had got on her high horse with me now.

"The right thing for who? For you? For Joe? Where does he fit into your perfect little plans?"

"The right thing for the universe Naomi, balance must be restored and maintained at *all* costs. I have already told you, you can choose not to follow this path and stay with Joe but in doing so the universe will fight to regain control. Can you live with what might happen because of it?"

"Yes. I can." I jutted out my chin in stubborn protest. The universe could fight all it bloody well liked but I would fight back with every ounce of strength in my body to keep Joe by my side. *If that's what he wants.* The knot of fear pulled at me again, what if he didn't?

"Very well then, if that is what you choose then bring Joe to me tomorrow and we shall see if he feels the same way. Those are the rules Naomi, you both must choose the same path. Like it or not you have been selected and only two choices lay before you now, I pray for everyone's sake you choose well...as I once did." Laney Marsh rose from her chair, nodded her head once in my direction and dismissed me, "Good day *Mrs Ferrantino.*" Her tone of dismissal wasn't lost on me, I sensed a tinge of jealousy in the way she had spoken my name. There was no doubt in my mind that part of her stupid rule of having to bring Joe to her was merely so she could see him again.

The Librarian shifted slightly, bringing my attention back to her.

"We shall see you both tomorrow then?" She asked very politely.

"Do I have any choice?"

She smiled sympathetically at me and that gave me my answer. I walked toward the library's exit and out into the hallway without waiting for the Librarian to escort me although I could hear her scurrying behind me. When we reached the front door she scooted in front to open it, I walked out without a backward glance, flinching as the heavy oak door shut hard in my wake. Now I had the hard task of convincing Joe to come and meet Laney. No, convincing him to meet her wasn't the hard part, it was everything that followed.

CHAPTER
twenty-six

Ashes to Ashes

I'd been right, it had been easy to get Joe to agree to visit Laney. He'd seemed rather relived that I had asked him. He said he'd been worried because I'd changed my mind and had gone to meet Laney alone. Poor Joe, I gave him a sideways glance as we stood on the stone steps of Laney's manor. Joe couldn't wait to meet her and put this whole thing to bed. Of course, he didn't yet know the full story, he only knew my version, the one I had told him to get him to Scotland in the first place. He was in for a shock to say the very least. I'd decided to hold off on anymore of the details of how my own visit Laney had gone, let her be the bearer of bad news. As I stood beside him on the steps, I worried that I should've given him at least some of the truth but then he wouldn't have believed it anyway. He hadn't so far. Joe caught my gaze and smiled, taking my hand in his he gave it a reassuring squeeze. That small gesture said so much, 'don't worry love, this will all be over soon'. If only he knew. The door clicked and swung open, my heartbeat instantly increased. This was it, the moment of truth.

Expecting to see the sweet, sickly smile and blue eyes of the Librarian, I was shocked to be greeted by none other than the lady of the manor herself, Laney Marsh. My heckles were up in a second. I wasn't prepared for Joe to see his old love just yet, I had thought we might have at least a few minutes with the loyal assistant first.

"Hello Joe." Laney held out her hand for him, he hesitated and shook it then stopped suddenly, dropping her hand like he held a hot pebble.

"Melissa?" He barely breathed out her name but it clearly affected Laney, she beamed at him. I scowled at her, secretly thankful of the fifty years that had aged her since they had last laid eyes on each other. "You're so old." Joe said in total wonderment. I couldn't help it, a snort of laughter erupted from me and I tried to smother it with a cough. Laney's mouth went to a thin line, the laugh had not escaped her. Joe regrouped and stuttered, "I didn't mean it like that. I meant…you look so different, so very different. How is this even possible?" He shook his head still staring at her in disbelief.

"Come inside and I will explain everything." Laney said, her face softened again as she addressed Joe. Laney glanced at me and I swear I caught a look of malice in her eyes. Turning on her sweetest smile for Joe she said, "You haven't changed a bit, still as handsome as you ever were."

Then she reached up and patted his cheek! My blood boiled and I glowered at her, right now I hated her- for everything she was about to do to Joe and to me and for daring to touch him with such familiarity. She'd had her chance with Joe and she chose to let him go. Joe was mine and if she laid a hand on him again, I'd make her regret it- old lady or not. We followed her down the same dimly lit hallway that I had walked down yesterday and into the vast library. This time there were four chairs instead of two, the Librarian already occupied one of them. She stood to greet us as we approached. I couldn't bring myself to smile back, the nerves had taken hold of me and I had no room for manners. I wanted to believe that Joe would feel the same way about me as I did him and that he would choose to stay but I had no real idea how he would react when Laney finally told him the truth.

"Please, sit." Laney gestured towards the chairs, I took a seat but Joe remained standing.

"No thank you. I'd prefer to get this over with as quickly as possible." His tone was clipped and business-like, I could tell he was uncomfortable but there was something underlying in his manner that I couldn't quite place.

"As you wish," Laney sat and folder her hands in her lap, she addressed Joe directly, "where would you like me to start?" Joe shifted his feet,

"I want to know how it is possible that you look like you have aged fifty years and yet I remember you like it was yesterday?" Joe demanded, "Naomi's manuscript…it had you in it, why? *How?* Tell me Melissa or is it Laney? I need to know. Merda! I have so many questions I don't even know where to begin! Was I ever in an accident?"

"No, Joe you weren't. You have holes in your memory because your past never existed."

"But…I remember you and you are in my past."

"No, you are in *my* past Joe." I glared at Laney, could she be any more insensitive? I know she had to give him the truth but Christ, she could at least give it to him gently; she was playing with his feelings! I hope Joe told her to stuff it and that he wanted to stay with me because I honestly couldn't see myself working for this heartless bitch.

"How is that even possible?" Joe said.

"Because it's the truth. Naomi told you the truth, although she didn't know the depth of it. You are a manifestation of her making," Laney looked down at her hands and added, "as you were once mine."

"You're telling me I'm not real? I'm just some made up…*thing*…I don't feel, or need or want?"

"Only what you were created to feel Joe, you're born of a work of fiction and manifested through a gift that only certain people possess, like Naomi and myself."

"Bullshit! You can't sit there and tell me what I'm feeling now, the pain and the betrayal," Joe glanced at me, "the love, isn't real! I bleed, I breathe and my heart beats the same as anyone else, so don't you dare tell me I'm not real!"

"Yes, that much is true Joe, you do feel and bleed the same as any other human being and if you were to choose to stay in this life, no doubt you would love Naomi till the end of your days but,"

"No! No '*but*'... I love her," Joe pointed at me and a multitude of emotions swelled in my chest, I felt the familiar sting of tears begin to form and all I wanted to do was wrap myself in his arms. "I love her and it doesn't make any difference how it came to pass, it just did. And I'm glad of it, at least now my questions about my lost memories have been answered. Now I know the truth we can leave and just get on with our lives...right?" The uncertainty in his voice betrayed his confidence. I couldn't bear the gravity of what I was about to tell him, the first tear slithered down my cheek and closing my eyes, I shook my head in despair.

"I wish it was that simple Joe, I really do." My hands shook with emotion, Joe immediately knelt beside me, clasping my hands in his.

"Why isn't it bella? Nothing else matters but you and me. If I don't have a past, so what! We can make our own together, the future is what matters now."

"That's exactly why you have a choice to make Joe," Laney interjected, "the future *is* what matters and it lies in your hands. Yours and Naomi's." Laney proceeded to tell Joe the rest of the 'truths' she had laid out before me yesterday, presenting him with the very same choice; save our relationship and suffer the inevitable consequences or, restore the balance and give it all up for the sake of the natural order of the universe and all of humanity. Talk about Sophie's choice!

"So...let me get this straight, if I chose to do nothing, Naomi and I walk away and continue our lives together but the universe will fight to regain order?"

"Essentially yes, you were never meant to exist on this plane Joe. You were not born into this world like a normal human being, you are a creation of an entirely different kind. Your existence here has already begun to affect those around you and the ripples of change will only grow bigger and more destructive. I cannot tell you who it will affect or how, only that it will."

"And if I agree to…to go back…to die?"

"No! Joe you can't say that, please!" I pleaded, Joe squeezed my hand and kissed my wet cheek.

"Shh mia cara, the question must be asked. This is a life changing decision not just for us but for all the people you love."

"You wouldn't *die* per say, Joe. You would merely cease to exist." Laney explained.

"Would I feel pain?" His voice cracked a little and my throat tightened, I couldn't bear to hear him even discuss the matter.

"No, you just wouldn't *be*. You would be as you were before, fictional."

"Until you decide to use him again on some other unsuspecting woman!" I spat. "Joe, you can't let her do this to us, please? I love you, I won't let her use you like this. Whatever consequences might arise from us being together, we can deal with them when they happen."

"Bella…ti amo, I want nothing more than to be with you, I know how I feel, regardless of what anyone might think. Right now, I am my own person with my own feelings and I do love you."

"But? I sense a but." My heart stopped beating, just for a moment as I sensed his trepidation at knowing the full truth.

"But, I'm not sure I want to be responsible for whatever else might happen." I started to protest but he put his finger to my lips to quieten me, "Naomi, what if these ripples of change affect your mother or your sister...or even her baby? My being here has already separated you from them, what if it causes them harm? Could you live with that? Because I know I couldn't." And then my heart broke, because I knew he was right. I had been so blind and naive to think that these changes wouldn't cause harm, I couldn't take that risk and Laney had known that all along. I looked at her and for the first time I saw genuine sadness in her eyes. I understood now the choice that she had made all those years ago, who was I to think I could take on the powers of the unknown universe and win?

"Joe..." I sobbed and let my head fall into his chest.

"I know baby," He held my face between his hands and kissed my tears away. I couldn't believe this might be the end, "will you give us a moment?" For a second I thought Joe was talking to Laney, asking for a moment alone with me but then I saw he was looking directly at me and I realised he was asking *me* to leave *them* alone. I couldn't hide the hurt I felt and knew it must be evident in my expression but I got up anyway and followed the Librarian. Just as we reached the doorway, something made me turn around. Laney was watching me leave. The gleeful spite in her eyes made me shiver. Joe had never looked so vulnerable, sitting there with his head in his hands and his shoulders slumped, with that old hyena looking like she was about to devour him. Every instinct in me shouted at me to go and fight his corner and it took every ounce of my will power to allow the Librarian to escort me from that room.

I sat for what seemed like an age, in a small parlour off the main hallway, trying to listen in to any snippets of conversation from the library but there were none. The Librarian sat patiently opposite me on the very edge of her seat as if ready to jump up and stop me should I decide I'd waited long enough. As I looked her over she never shifted away from my gaze, just smiled politely and waited. I could not envisage working with these two for the life of me, the thought that I might not have any choice in the matter was sickening. What the hell would I tell my mum and Immy? And what would happen to mine and Joe's book bar? I loved our little place, I loved being in my flat in Lincoln…with Joe. Without him I had nothing. As much as I tried, I couldn't see any way out of this horrible situation. I wanted to scream at whatever power had brought me to this place. I didn't want this. I just wanted Joe.

I heard footsteps in the hallway and I shot out of my chair, the obedient Librarian following. Joe waited there for me, alone. Laney had remained in the library, thank God.

"Come on bella, let's go." He took my hand and began leading me towards the front door.

"What did you say to her? What's happening now?"

"You don't need to know mia cara, I just needed time to get things straight in my head without you there, you're such a distraction," Joe smiled down at me and blew me a kiss.

"Don't do that. That's not fair Joe, now isn't the time for jokes. I want to know what's going on." We got to the door and Joe yanked it open before the librarian even reached for the handle.

"Goodbye." He nodded at her politely, I just ignored her. I wasn't in a very polite and forgiving mood. The shut behind us and I whirled around in front of Joe, halting his steps.

"Joe, for Christ's sake tell me what is going on?" He hesitated a moment and then gentled his tone,

"We have a few days or so to sort things out."

"Sort things out?"

"Si, talk and think things through before we make a final decision. OK?" I sighed with relief, there was still time to find a way out of this mess, still time to be with Joe and somehow make it work.

We walked the long trek back to Crovie and our holiday cottage hand in hand and in complete silence. Neither of us wanting to break the spell of just being together, neither of us wanting to confront the choices that lay ahead. Joe took off my coat and hung it on the door hook as we entered the cottage. I went to the kitchen and put the kettle on,

"Coffee?" I asked and then promptly burst into tears at the triviality of my question. Joe came to join me in the kitchen.

"Hey now, come on bella. Don't cry." Joe pulled me into a tight hug and smoothed my hair with his hand.

"I can't lose you Joe."

"I know baby. I don't want to be without you either."

"What are we going to do?"

"Well, for now, I'm going to light the fire and make us dinner and you are going to take that beautiful body of yours to bed and rest. No protest! It's been an upsetting two days for you. We can't make decisions without a clear mind, so off to bed. I'll come wake you in a short while OK?" I agreed and reluctantly made my way to the snug bedroom. Despite the anguish that tore at my very soul, I fell almost instantly into an exhausted sleep.

I woke up some considerable time later. I knew several hours must've gone by because it was dark enough to be late in the evening. A tiny sliver of light crept under the bedroom door. Joe wasn't in bed with me so I got up and made my way sleepily towards the lounge, following the warm, amber light that must have come from the wood burner.

"Joe? Why didn't you wake me up babe? Did I miss dinner?" I rubbed my hands over my eyes trying to wake up properly, I felt ridiculously tired. The lounge was empty but for the last flickering embers of the fire. "Joe?" I called en route to the kitchen. When I didn't find him in there or the bathroom I assumed he'd gone out the back for more firewood. I sat on the sofa and wrapped the soft throw around my now shivering shoulders, the fire had almost died out and a chill crept into the room. The flutter of paper caught my eye and I leaned forward to pick it up, it was a piece of the page of manuscript that I had torn up in anger. The sight of it brought feelings of fear and dread at the decision Joe and I had yet to make. I became impatient and suddenly wanted it over with, Joe and I needed to talk right now. I couldn't take living in fear of if or when it all might end. I needed a plan, a process to follow, I was so tired of winging it. Where the hell was Joe? I got up, keeping the throw around my shoulders and opened the back door,

"Joe, are you out here? Can you come in now? I need to talk, and bring the wood in will you babe? It's bloody freezing in here." I got no reply, it was pitch black outside and there was no wind today but it was raining again. I listened for a reply but got none. Maybe he'd gone out to see our landlady, Moira to settle the bill for the cottage. I decided to see if Joe had left me a plate of dinner, I hadn't realised until that moment that I was hungry but Joe's cooking always got my appetite going. I turned on the kitchen light and scanned the worktop, there was no dinner that I could see only a sheet of paper. I could see there was writing on it and knew it was a note. I'd been right, Joe had gone out. I picked up the note and began to read, no more than a few lines in and I began to shake. I ran back to the lounge towards the fire and my eyes fell upon my old satchel. It was open on the floor…and empty. I didn't want to look, I tried desperately not to but I couldn't stop my gaze travelling to the wood burner. Why hadn't I noticed the burner door was open just now? Why hadn't I noticed my satchel on the floor? I was too late. There was nothing I could do to change anything now. Joe had left me no choice. I knelt in front of the burner and looked despondently at the large pile of smouldering ashes that had been my manuscript. The letter fell from my hand and fluttered gently and softly to the floor. My whole world crumbled and I felt my heart break into a million pieces. I was painfully numb. I had nothing left. I was alone…and Joe was gone.

to be continued...

Acknowledgements

To my editor Ewelina Rutyna, for taking a chance on me & for telling it like it is. I couldn't have done it without you.

Ednah Walters, for writing the best book boyfriend a girl could ever want & for your enthusiasm, friendship & support throughout this journey. Because of you I wrote a book!

The Pink Ladies & Shawn, for always listening & being willing guinea pigs. Not to mention putting up with me for so long! You're my kind of bonkers.

John Douglas of JCDPhotographic, thank you for a lifetime of friendship & all your design input.

Bridgette O'Hare of Wit & Whimsy cover design, working with you has been a real pleasure- thank you for making my book look so pretty!

My druidy wingman, Lorna- your advice and opinions have been as invaluable as your friendship.

Jocq, Meghan, Samantha, Carla, Emma, Daniella, Fran & Alysson you've no idea how much your input has helped. Thank you all so much. I can always count on my 'bookies'.

To MY one and only book boyfriend- muse, friend, sounding board, heartthrob, dreamboat, comedian, outrageous flirt and willing accomplice- this one is for you!

Printed in Great Britain
by Amazon